Alex in Wonderland

ALEX MACDONALD

New Star Books
Vancouver
1993

Editor: Rolf Maurer
Production: Audrey McClellan
Printed and bound in Canada by Best Gagné Book Manufacturers
1 2 3 4 5 97 96 95 94 93
First printing, May 1993

Publication of this book is made possible by grants from the Canada Council, the Department of Communications Book Publishing Industry Development Program, and the Cultural Services Branch, Province of British Columbia.

New Star Books Ltd.
2504 York Avenue
Vancouver, B.C.
V6K 1E3

Canadian Cataloguing in Publication Data

Macdonald, Alex, 1918-
Alex in wonderland

ISBN 0-921586-28-0
1. Canada – Politics and government – 1984- – Anecdotes.* 2. Canada – Politics and government – 1984-   Humor.* 3. Macdonald, Alex, 1918- I. Title.
FC173.M23 1993   971.064′7′0207   C93-091481-3
F1026.4.M23 1993

Contents

Preface

This preface must serve as my defence for having written this book — a short defence, for long-winded ones almost always convict.

I write because, looking around on this big rock, flung off by a dying star five billion years ago, what I see ... Well, let's say the omens are not that propitious. More stress, not less; underemployed human capabilities; a general erosion in values (whatever happened to the notion that people get what they deserve?); growing, rankling inequities in wealth and opportunities ...

You want specifics? What? Here, in a preface? Patience, gentle Reader. Details will follow, scenes you'll be able to listen in on. You'll get the chance to practise safe reading, taking this book to bed. Suffice it to say now that any god, sitting on a cloud and looking down on Earth, would be appalled. He'd sigh, and say, "What a mad world." And she'd probably add, "What a wicked world."

I write because mean, destructive things are happening for no good reason. And I'm immodest enough to think I could — well, if not stop them, at least start the process of stopping them. There's no need for us to stumble, like sleepwalkers, into a future not of our own making, driven by me-first economics.

There's no need for undernourished children anywhere, especially in our rich country. Modern science (how it has outstripped social progress!) can grow tomatoes in greenhouses in Greenland, using stored sunlight and recycled materials; or put a clicker in your hand to turn your living room into an office, playpen or school. That same science, managed well – by hard heads and soft hearts, *not* the other way around – can provide for all. So I write, putting aside my natural modesty. Modesty is an over-rated virtue anyway.

I've done my best not to preach, but to make happenings the message. I show you word-pictures which, I hope, have hidden in them solutions. I present characters (some odder, even, than me) for the same reason. I write to reach social democrats, whatever their political stripe. You can't be sure, on some issues, who's left in right field, and who's right in left field. The true social democrat is simply one who puts the common good first, without a lot of salaaming to special interests. And one who does not go for free-for-all mud-wrestling as the way to settle questions about income distribution, much as the slippery and the strong enjoy such methods.

Social democrats, of course, must be ready to take a lot of flack from the privileged. Wasn't it a Mac (Machiavelli, one of the Italian Macs) who said that those who would initiate a new social order must expect to draw fire from those "who profit by the old order"?

One thing I will admit to, and that's making use of my senior's pass to exempt myself from some of the current rules about political correctness. Not that I go overboard – not like Dominick, a former student, born a Maltese falcon. From Malta, he emigrated to Australia, where (he says) he was looked on as a wog – a "wily oriental gentleman" – and thence to Canada, to be regarded as a white caucasian male. And Dominick treated all this as something to smile about. You're sure not one to equate pompous bigotries with profundity, are you, Dominick?

An earlier writer of epistles caught what I like to think of as the essence of social democracy. That was Paul, who wrote to remind the Ephesians that they were "members of one another." (Unfortunately, Paul spoiled things, for me at least, going on to advise those Ephesians "wherefore, putting aside all lying." All, Paul? Ah, me! No one ever looking me right in the eye and telling me a whopper? No one letting me down easy with a white lie?)

Still, I could dedicate this book to Paul ... or maybe to Clyde Gilmour, "a Toronto broadcaster." You were tweaking us, weren't you, Clyde, when you tickled the ivories and crooned that ditty, "Ain't *no*body goin' to share my jelly roll with me"?

No, I will do the right thing, the proper thing, and dedicate this book to my wife, Dorothy, who has always understood me. And now, she even trusts me! That it should have come to this!

And I thank Elizabeth Godley for editing my stuff, but not editing me out of my skin. Elizabeth, so fine a writer yourself, how could you be so patient with me?

As for you, sagacious and honoured Reader, be of good cheer. Social democracy is not dead, just sick in bed. Just you watch — it'll take up its bed and walk.

CHAPTER 1

Alex hitches a ride in a limo with the auditor-general.
The bar stays closed. Alex learns how to slay social
program-eating debt monsters — and how to change
human nature (with help from Katharine Hepburn).
And Alex stands corrected (but only partially).

Dear Reader,

It is late on a winter's afternoon, in the Year of Our Lord 1991. We are at the airport in Ottawa, where I am waiting for my bag at the carousel. Suddenly, who should stroll up but this hearty, bustling guy with his hand out. Apparently he has penetrated my disguise as an absent-minded professor.

"Aren't you the Honourable Alex Macdonald?" asks he.

"I used to be," say I, "but now I'm the formerly Honourable Alex Macdonald."

Ah, now, who could this hearty fellow be? Why, none other than the auditor-general of this great land, Mr. Kenneth Dye. I'd met him long ago on a sunny day at our family cottage at Buccaneer Bay, in beautiful B.C. He'd taken at once to my daughter Christina, then 11, and off the two had wandered in deep conversation, our cocker spaniel tagging along. I have to disagree with that crotchety old W.C. Fields — I *like* people who like children and dogs.

Since that distant day, Kenneth has somehow become our auditor-general (I think he knew Pierre Trudeau). And I have more time for him than ever. Here he is, in Fat City,

1

doing time running down scams, boondoggles, loopholes, bungles – you name 'em, this town's got 'em.

Ken's work is never done. It goes on and on, like the work of Hercules, who did his bit, long ago, cleaning up the droppings of 5,000 swine in the Augean stables.

Still, one look and you know this man likes his work. And me? I'm cheering him on. Who needs waste and wastrels? Certainly not Canadians. We live in the most debt-ridden country in the western world, with our government so strapped for cash that things like a national day-care program for working mothers have floated out of reach – they were nothing but airy election promises.

Maybe you, gentle Reader, have noticed those debt monsters crouching at the doors of our parliament and legislatures, devouring unborn social services and nibbling away on the live ones – the very services that help Canadians to like each other better!

Ken kindly offers me a ride into beautiful downtown Ottawa, and I jump at the chance to rifle his mind. The old fellow has just made another headline: "NATIONAL DEBT THREATENS THE VERY ABILITY OF GOVERNMENT TO GOVERN."

Can it be that bad? I'm afraid it is. With the federal deficit going up by $100 million every day – with the interest on that deficit costing us another $100 million every day . . .

When my little grandson Andrew first rubbed his eyes in the light of day, he owed $15,000 in federal debt – never mind provincial. Yes, some of that is in long-term pay-off investments, but most goes for indulgence now. By the time Andrew's little brother arrived, they each owed about $18,000. They were born into a kind of debtor's prison, where the bondholders also hold the keys.

What's going on (and this is what gets me) is a continuing transfer of wealth from interest-payers to interest-receivers. A transfer, mostly, from those with less than enough to those with more than enough.

And while a dose of inflation eases debt loads (though

not our foreign debt load), you know who that hits hardest
– yup, those with less than enough.

So I gladly accept Ken's offer of a lift, quietly resolving,
since I was given two ears and only one mouth, to listen
twice as much as I talk. You will see, dear Reader, just how
well I managed that.

First, to draw Ken out, I think to put him in a good mood.
I say, "You know, Ken, I'm here as a guest of the friendly
Canadian taxpayers. What with the lift my daughter gave
me to the Vancouver airport, and your lift downtown now,
the three of us are saving the taxpayers a few bucks."

At first, this seems to go down well with the auditor-general. They don't call him Mr. Trim-the-Fat for nothing. But
then he appears to pass some gas.

"Why on earth," he wants to know, "should the taxpayers
give you, Alex, a free trip to Ottawa?"

I tell him I've been invited to address the Canadian senate
on Canada's Constitutional Crisis. Ken is not mollified. He
starts muttering.

"You, to the senate? I thought your idea of senate reform
was more mercy killing. I thought you had no use for those
old boys – that you thought Canada didn't need *two* parliaments? How could *you* tell the senators anything they haven't
heard a dozen times? And what about the costs of all this
constitutional talk-talk? Hundreds of millions..."

"Ken, Ken, you're so impatient," I reply. "Our Canadian
Constitutional Crisis will all blow over in another twenty or
thirty years. Meanwhile, I intend to tell the senators all I
know about the constitution. And that could take me up to
ten minutes. I'll have them tapping their canes. And I'll meet
some old friends I haven't heard hide nor hair of since they
were made senators... Except I will miss one. Sadly, old
Senator Freddy McGrand of New Brunswick won't be there.
He woke up in a testy mood last week, said the heck with
it, and took early retirement – at age 91."

Ken, musing, says, "I hope alarm bells don't go off while

you're speaking. The senators installed those bells under their desks. Come a seizure, or a terrorist, and they can push their buttons without the bother of calling a page."

"I hope so too – no bells – someone in the gallery might think one of the senators had escaped."

At this point, Ken's driver appears and puts my zipper bag into the trunk of a long white limo, under the antenna. And off we go – but with the bar closed. Ken seems a little sheepish about the limo, and murmurs, "You know, Alex, in my job, time is money."

"I guess it is," I assure him. "But at my age, it isn't."

We drive past roadside snow drifts. This town lies under piles of snow, as well as piles of debt. It'll be months before the crocuses and potholes appear.

I ask Ken if he'll be given a second term as auditor.

"I can't be reappointed," he replies. "And that's as it should be – so there's no temptation to go easy on the powers that be."

"You must be the only public servant in Canada not angling for something more," I tell him.

"I hope to come back to Vancouver later this year, if I can afford to. The house I sold on the North Shore would cost me a million dollars now."

"Don't tell me – a million? More, I'd say. And you know you're not the worst of the victims, Ken, not by a long shot." I'm getting heated up, starting to take off like a red-hot missile. I get diverted from the subject at hand.

"What's up, Ken, to price homes out of the reach of young families? Sucking so much goodness out of family life – is it the price of nails? The plumber's wages? Have we run out of land, or what?"

Ken: "Well, land *is* in short supply."

"Yes, in places. And Mother Nature isn't making any more of it. But what we've done is let the provision of shelter be a big-buck money-maker for a few lucky ones. I'd like to have a scourge and chase speculators, flippers and usurers out of the housing business faster than the good Lord threw the money changers out of the temple."

"You haven't changed, Alex..."

I keep on, showing no mercy to my captive audience of one. "Who wins in a real estate boom, Ken? Not your young first-time buyers. Not tenants. I'll give you a winner – and a loser. You be the judge, Ken. You decide if we're mad – or just bad."

So I give him a winner – an agent. This Malcolm fellow I know tells me he's sold 65 homes worth a total of $25 million in the last seven months. He's 35 years old, motivated, ambitious, persistent. He works out of his Porsche, a phone in his ear, Gucci loafers, blue silk shirt.

"How much will you make this year, Malcolm?" I ask him.

"Seven figures," says he, "low seven figures." He's not one of the salespeople who make so little they can't stay in the game. He says he'll own the Mona Lisa one day – and maybe he will. He has no idea he's not doing good by doing so well. It's hard not to like him.

But there's a loser, too, in this game. He's a union-wages handyman I see around the court house. Good times are bad for him; says the rent on his flat in Vancouver's West End has doubled in the last year, that he's paying out 50 per cent of his income in rent, that he and his wife can barely make ends meet. Just $17 left at the end of last month, he says.

"So you know what, Ken? The law of economics decrees that this guy has to move far away from where he works. But me, I believe in a higher law."

"I'm sure you do."

"I'd sure not leave housing to the blind furies of the market. Would we do this with education? Or health? Well, the homes we live in, and pay for, have a lot to do with health, of body *and* mind – and a lot to do with how well the kids do in school."

The auditor quietly shifts the conversation. He's a decent

sort, really – not a radical like me. He makes the point that deficits also push up housing costs, because government borrowings push up mortgage interest rates. He goes on to say that a 1 per cent rise in interest rates costs the minister of finance an extra $1.6 billion a year in his budget.

Then he gives me a little jab. "I didn't expect you, Alex, to be so concerned about deficits. Don't socialists give priority to spending programs? Are you out of step with your colleagues?"

"No, though some of them are out of step with me," I say. "I've got stuck in my head some of the hard-headed ideas of old socialists like George Bernard Shaw. He'd come out with things like, 'We can have liberty and socialism only when the daily debt is paid by the daily labour.' "

"But how," asks the auditor, "are you going to get Canadians to take less today in order to have more tomorrow? They seem to want it all now – if not yesterday."

I can't help glancing toward the limo bar – or the place where the bar should be.

"Nothing to it, Ken. It's just a simple matter of changing the ways of making our livings. Right now, we do it in ways that positively encourage greed. We put buying and selling for profit at the centre of our social transactions. That's what screws up our priorities and skews our values."

"Sounds like you want some kind of revolution . . . "

"Well, yes, as a matter of fact, I do. But a step-by-step one – moving toward new ways, new values. There needn't be that much difficulty about it. We've got to think up simple, practical devices that'll do the trick."

"Such as?" Ken asks.

"Well, take your farmer. Farmers who get together to sell their produce cooperatively, instead of cutting each other's throats, are better people for it.

"Or take the devices that make it easier for people to be found out. They improve their morals. The installation of surveillance cameras in banks, for instance, has done wonders for the moral values of robbers."

"Oh, my," says Ken. "You socialists have this rosy view of human nature. Do you really think you can change it?"

"No, I wouldn't think of fooling around with Mother Nature. But change human *behaviour* – why not?"

"You remind me of Katharine Hepburn," Ken says. "Remember that movie, *The African Queen*? Katharine thought she could make a better man of the old reprobate, Humphrey Bogart. They were alone on a river boat in the Dark Continent. Humphrey starts coming on to the school-marmish Hepburn, breathing hard and muttering, 'It's only natural.'

"Miss H., however, has another idea. 'Nature,' she says primly, 'is what we're put on earth to rise above.' "

"Thanks, Katie," say I, to myself, and to Ken, "Canadians don't have to rise that much above our natures. Good stock! I'll give you a couple of examples to buck you up. One from the East Coast, one from the West. Canadians who insist on the right thing being done."

So I tell him about the federal wharfmaster at Bedford Harbour, Nova Scotia. (Pat Nowlan, MP, my Red Tory sometimes tennis partner, told me all about him.) Seems this wharfmaster was a Liberal and expected to be fired when Joe Clark won for the Conservatives in 1979. After all, turnabout is fair play. Instead, the Conservatives abolished the position – there hadn't been a ship through there in years!

"Our Liberal was deeply offended. What would his friends say? He fired off telegrams demanding he be sacked. At last, Joe gave in and fired him, satisfying his sense of propriety."

Then I told him about a West Coast lawyer, Scott van Alstine, in Nanaimo. In 1988, he had run for the Conservatives and lost by a respectable margin. But they never gave him a thing – until one day the phone rang. An Ottawa voice says, "Mr. van Alstine, we have three candidates for

postmaster in Nanaimo – McLean, Jones and Robert. Which
would you prefer?" Said van Alstine, "Never heard of any
of them, and I don't give a damn what you do." To this,
the voice replied, "Would it . . . would it be all right, then, if
we fell back on the merit system?"

"So there you go, Ken," I say. "The true Canadian grain
takes a lot of bending – it's as straight as a furrow!"

I can see that the auditor-general is deeply impressed.
"Yes, the Canadian grain," he says. Then he let fall something
about the late, great sage, John Stuart Mill, about how he'd
said the worth of a state depends in the long run on the
worth of its citizens.

And then he comes back at me. "Where do you really
get your 'save for a rainy day' attitude from, Alex? Is it the
Scotch in you?"

"Could be," I confess. "And I don't mean Black and White"
– with a glance at the limo bar, still firmly closed – "I've
got some good-granny values left – most Canadians have.

"And you know, Ken," I continue, "you sure give Canadians a lift with your exposés. And say, I like your proposal
of free phones so Canadians could call you with their litanies
of government boondoggling. Did it go through?"

"No. The people on the Hill didn't think they'd like the
sound of my whistle blowers. I think this idea would have
paid for itself in no time – but the Conservatives didn't like
it because they were in government, and the Liberals didn't
like it because they expect to be."

"Too bad. We'll just have to get along with the odd sal-
utary leak," I say. "Or perhaps an act of parliament to protect whistle blowers, save them from extinction – like trum-
peter swans."

"Sometimes," Ken says sadly, "the whistle blows too late."

"You're telling me! I see headlines – one went something
like this: 'FEDERAL BUSINESS-LOAN CORPORATION ADVANCES
MILLIONS TO START THREE STRIP CLUBS IN HULL IN PLAIN
VIEW OF PARLIAMENT HILL. *Minister says he saw nothing wrong.*

Voyeurs turn out to be Conservative bag men with bags under their eyes.'

"Ken, that should have been exposed sooner. Things like that cause widespread psychological damage to taxpayers – to their concern for others and their care for tomorrow. It tests their Christian charity. Sure, they know well enough what Saint Thomas Aquinas said, in the 13th century: 'To pay taxes is to provide for the common good from the common stores.' But things like that get them tired."

"I suppose so," says Ken. He's really sad now. He drops me off on Parliament Hill at the senate door. I can breeze past the security commissionaires there easily. They take me for a cigar-waving passive senator, dropping in to pick up his cheque.

I hurry to the round parliamentary library, to make notes of everything the auditor got in edgewise. Around me rise circling galleries of white pine and cedar, thronged with noble volumes glimmering in the lambent light. The galleries meet in a baroque dome decorated with wrought iron. Ah, the delightful society of books. They don't talk back.

This library escaped the disastrous fire of 1916 that destroyed the adjacent parliament buildings. The rebuilding of parliament was completed after Mackenzie King became prime minister in 1921. King appointed my uncle, the Honourable J.H. King, minister of public works to finish the job. There had been construction scandals, and Mackenzie King wanted to make sure that only Liberal contractors of unimpeachable integrity would get the work.

Old Mackenzie King wouldn't have needed an auditor-general poking into his accounts. In 1944 he travelled to Washington by train, in a lower berth, to sign the Bretton Woods agreement. He was not a big-time spender like our Brian M., with his million-dollar foreign sorties. This PM flies Challenger jets to penthouse suites with an entourage of image polishers, ghost writers and court jesters...

Later, I go for a simple supper in the parliamentary restaurant (where you find neither tripe nor snipe on the menu), and do some table-hopping amongst ranking honourables and parliamentary foot soldiers. And I make a point of *not* spreading the word that Ken's next audit is to be Parliament Hill. I wouldn't want to spoil anyone's dinner.

Well, ever-so-patient Reader, I've pretty well emptied my head now. Don't cry; I'll get a fill-up and give you more. I *have* to! There's something wrong with the picture I've painted so far. I seem to have laid all the blame for debts and waste on governments, politicians, and even voters. While what can *really* do us in are the misappropriations of the wrong things, and the scams in the private grab-as-grab-can world of the financial elites. We don't hear as much about them, do we?

So to straighten up my picture, I'll give you one story, just one, for now. About Goldenballs. You can decide how far he's in or out of the norms of what's going on.

I first heard about Goldenballs in a London pub, oh, about three years ago. After making a pit stop, I sat down at a table with a printer. He'd lost his job at the London *Times* after a bitter strike, and was working part time in Fleet Street. Something in the newspaper he was reading upset him. He'd take a swig of his beer and another look at his paper, getting hotter all the time.

"Look at this, old chap," he began. "Sir James Goldsmith, international privateer, net worth a billion or two, has sailed back to England with a $21-billion bid to take over BAT, Britain's largest conglomerate."

I decided to draw him out by playing the part of a seedy colonial academic, badly in need of educating – duck soup for me.

"Ah," I said, "Sir James. Oxford man. Man of substance. No penny-ante sort that one! BAT also controls companies in my own country – Canada Trust, Shoppers Drug, tobacco interests, gold stocks . . ."

"Goldenballs, they call him, and not for his stable of

horses," said the printer. "When he's not gambling with chips, he's gambling with people."

I said, "I suppose he's returned to England from the West Indies because Margaret Thatcher has created a climate in which capitalists like himself can flourish."

"Climate," the printer sputtered. "Yes, scattered golden showers, falling on the likes of him. He 'created' $3.7 billion just by announcing his take-over on TV – manipulated the stock up."

"Yes, they say nothing makes money like money."

"You don't make money like that doing good deeds," the printer said.

"Well," said I, "Sir James is a greenmailer – a man has to make a living."

"He pillages companies and runs. Like a pirate. He'll sail back to his tax-free hideaway in the Bahamas on a Concorde loaded with gold bullion – Long James Goldsmith. Should have a black patch over one eye and a parrot on his shoulder. He'll rest up and raid again at the expense of the British working man."

I tried to explain to him that what Sir James was doing was perfectly legal.

"Sure it is. It is grand larceny within the law. And if an illiterate kid from a broken home knocks off a post office, he'll be within the law too – doing hard labour, not hard living."

I don't tell the printer this, but Sir James also made a take-over run at Goodyear Tire, with plants in Canada as well as the States. Was he attracted by its Rubbermaid division? Goodyear paid a bitter price. It bought back a lot of its own shares at a cost of $2.7 billion. Debt-stricken, the company terminated 2,000 rubber workers in Ontario while Sir James sailed off with $80 million in pirates' loot.

In 1990, Sir James and associates also went for the gold with a run at the Toronto mining company, Barrier Resources. How they did on this, I don't know. But I did catch

Sir James on telly, proud as Punch. Turning acquisitiveness into a virtue, he was.

"All in a day's work," he said. "I make businesses productive even if they fold. Bees don't make honey to do good."

What will do us all in, impatient Reader, is our steadily decreasing rate of public and private saving; our decreasing investment in people and things that can make a better tomorrow. An economy of "everyone out for all they can get" and of "anything goes" doesn't save enough.

CHAPTER 2

Old Alex, like some seeing-eye God, looks down from 33,000 feet on a still-virgin country pregnant with possibilities, but with its values raped by a preoccupation with Mammon, among other deviltries.

Dear Reader,

A retired Ontario policeman got me thinking recently about Canada's values. I chanced on him at the Toronto airport, where he was pushing lottery tickets at a small table. His sales weren't that brisk, thank God, and he was glad to talk to anyone, even a non-buyer, and bare his soul.

He allowed, with a rueful smile, that a short while ago (half a century, no more) he had been busting people for buying Irish Sweepstakes tickets. Now here he was, peddling Lady Luck to their sons and daughters.

What a falling off in Canadian values! Lucky suckers, getting something for nothing, winning jackpots neither earned nor deserved. It's these "gimme" times. They are infecting the good old pillars of Canadian decency, the ones this country rests on. We need them, strong and firm, more than ever.

What's that you say? I use words like "values" without saying what I mean? Okay, okay. Values – the good ones – tell people what's right and wrong, and give them the willpower to right wrongs – and to stand some pain for long-term gain – and to feel some concern for others. A *liking* for different opinions, various skin colours, different

13

religions. You get the idea. Just don't tell me values are airy-fairy things that don't pack practical consequences.

Anyway, thanks to that ex-policeman, I boarded my plane quite het up about moral slippage. My aerial whale, a 747, was about to shoulder its way, shuddering, into the skies over Toronto and then rev down a bit and level off for its race with the sun to Vancouver – and I would muse on, flooded with concern for my country.

Westward-ho, with the earth below! Mother Earth – though I'm sorry to say we have no right to call her Mother, the way we've been treating her. Pillaging her treasures pell-mell . . .

Take this whale I'm riding – please. It has consumed, to get to this height – let me see, with the help of my handy pocket calculator – yes, precisely the same amount of energy that 1,019 slaves put out in one 16-hour shift building the Seven Towers of Thebes.

And trailing behind this whale, as we climb above Toronto, is a dirty brown plume of exhaust gases. Not, I'd have to say, an appropriate parting gift to leave such a fine city, with so many lifestyles, some of them positively bizarre, at least to a man of my age. Modern Man (or Person, I suppose, is more politically correct) is burning up in a couple of hundred years the fossil fuels our Mother Earth spent a couple of million years to make. Kind of arrogant, I'd say, Man is. He's the cleverest of the animals, by a long shot – but maybe not the wisest.

What's the big rush? This spending binge we're on has us spending oil and gases and trees and fish like there's no tomorrow. And there will be no tomorrow if we don't slow down! Gobbling with a hearty appetite the substance of the earth, mostly to show off.

As I, like some modern Jonah, circle over Toronto in my whale, I look down from the window. I can see where my Granny Macdonald passed the last years of her life. Strong granny values she had! We named our daughter Christina after her. She left the farm near North Bay when she lost her husband, and moved into the big city, Toronto, with her unmarried daughter. Sorrowfully, she would outlive all her fine sons, and die aged 107 in 1946. When I was a student at Osgoode Hall, I would visit her on a Sunday in her tiny house on Logan Avenue. Her life was founded on hard work, thrift, mending and saving. She'd keep scraps of left-over threads, bits of wool – wouldn't think of throwing them out. If I'd say, "It's a fine sunny day, grandmother," she'd say, "Och, we'll pay for it."

And pious? No food was cooked on the sabbath, not a dish was washed. A cousin of hers, Dan Macdonald, caught heck for rinsing out his shirt on a Sunday. In Toronto in those days, even Eaton's store windows were draped on the sabbath against the covetous eyes of passers-by.

But in Toronto now? Everyone is hit by the good consumer messages, "Throw it away! Buy another!" I've sat on the hard slat benches at Eaton's Centre – carefully engineered to get you up and shopping. I spoke to one Toronto insurance man who bought some jeans for his 13-year-old daughter at the K-Mart. "Oh, Dad," she said, "I can't wear those! No brand name! Everyone at school will notice." This youngster already has two part-time jobs to bring in spending money. TV has done its work – I shop, therefore I am.

And the economists say if we stop shopping, we'll all fall down. They have no imagination. Most of these economists can't even dream of a society with fairly paid jobs for all who can work, turning out useful goods and services. They seem to think that's not in the natural order of things. What dummies!

But now, dear Reader, we are in a sky-bus high over Ontario. This province is (laughably) the centre of gravity (if not sobriety) of the second-biggest country in the world – area-wise, that is. This Ontario, with its hinterlands – i.e., the rest of Canada – can make it really big in the 21st century, if ... IF it dusts off and uses the best of its pioneering

values. Such as the principle "all for one and one for all."
Our early settlers would never have been able to beat the
cold and the distances without putting that principle to
work.

Ah, I see a flight attendant edging her cart closer to my
seat. I could use a pick-me-up, pinched as I am into a sec-
ond-class seat and paying my own way! Where, oh where,
are those taxpayers who were so friendly to me in my political days? Oh well. "Pull yourself together, Alex," say I to
myself. "Remember the Highland ethic of your wild Scottish
ancestors: 'To endure without complaint and without dependence.' "

Besides, I'm travelling with a fine class of people – ordinary Canadians, and every one of them extraordinary. Not
that I mind hanging out with millionaires, but they're always
sticking me for change to buy a paper or something. They
think carrying cash is not in keeping with their status. There
are no millionaires in this cabin (I don't count myself). I
know, because only black raincoats are stowed in the lock-
ers. Millionaires wear beige.

You must stop distracting me from what I want to say!
That values make good institutions and good institutions
make better values. That Highland ethic survived the Atlantic
passage and settled on the Old Macdonald Farm – the farm
some where below me now, on the eastern shores of Lake
Huron, that was carved out of the bush in 1846 by Macdonalds and Nicolsons. It raised eleven bairns.

My grandfather, John Macdonald, came to Canada as a
three-year-old. His parents stowed him in an ox cart for the
last leg of the long journey – from Hamilton to Lucknow,
over trails in the primeval forests of Old Ontario. My father
was the seventh of the eleven children. He was into farm
chores as soon as he could toddle. He was christened Malcolm – Ontario farm boys didn't get middle names then.
Later, he gave himself one to become the impressive Mal-

colm Archibald Macdonald, Chief Justice of British Columbia
– "MA" to his friends.

No high-paid doctor attended his birth. Only a kindly
housewife from nearby. There was none of your "luxury's
contagion" on that farm, to borrow Robbie Burns' phrase.
But there were books – the family Bible, as well as a volume
of Burns' poetry, dedicated to "the Sons and Daughters of
Labour and Poverty." "And oh," wrote Robbie, "And oh,
may Heaven their simple lives prevent / from luxury's contagion weak and vile." The Macdonalds were a dispossessed
family, one of many Scottish families driven from their hum-
ble crofts and communal holdings by English aristocrats
who (mis)took their land for sheep runs. Sheep ate men.

In Ontario, they encountered another dispossessed people: the Ojibwa. The Ojibwa lost their lands by Treaty 45,
written on half a piece of parchment. Sir Francis Bond Head,
lieutenant-governor of Upper Canada, wrote up the treaty
when he was on an outing in 1836. He held a pow-wow
with the Ojibwa and must have spoken with forked tongue.
The Ojibwa put their signs on the parchment. One-and-a-
halfmillion acres passed to immigrant settlers.

What an unpaid debt the rest of us owe those who settled
in Canada thousands of years ago. I want it paid in equal
rights *and* opportunities, without discrimination or segrega-
tion, with Native Canadians living amicably side by side with
the others, all enriched by borrowings back and forth.

A tough people settled Old Ontario: the Scots; United
Empire Loyalists fleeing the unruly American Revolution
(that's my mom's side); soldiers from British regiments who
fought off American invasions and were rewarded with land
grants; hungry Irish peasants driven by the failure of the
potato crops, which their English landlords did little to
relieve. So many . . .

Anglo-Irish ancestors of my wife Dorothy's received land
grants in the Ottawa Valley. One settler was her ancestor,

Colonel George Thew Burke. His portrait hangs in our house. In 1821, he became the first Member of Parliament for Carleton County. Earlier, as a young officer in the Irish Fusiliers under the Iron Duke of Wellington, he fought Napoleon. Then, oh my! The Protestant colonel took to wife a Catholic Irish colleen. How the gossips must have talked behind their hands about that. (Religious toleration was a scarce value in those days. Much scarcer than it is today, thank Allah!)

Then, a posting to Canada in 1812. Did he want escape from the wars? Or to flee the murmurings? Well, in Canada he quickly found himself fighting the American invaders in the War of 1812-14 (will they never let us be?). He was wounded at the battle of Queenston Heights.

Then he was assigned to protect the Ottawa Valley from surprise attack by American rivermen. Thus he founded the military settlement of Richmond, fifteen miles away from the Ottawa River. In bitter winter cold, they, families and all, cut the trail that is now the Richmond Road. In a small museum in Richmond, you can see some of the military issue they carried: axe heads, window panes...

I have seen the colonel's silver snuff box. He carried it in a vest pocket and claimed it saved his life. You can see the dent the bullet made.

Now the Protestant colonel lies in the Catholic cemetery in Richmond. Dorothy took me to see his tombstone; her mother had it spruced up. Last rites were said over the colonel in the Episcopal Church in Ottawa — then spritely Catholics spirited away his remains to lie in Catholic ground. And he never said a mumbling word.

There was a word of advice left behind for us by the colonel's uncle, none other but the great 18th-century philosopher-statesman Edmund Burke. "People," Edmund said, "will not look forward to posterity, who do not look back to their ancestry."

His nephew, Colonel Burke, was just one of all those who made this impossible country, working together, helping each other.

So in 1906, when hydro-electric generation came along, Ontario opted for public ownership under Ontario Hydro. Their decision flowed as naturally as maple syrup from that cooperative spirit that animated the rural communities. Hydro of the people, by the people, for the people.

Then – and now. Now I'm looking down on the farms of west-central Ontario – plush green or striped brown. So neatly laid out on the survey lines of the Old Back Concessions. So prosperous they seem, and so huge the land. Too huge to spoil? Once we thought so . . .

I can't quite make out the contented Ontario cows munching on Ontario grass. But I know they're down there, with the queenly self-assurance of inhabitants of this, the most pampered province of the Canadian confederation. Ontario, StatsCan tells us, has 260,000 triple-toileted families. Toilets make philosophers. Though, we are also told, the sitting time in Toronto, by the latest count, is less than the national average. Too hectic a pace in that town, eighth-largest of the world's Italian cities.

Soon we will leave Ontario. We are westering fast, although the sun, our creator and our destroyer, has just about caught up with our plane. She'll have snuck ahead before she beds down in the Pacific.

I see down there rocks and trees, lakes and rivers; yes, water, water, everywhere. What a country we've inherited, dear Reader. What with raindrops and snowflakes, it has more fresh water than any other country. A Canada of 30 million people and almost a third of the world's running water. Wait and see – our fresh water'll be more precious than oil.

Fresh! If only our water *were* fresh. Alas, now, some of those lakes down there glow with a ghastly acidic hue; some of those rivers serve as sewage drains. Better we deal with that, but *fast*.

And better, too, that Canadians stop complaining about the weather! Even I have complained about rainy Vancouver when I can't see through my sopping glasses. I should stop; besides, there'll soon be automatic glasses-wipers on the market.

I look north – the vast land stretches beyond sight. Boreal forests give way to tundra, tundra to snowscape – snows in varieties only the Inuit (who have 70 words for it) understand. Then Arctic ice – and our ice is water! In 100,000 glaciers, Canadians have one and a half times as much fresh water as we have surface water. Water locked up in our Great Northern Bank. Frozen assets, some day to be drawn on – but not drained.

The vastness. "I knew a man whose school could never teach him patriotism, but who acquired that virtue when he felt in his bones the vastness of his land and the greatness of those who founded it." That was Pierre Elliott Trudeau – remember him? Who would have thought the old fellow to have so much poetry in him? And moments of wisdom? You know, I suspect (something always difficult to prove) that Trudeau is an intellectual.

Now we're flying over Manitoba. Away back, in the Hungry Thirties, on a small-holding near Brandon, the Reverend Robert Grant MacKay contrived to bring up his brood in the Great Depression. He preached and held Bible studies. His was a busy Sunday, giving as many carefully prepared sermons in as many Presbyterian country churches as he could get around to.

I know about the Reverend MacKay from his daughter, Jean Fahrni. She lives near us now, makes the best bean soup anywhere, and at her parties I have the privilege of talking to Bill Reid, our great Haida sculptor in wood, argillite and bronze.

"A wise man," MacKay told Jean, "can prepare a sermon

in six days. A dunce can prepare a sermon in no time at all."

Those Canadian kirks didn't pass a tin pail around for the collection, as they did in Scotland. Tin lets everyone know if it's a shilling or a farthing tossed in. No, the Reverend MacKay was paid for his sermons with a roast chicken. Or with sour cream – cream wasn't fresh for long back then, with no refrigerators. Jean soon learned how to put sour cream to good use. She'd cook sour-cream pies, or biscuits, nutritious and delicious. Or use it for cakes and salad dressings.

Ring Day was a high old time for the MacKays and the neighbours. About 25 farmers would get together each Ring Day, taking turns at bringing a cow to be slaughtered. Everyone shared in the cow, its beef, heart, liver and tail. Sometimes, Jean said, the Reverend MacKay would be given the offal to take home in thanks for his labours.

Those farmers tended the land with loving care, like careful gardeners. Crop, fallow, crop – no pesticides, no insecticides. The values they lived by were simple: helping each other out at harvest, mending, saving – and working hard. Jean remembers raising her voice in a hymn written by Anne Walker, an Ontario girl of 18. Jean would sing, "Work, for the night is falling / when man works no more." To work, to provide, to save. These pioneering values, and a sense of duty, shaped early Canadian lives and communities.

A friend of mine, who grew up in Winnipeg, told me of three fathers, all heads of families, who came to the point where they could not carry out their obligations. All three lived on Somerset Street, in Winnipeg. In the Hungry Thirties, when they couldn't pay their bills or put food on the table, they lost their feelings of self-worth. All three took their own lives.

Has there been a decline since then, dear Reader, in the general sense of obligation to others? I think so.

Prairie farmers in the thirties created the Canadian Wheat Board as an expression of their values. The Tory prime minister of the day, R.B. Bennett, added the finishing touches. Through their board, the growers have served the markets of the world in an orderly, cooperative way, with better returns for their crops.

But the growers' Wheat Board is at risk today, about to fall prey to go-for-it values. And it was a Macdonald who helped put cooperative marketing at risk. The Hon. Donald Macdonald ended his 1985 Royal Commission Report by advocating "free trade" with the United States. Had he any idea where that principle would lead?

I had a chance to gently upbraid this namesake of mine in London not long ago. A security guard escorted me into his presence. He, a former Liberal cabinet minister, was then Canada's High Commissioner in London – appointed by a Conservative prime minister. That in itself was enough to make me suspicious.

Still, Old Macdonald was in a jovial mood when I was shown in. We agree, for one thing, on the spelling of our surnames. (Not everyone knows that the McDonalds are the illegitimate children of Macdonalds.)

I gave Donald a copy of my book, *'My Dear Legs . . .'*. He thumbed it, scanned the pictures, said I was all wet but promised to read it. What! With his finger he'll read it?

"Well, Thumper," I began, "you've come a long way since we did business in 1973. You still thumping them in the squash courts?"

"I got that tag from my debating style in the House of Commons," he replied, a bit haughty.

"A long way, since we were energy ministers, you in Ottawa, I in Victoria. You with your National Energy Program, I with the B.C. Petroleum Corporation. Both of us for regulated prices and supplies of natural gas and oil for the good of Canadians . . ."

"Some ripen with the years – others stay green."

"A long way, Thumper, from then to free trade. You know, you may have helped to kill the Canadian Wheat Board."

"I didn't want agriculture in," he defended himself. "Anyway, now trading blocks are forming in Europe, Asia, America. They will block Canada — we must join one."

"And leave our resources to the play of market forces?"

Pause. You can always tell a Scot, but you can't tell him much.

Thumper, irritated: "I should report you to the Clan, Alex." Then, "Where were your people from in Scotland, anyway?"

I told him my name comes from Inverness — that I went back once, got up in a tavern and announced I'd buy a pint for any Macdonald present. The whole place stood up, Mackenzies, MacKays, McLarens . . .

Thumper replied that in London, it's the Englishman who stands drinks all round. The Scotsman stands six foot four. Then he uncoiled his own six foot four with a cheerful, "Until we meet again!"

Since I spoke with Thumper, the dread "market forces" are snatching oats away from the Board's jurisdiction. Speculators will bid for oats at the growers' expense. There's a man with a hoarse voice and a sophisticated computer in the pit of the Chicago grain futures exchange. He's buying rye and canola and soybeans that are still in the ground. He's placing bets against a farmer — he makes a big score if drought or hunger push up the price.

There's an evil wind rustling the prairie grasses. Global economics are dethroning reason as the arbiter of how people live and get by. If they're not checked, they'll make people's futures for them, instead of people making their own futures.

Yes, back then, in Saskatchewan, the cradle of Canadian socialism, Tommy Douglas spoke of a better way to go. "Why," he used to ask, "must it be 'every man for himself,' as the elephant said as he danced among the chickens?"

Now the afternoon light is beginning to fall over the

flatlands. Saskatchewan is snow and dun – not as green as it should be. Bad warming winds? It may be too brown later on.

Sunlight filters down onto the prairies, irradiates the soil and escapes. But its escape is increasingly trapped by an invisible shield of man-made gasses and particles. Water tables fall. Where it once took 55 acres to feed a cow, it takes 200 today. A degree or two of temperature rise can return the Palliser Triangle in the southwest to the desert from which the settlers rescued it.

Yes, back then, the family farmers fought soil erosion and desiccation as best they could, like careful husbanders. They built dams and sloughs and windbreaks.

Now, the markets turn the heat on for quick returns – for maximum production, by capital investment and product specialization; on company farms with toxic pesticides, too much fertilizer, and foreclosures. The land and the farmer get it where it hurts. (Old T.C. Douglas used to tell of a sign in an early Trans-Canada Airlines plane: "Don't flush the toilet over the cities." Said Tommy: "The farmer always gets it in the neck.")

The Ukrainians who came from so far away to break the soil in Saskatchewan and Alberta couldn't foresee that today two forces – cooperation and acquisitiveness – would be locked in dubious battle on the plains.

In 1904, the first of the Fedyks burrowed in the sod near Vegreville, like ground-hogs, to keep body and soul together through the bitter winter. Their wealth was a team and a wagon, an axe, and a dog to run down tasty prairie chickens. Tillie Fedyk McGee (a Vancouver-East resident who helped me win my first election in that riding – I didn't run on the west side, where I live, being too well-known there) recalls, as a child, going 40 miles into Vegreville to exchange grain and vegetables for salt and sugar. Money was not the medium of exchange. Horses were scarce; the family had to train wild colts to travel to town, and her young brother was killed, caught in the harness of a runaway.

The Fedyks, parents and children, cleared three acres of poplar bush a year. A horse pulled out the stumps; the roots were pulled by bare hands. That was long before the oil patches – and long before Ukes were electable. Now, a hungry world needs the fertile prairies. That world is losing one hectare of arable land every fourteen seconds. Its population rises by 25 humans every ten seconds. It's a world where 37,000 children under the age of five die every year from malnutrition and preventable diseases.

To leave the land as rich as we found it – and the forests too. Surely it's possible, with forethought and planning?

Now, far beneath my 747, the Rockies are pushing up turbulently, reminding me of a summer I spent climbing their peaks. I was a helper on a geodetic survey party. That was long ago, when British Columbia seemed to be forever young. (And, at 15, I did too.)

Two of us would pack the transit, lights and batteries, food and tent, to the top of a snow cap. On clear nights, we'd point our lights at other transits on far-away peaks. Before dawn, we'd crawl through a sphincter in the tent, well anchored in the snow and rounded to withstand the winds. Supper we made on a portable coal-oil stove. In my sleeping bag, I surreptitiously tied myself up in my boot laces, for fear of sleep-walking in the snow and into some abyss. Nothing but an infinity of wooded mountains tumbled around us. In those days, this geography – if I thought about it at all – seemed too big for plundering.

Beyond the Rockies, the sun has dipped in the Pacific. B.C. lies below in a twilight zone, between its British past and multicultural future. Its three millionth child just born, and in lawful wedlock, yet! A province humming a harmonious tune – to be continued, I hope, with the help of a valuable value – no tolerance for intolerance.

Down, down, through the deregulated skies, I can just make out where Kelowna should be. Canadian Airlines flies the Kelowna-Kamloops-Vancouver routes. But with deregulation, five years ago, opportunity beckoned to a Mr. Barry Lapointe. With some government aid, he bought two Convairs, stretched them, and beat Canadian's price of $135 for a one-way ticket by charging only $105. This set off a price war until Canadian, with deeper pockets, offered a $35 fare! Lapointe was driven from the market. He flies freight now, I hear, to wherever.

What did this Darwinian price war do for consumers? Yes, it was great — for a while. But Canadian, and its employees, were wounded, making the airline easier prey for a foreign take-over.

Soon we're over the Coast Mountains with their rich mantles of timber. But the bearded giants of the coastal rain forests have pretty well fallen now. Yellow cedars 500 years in the growing have become tourist attractions. Old-growth Douglas fir is disappearing. Over-production is the rule. Without new priorities, a tripling of spending on forest conservation, skilled forest stewardship, B.C.'s chief industry faces catastrophe.

In 1906, my friend Wally Cook, faller and bullbucker, was born in Tent City, Jericho Beach, Vancouver. His mother, in her late 40s, delivered Wally with help from Dr. Pollen, who had an excellent name for a pediatrician. Wally first worked in the woods with "axe men," with "doggers" who hitched the logs with iron hooks, with "bull punchers" who prodded teams of yoked oxen. It took five men several days to fall and buck a forest giant. Today, one faller with a power saw can do it in two or three hours. Soon, B.C.'s fibre farms will be in great demand. How many forest acres does it take to publish an edition of *Playboy*? Or this Sunday's *New York Times*?

Now our plane is making a wide circle over the Strait of Georgia to land into the wind. I see Buccaneer Bay, on Thormanby Island, in the darkness. Dorothy and I have a cottage on that island, which is still much as nature made it.

Sixty years ago, fathers came to Thormanby to spend weekends with summering wives and children. They came on a single-stacker Union Steamship, the *Capilano*, which hoved to by the beach to the sound of children calling, "Daddy! Daddy!"

Today, travel to the island is by car, ferry, outboard. The Daddy Boat took a little longer to get there. But on its decks was leisurely congeniality, and it was easier on Mother Nature.

If you, gentle Reader, put your ear to the ground, you'll hear the Earth murmuring, "Gently! Gently, sister, gently, pray! Slow is better — less is more!"

Consider the lifestyle of the Canadian beaver. The beaver, our largest rodent, takes her time. A short day-shift, gathering sticks and mud for her dam; some tidbits for dinner; then off she (or he) paddles to play with the kits, crooning to them the song of the Lotus Eaters. "Why, oh why, should life all labour be?" We could sure use the beaver's philosophy to make the world go around. Work, like manure, should be evenly spread.

CHAPTER 3

Alex walks Parliament Hill where once he sat; hears money talking in whispers off-stage; sees Canadians sailing from Democracy (rule by the people) to Plutocracy (rule by the wealthy); and hollers, 'Reverse engines! Change course!'

Hey, dear Reader! I'm back here among the Hill people, observing their strange rites and practices. So glad to have you along, this chill February day in 1992.

What pulls me back to this Hill where I sat as an MP so long ago? I feel like a gambler who can't stay away from a roulette wheel, though he knows it's not working right.

Strange, the way I keep turning up here. You don't think that part of me yearns to run again for MP? Could be. The other day, I was in my old constituency, Vancouver East. Some old-timers came up. Instinctively, I stuck out my hand, like a candidate, and proceeded to introduce myself.

"I'm Alex Macdonald, used to be your MP."

"Oh, we know, Alex. We were just laughing about that. You going to run again?"

But all I say to them is, "Me? In my ember years? Run for the border perhaps, for the bathroom for sure..."

Still, I can dream ... How nice it would be to feel important again! But dreams aside, I know that sitting in Parliament now, I'd not have as much keenness and hope as I had years ago, when I was a young CCF Socialist member.

How old-fashioned my CCF colleagues were! They'd caucus and decide what was right to vote for, whether the voters followed them or not. That's how they came to be called "Canada's Conscience." But that was long ago, in a different space. Since then, my youthful idealism has taken a lot of punishment from hard realities.

Today, parliaments have two roles to play. First, they are the democratic bear pit where the great games of adversarial partisan politics are played; continuous election campaigning between elections. Second, parliaments are a forum for the deliberative, consultative search for answers to the needs of the times, let the votes fall where they may. These days, the first role obscures the second.

And worse. Democratic government itself is losing its power to do those things for people that they can't do for themselves. Control is slipping away into private corporate boardrooms and into the hands of politically strong interest groups.

And as for politics, more and more it's becoming a case of winning at the expense of leading.

How I carry on! By the way, gentle Reader, should you detect (most unlikely) a smidgeon of the old CCF self-righteousness in this writer – just put it down to his second youth. And if anything I say bewilders you, it simply means you are paying close attention.

If you're wondering how I travelled to Ottawa – alas, it was on my own slender means. Not ticketed by taxpayers, nor by lawyers – a year or two ago, I got a free trip here from the lawyers, to debate with John Crosbie before the annual convention of the Canadian Bar. What an experience!

I had to argue "that there are too many lawyers in Parliament." And before *that* jury! Judges, wannabe lawyers, benchers and sons of benchers. It was awful and I enjoyed every minute. Though what could I say? If I said lawyers do string things out, I'd be hooted. (Well, I did and I was.)

I'd have got off lighter if I'd said it takes one lawyer two minutes to change a light bulb and two lawyers twenty minutes to change one.

On the other side, oh horrors, was the minister of trade, John Crosbie. He only once alluded to the subject of debate, claiming there were only twelve lawyers (left?) in the cabinet. Then, eying me, he attacked socialism. "Like cod-liver oil," fulminated the Codfather. "Not pleasant to take but somehow supposed to be good for you; only good for keeping the old parties regular." And then, inebriated by his oratory, he attacked his own debating partner, Ray Hnatyshyn, then minister of justice, calling him a "spelling mistake."

Luckily, I had Jean Chretien as my partner. Speaking at once in both official languages, Jean said Crosbie himself was living proof that there are too many lawyers in parliament.

I'm off the point. Where was I? Oh, yes, power bleeding away from elected governments. Did I ever get a case of that on this trip, over coffee with Bill Blaikie, MP. He told me about a give-away by this parliament, just a while ago. A give-away of plant-breeder rights to private corporations. A bill was passed giving patent rights over seeds, pesticides, fertilizers . . . Now the companies are competing to patent anything biological, and trading patents amongst themselves. At the end of this process, what will we have? One big international bio-tech combine? How many competitors will be left?

During the debate, some company lobbyist asked an MP: "What's the difference between patenting a tomato and a light bulb?" None, as even dim bulbs know, in the blind eyes of mar- ket forces. And those forces won't quit. Germ plasmas, pat- ented genes, even fusing eggs to make geeps from sheep and goats; any life stuff discovered under the weird lights of their laboratories – all patentable simply as processes. Really scary interference with nature's laws.

We are backing into the future, gentle Reader. It was not

so long ago when Canadians were proud to see the University of Saskatchewan present canola seeds to a hungry world; when the Dominion Experimental Farm in Ottawa bred Marquis wheat as a public service – early maturing, resistant to rains, snows and cold.

Salaried Canadian researchers, as good as they come, unlocking nature's wonders. Must people be overpaid and underworked to do their best? Ridiculous! Certainly not Dr. Jonas Salk. He isolated the polio vaccine in his lab in 1955, and saved thousands of lives. But he wouldn't take royalties on his wonder drug, and insisted all qualified labs should have equal access to it. No patent-enriched shareholders.

Later that morning, I headed over to the office of Pat Nowlan, Conservative MP for the Annapolis Valley. Pat's my serve-and-smash tennis enemy, and one of the longest-serving members of parliament. He sometimes forgets to check his conscience at the door of the House. Pat's long political career is in deep trouble. He hasn't played the game of "follow your leader" like he was supposed to. He has broken his party's ranks and is paying the heavy price. Pat's trouble began way back in 1976, when he ran against a Mr. Brian Mulroney for the Conservative leadership, and was reported as saying, in Montréal, that "Brian's never been elected. Not even as dog-catcher in Westmount."

Comes 1984 and Pat is waiting his turn for the courtesy call on new PM Mulroney. A whisper to him from the PM's press secretary, Bill Fox: "Don't mention anything about dogcatchers." Wonderful, this long memory of some pols for anyone who has crossed them; combined, all too often, with the fine art of forgetting, when occasion calls.

Half way into the dog-house, Pat voted against his leader's Meech Lake accord. Now he might as well be in that cold northern lake, without the proverbial paddle.

(An aside. I used to drop in to see Ed Broadbent, the NDP leader. This time I have to miss his company. Ed has made a peaceful and a sweet retire. After testing positive for Meech, he has a government job in Montréal studying international affairs, of which there are quite a few. Not that Ed ascended to the cushiest of the Meech Valhallas. A Brian Smith made that pinnacle – a man who took my desk, car, etc., when he became attorney-general of B.C. This Brian got his Premier Zalm, who dislikes French on corn flake boxes, to walk on Meech Lake. For that feat, he got the thickest topping on his legislative pension: chairman of CN Railway, with its water hole in Paris. End of aside.)

Pat's political future may be behind him, but he's still his ebullient self.

"I can do without the perks that come with being in with your party whip," he says. "Okay. And so I'll not be on some committee that goes offshore to study democracy in Turkey. Okay. And so I'll not get on the list to be recognized in question period. But – and this is too much – now it's law that party leaders have to sign the nomination papers of anyone running for their party. And the PM has just said he won't sign for one of his MPs, Alex Kindy, because he voted against the GST."

"But you'd easily win renomination from your riding association, Pat."

"Sure, sure, Alex, but now I can't run without the PM's approval. That law is supposed to be about election expenses. In fact, it puts the bee on party members to toe the party line. Play up and play the game!"

(Which now sets yours truly to pondering that parliament, by some strange osmosis, is becoming like the commercial world outside. There, you say the wrong thing, break the conduct code, even the dress code, and your career track is muddied.)

To Pat, I replied: "Ah, but was it not ever thus? Didn't the Honourable Mikado sing 100 years ago:"

> When MPs in the House divide
> If they've a brain and cerebellum too,
> They have to leave their brains outside,
> And vote just as their Parties tell them to.

To which Pat responded: "No. It's getting worse."

And I got right off the point here (as I do sometimes), and said: "You know what, Pat? Our late Canadian philosopher George Grant wrote something like this: 'Socialism is a variant of conservatism. Each seeks to protect the public from private freedoms.' "

Then I added: "Almost twelve thirty! Are you taking lunch, Pat?"

When the parliamentary lunch bill is presented, I put my hand in my left pocket, only to be told by Pat that socialists keep their hearts on the left and their money on the right. Without missing a beat, I regaled him with the story of the Scot and the Irishman who had a genial meal until the bill arrived. Then the Scot was heard to say, "I'll luke afta thaat." The next day, a newspaper headline reported: SCOT SUES IRISHMAN FOR VENTRILOQUY. By this time, Pat had paid the bill.

Serve-and-Smash left to sit impatiently among the government backbenchers in the House. These are the lowest form of parliamentary life. Their leaders do not expect them to bark — just to wag their tails nicely from time to time.

As for me, I toddled off to the galleries to take in question period. Can't stay away. This hardened political sinner still loves the great game of politics, the players with their strut and fret, and their careful maneuvering to one-up their opponents.

Yes, I like question period — though, sadly, it's a show without surprises these days. As in a sit-com, you know what's coming. Governments take credit for good news; oppositions blame them for bad. Opposition members ask questions that are carefully drawn up so as not to offend any possible supporters. They wax indignant. Government ministers pride themselves on the artful way they dodge the questions. Still, if you listen patiently to what is *not* said, question period remains, digs and slurs withal, wit and half-wit, the centrepiece of democratic government.

I take my seat in the bleachers and munch my post-prandial cigar until there's a tap-tap on my shoulder by an attendant. No smoking – and no munching either, I'm told.

Gosh, last time I was here, my niece Mollie was with me. I remember her looking down and saying, "And this is where they *make* the laws?"

And her wise old uncle gently corrected: "No, this is where they *pass* the laws."

As I sit down, Bud Bird, MP, Fredericton, rises:

"I have the honour to present the report of the all-party parliamentary delegation to Brazil and Chile."

My, he looks well. I seem to recall last year a report from Pyongyang. It has been reliably estimated that 1.56 per cent of the world's 70,000 parliamentarians are airborne at any given moment . . .

Ah, now – Mr. Speaker rises in his throne with the pages to call "Questions." This you'd enjoy, Will Shakespeare, even though you said, "And this Great Stage presenteth naught but Shows." How could you know?

Sheila Copps is first up for the Liberals. She has matured since her brat-pack days, when hers was the longest shiv. She has ripened like an apple, and today wears her statesperson face. Still, she sure lights into the health minister. And she's on to a big, never-to-go-away Canadian issue: How much national funding of provincial social programs? What national controls?

Sheila: "This uncaring government – cutting medicare dollars to the provinces – strangling health plans – we know what you're up to – ten different plans – two or more tiers of health-care delivery – top for the rich, bottom for the poor."

She herself is arrayed in radiant virtues, like the lily. She is clad in worthy values: "balanced budgets ... low taxes .. . better services."

But, aha, see how she shies away from talking about how to raise the dollars. Bad politics, she figures, for the opposition to get into *that*.

The minister (or someone for him; I see only his back) genially replies with an "any dope knows better" air. "Transfer funds capped? Yes, but more 'tax points' for the provinces." No, I don't hear him say how this will net out in dollars to various health plans. Bad politics, he figures to get into *that*.

Alas, his z-z-z charisma is not up to Sheila's. I wish he'd say aloud what I can hear him saying to himself, through the back of his head: "Ding-a-ling! Off my back. I'll see you off! Change places, you'd be in my financial bind and you know it. And you know damn well, too, there's a global economy out there grinding down social services."

And up here, I hear (me to myself): "Feeling the heat from the well-heeled health industry lobby, aren't you, Mr. Minister? That industry hankers to run health in Canada as it does south of the line ... Hates, it does, to have to sell its lift-up beds, prosthetic legs, antibiotics, to one big buyer like the Ontario Medical Plan, that haggles over prices; prefers to knock over private hospitals that might even be owned by some dear associates. Crouched, that industry is, for a power grab."

And just imagine this. I see an old guy in front of his TV in Medicine Hat taking all this in. He's munching peanuts, talking to himself. "Hey, Sheila? Minister? Did either of you come clean? Each spotless, eh, and the other smudged? More to it than either of you let on. That's what I think."

Next come two new players. A high point in the theatre of democracy, Dave Barrett and John Crosbie get down for a go-to. When either of them borrows your ears, they don't let go. Not with them will parliament lose its audience.

The topic: Free trade – with Mexico, yet. And under cover of this exchange a timeless clash of philosophies.

Dave: "Mexico now, Latin America tomorrow? Do you know, Mr. Minister, that a Mexican factory turns out dashboards 36 seconds faster? Pays only $2.20 an hour? Is dirty? Has no company cafeteria? You're levelling down, not up, Mr. Minister."

Dave knows that rule, gentle Reader: Never ask a question in parliament unless you know the answer. And Crosbie knows the other rule: When in doubt, make up both question and answer.

Crosbie feigns indignation. He feints. "Where have you been? Don't you know I've just won a great Canadian victory: A seat under the table at the Mexican talks? Your question lacks decency, specificity and truth."

Loud claps from Conservative members. An approving smile (mouth, not eyes) from PM Brian Mulroney. Will that smile be the last we'll see of him, like the Cheshire cat's? At the same time, Brian is keeping one eye on Joe Clark, and Joe is keeping one eye on Brian. In parliament, your political opponents are across the aisle. Your political enemies sit around you.

Crosbie lifts off with gusts up to 130 words a minute. Talks in a Newfie brogue. I catch only the sense, not the words. But I can imagine what he's saying. "Unfettered markets! Their capricious effects are good for you! Praise the dollar! Study the Good Book intensively, as I do every night! Cupiditas, and Cupid, too!"

This is the man who said (in our debate), "The intelligence of politicians is so low, the voters have to stoop to reach it." But just try to lay a hand on Crosbie in debate! You're never sure when he's poking fun at you, himself – or both.

Still, under the question and answer lies a grave Canadian issue, one that's not going away.

Crosbie: "Let trade run free for more, better, cheaper

products; each country making what it makes best, using resources efficiently, uprooting domestic monopolies."

Barrett: "Let elected governments see to it that trade runs in ways that promote social objectives; the provision of fair employment opportunities, as well as inexpensive goods and services."

Of course, I'm with Barrett. Who's to run things? For what ends? Pat Carney, Crosbie's predecessor, told an Alberta audience that "What's good about U.S. free trade is that Canada can never again have a national energy policy. The agreement ties the hands of governments." Oh my!

Oil, gas, anything with a price, freely bought and sold anywhere, with free-flowing capital. That's what Free Trade is all about – the corporate agenda that only a social democratic alternative can stop.

Look, Reader! There's David Kilgour, MP from Edmonton. He can't sit still! He's itching to ask a question. Sat for ever so long as an independent, not on any party's lists to ask questions. De-listed, he'd been, by his own Conservative caucus for voting against the GST. Kilgour became an unperson, shopping for a party. Now, a Liberal at long last, he wants up.

But they're still afraid of him. David might bring up "double-dipping" again – i.e., MPs retiring into a plush government job to top up their parliamentary pensions. Bringing that up in this club is like suggesting skinny-dipping at a Methodist retreat.

And now a question of Barbara McDougall, minister for external affairs. Slowly she stirs. Was she dreaming of a run for Conservative leader?

"How come," asks an NDPer, "a U.S. nuclear sub is allowed to poke its nose into the Canadian waters of Dixon Entrance, on our north-west coast?"

"Another wahn," drawls Barbara. "But it's just acoustical testing, not nuclear." (You don't catch Barb with her briefings down.) "Ah-nyway, those subs have an excellent safety record." (Safe! Then what's their *raison d'être*?)

When Barbara was immigration minister, the Supreme Court of Canada, pushing its growing power against the authority of parliament, in an unlucid moment (a rare one, lucky for us) struck down Canada's internationally approved immigration procedures. Said our high court, inquiries by trained adjudicators into the merits of would-be new Canadians were just not good enough. No, all would-be's, if they somehow get to touch Canadian soil, must have an adversarial hearing and a lawyer at their elbows (or at least a "consultant" – with either, the cost is much the same, averaging $1,000 a case, usually paid by our treasury).

That decision set off an explosion in the immigration department. Seventy-five new "judges" had to be found, but quick. An extra $170 million had to be found. Legal truth, perhaps, but what consequences? Waiting lines of would-be's and refugees elongated exponentially. So long they grew that the government said, "Will all those waiting please sit down and stay. We're going to have to start all over again from scratch."

Some said this was one more case of individual rights trumping the public good. Others thought that the Court, with one deft stroke, had solved two nagging social problems – unemployment among lawyers and other legal beagles, and "judge" jobs ($80,000 a year) for restless Conservative Party stalwarts.

Yet here am I, worrying about someone, somewhere, badly wanting to be a Canadian, with all the merits, who can't get into any waiting line at all because of the congestion at the front of it. More law, dear Reader, sometimes brings less justice.

Oh, my. There's Alan Redway, glum in the back benches. Wants to get back his job as housing minister. Wants questions to *him*. He had a great fall from cabinet for telling a joke about guns at an airport security checkpoint.

Hey, Alan! Gun jokes are all right in the House – but not at airports. Jokes like the gun law passed in the House, leaving shotguns, rifles and semi-automatics still easy to buy. And limiting ammo clips on handguns to only ten shots – to improve marksmanship, I suppose. You'd think that Canada was trying to out-do Texas, where gun deaths have now surpassed auto fatalities.

Hey, William Kempling just came in. MP from Burlington, Ontario. He's the one who called Sheila Copps a slut, or something like that. Imagine that slur coming from an MP who believes the rooster should be removed from the hens on Sundays!

Oh, oh. There's Lucien Bouchard. Wants up too? He sits in a back corner of the House, after leaving the cabinet to join the separatist Bloc Québecois. He is no longer (can't be, now) the genial fellow I met in Paris when he was our Canadian ambassador. A separatist drawing federal cheques must not find much funny about anything. In fact, if nationalism is not serious business, it evaporates. Did I hear right? Who told me that the Bloc caucus had to "admonish" one of its members, who was caught smiling between meals?

Will you miss your Bloc colleague, Lucien Lapierre? Lucien is taking early retirement – at age 36 – to pursue a career in Montréal. His move is cushioned by his lifetime MP pension, worth $4 million if he takes care of himself.

Next, I see Kim Campbell rise, minister of justice. She's MP for my house, and – know what, Reader? – I'll be sorely tried not to vote for her (and not just because she came to my class to talk to my students). She repealed, mostly, the old consanguinity laws, which forbade a man from marrying his aunt, grandmother, etc. Now, a man can marry his own niece! (But Mollie, if you're reading this, not to worry, child! Your uncle is trying not to use a proposition to end this sentence with.)

Kim has climbed from school trustee to justice minister in five years. And still hungry? A political appetite that grows by what it feeds on? Photographed with naked shoulders above legal briefs – and naked ambition showing too? She has the leadership yen, all right – that quality sports stars call 'desire'.

Kim makes a serious announcement. She is allotting $5 million for an inquiry into the wrenchingly rising levels of abuse against women. Dawn Black, NDP, gets, I'd say, an assist on this. There were 100 murders of women, Dawn says, in Canada last year.

If your commissioners, Kim, get to the bottom of this rising violence, they'll radicalize themselves in the process. They'll find that greed economics running hog-wild has more than a little to do with it.

Ah, too bad. No question to Jean Charest, the environment minister. The beamish boy of the Conservative party. He sits quietly gazing into his political future. Good Franco-Irish looks. No need for Jean to pick homely colleagues to sit among to enhance his beauty. (A trick the Queen of Sheba used to use. She would sit between two baboons to highlight her own beauty.)

Question period is over. Now I'm downstairs in the foyer outside the House. After question period, it's media scrum time. Lights, cameras, mikes, notebooks in a jostling melee. Parliament's voice transmitted to the eyes and ears of the Canadian masses. MPs edging hopefully toward the limelight. The PM's back is seen ascending a staircase.

What will be the catch of the day, to serve for Canadians' supper?

I mosey over to Mr. Speaker's office. John Fraser leaves his throne right after question period, for relief. I take leave to drop in. After all, in the Scottish Hall in Vancouver, we are of the same visible ethnic minority.

John regards me as harmless and slow to mature, like

Limburger cheese. Last year I tendered this Mr. Speaker some sagacious Scottish advice. He's in a Charter pickle, what with no longer being able to open Commons sittings with a Christian prayer. Try, said I, the thanks of Clan Macdonald when the Chief takes his place at the head of the table: "Almighty God, grant that we may be worthy, in some sma' degree, of the esteem in which we hold ourselves. Amen." He doubted this would withstand Charter scrutiny.

Today John sits me down. Coffee is served. I am the soul of deference when I address Mr. Speaker. He is, you know, just a cut above, or below, a judge.

"Mr. Speaker," I put to him, "this old parliament you have working to rule – how old is it? Nine hundred years? Due, I'd think, for more than a tune-up; more like a major overhaul."

Mr. Speaker replies that the Committee on Standing Orders is modernizing procedures all the time, and new rules will improve the deportment of members.

"The deportment of members! The public seem to want that. Why, when I was in the gallery, some dingbat called another one 'crazy'. Can you call an MP 'crazy'? I thought you had to say 'eccentric'."

Mr. Speaker: "Order. You are employing unparliamentary language."

Me: "I withdraw the offending words. But [changing my course]... What do you say, Mr. Speaker, to David Kilgour? 'Presiding over,' he said you were, 'the most tightly disciplined parliament in the world.' Whips cracking whips, leaders anointing, striking committees, critics' roles ... like a boys' school, with prefects and fags, play up and play the game? Poor Kilgour lost his office space near the stairs for talking wrong. Couldn't get a flight to Moosomin, even without the wife or kids, until he joined the Liberal Party."

Mr. Speaker: "I hope you are not imputing unworthy motives."

Me: "Never! Not me! I'm imputing too much partisanship.

What are people saying about their MPs – 'Always at their party's call, never think for themselves at all.' "

Mr. Speaker: "That observation is older than you are. Let me say, we are changing the rules to allow more free votes in parliament . . . "

Me: "Your old parliament – "

Mr. Speaker, cutting me off: "You are becoming tedious and repetitious."

Me, persevering: "Your old parliament should have fixed term elections. Every four years on a set date. What kind of game allows one player, the PM, to call an election for the one moment he's popular and has a salable issue? Makes it easy, eh, for the government whip to keep his members in line: 'Vote as we say, or you'll be on the hustings facing angry voters.' "

Mr. Speaker: "But if a government were defeated in the four years, who would carry on?"

Me: "Oh, the House would just have to come up with another PM. After all, Mr. Speaker, it elected you, though it took twelve ballots and God knows how many hours to do it."

Mr. Speaker: "The last comment will be expunged."

Me: "And how many times have you been elected to parliament? Five terms? Six? Why not just two terms for MPs? Make 'em deliberate more, ingratiate less – "

Mr. Speaker: "My God, Alex, you'd end my career – retroactively!"

Me: "Another thing. Why doesn't Canada look at proportional representation? Europe, every new democracy goes for that. Not this first-past-the-post, where governments and candidates get elected by less than half the voters. Where there's an opinion, at least 5 per cent in a region, why shouldn't it elect 5 per cent of the seats? More parties in parliament! Say, two on the left, three on the right – even Greens. What's wrong with that?"

Mr. Speaker: "Your party would go for that? Doesn't it want strong government to ruin things in its own way? That's what you want, Alex."

Me: "... But where does that leave ... a Rhino friend of mine? He wants his ideas tested in parliament. He wants, oh yes, a law to make everyone drive on the left, not the right – introduced in stages. First for buses, then trucks, then cars. And let's see ... "

Mr. Speaker: "We need more nutmegs in parliament!"

Me: "Better fools than rogues. How many rogues have been found out in this one administration? Twelve? Fourteen? Even twelve fallen angels is more than bad luck."

Mr. Speaker: "I must admonish you."

Me: "Admonish all you like. Why, that all-party Board of Internal Economy ruled that *it* would decide when an MP was misappropriating public expense money. My hairdresser said this is a double standard!"

Mr. Speaker: "Order. You are making personal allusions. Where are the rogues now? Where are the bores? We are limiting speeches to fifteen minutes."

Me: "My God, Mr. Speaker. What are you doing? A good bore can't clear his throat in fifteen minutes. You'll drive them out to practise in country halls. It's started already. I heard of a large-calibre New Brunswick bore who droned on and on, addling his audience, numbing their buttocks. Even the chairman slumped beside him. On and on, until a farm hand at the back, sucking on a bottle of wine, was so frazzled he hurled his empty bottle at the bore, but hit the sleeping chairman instead – right between the eyes. There was the chairman, sinking slowly under the table, crying, 'Hit me again! I can still hear the swine.' "

Mr. Speaker: "Only in Canada."

I'd prescribe two pills for Canadian democracy. Old Doc Macdonald's remedies. Easy to swallow, if we have enough desire to clean up politics.

The first pill would dissolve the money in our money-politics. No more campaign "donations." None. In their place, modest public subsidies to parties and candidates for their leaflets, lawn signs, meeting halls and so on. But not for paid political TV hype ads! God, they're deceptive. Empty of content. Sound bites. Attack politics. Who needs them?

As it is, how many millions in special-interest donations does it take to form a government? The three parties raised $55.6 million in the 1988 general election. And how much does it take even to win some national party leaderships – two million? What, I ask you, is the difference between contributions and influence-peddling? A fine? Possibly. A fine line? That's for sure.

Who pays the piper? Rather, who'll be the pipers, and who the pipes?

(A Coquitlam alderman I know told my class one day that a municipal contractor had left $300 in an envelope under his door when the alderman was running for re-election. I advised him that, to avoid temptation, he should return the envelope to its sender, but with a note saying that $300 is too big for a gift and too small for a bribe.)

The other pill? Regulation – and funding – to assure full, fair, free-swinging, wide and deep political discussion. Panels. Inquisitions. Prime TV times, set aside as a condition of licences ... Who owns the airways, anyhow? Discussion monitored. And fostered by selected juries of respected citizens.

Newspapers, you ask? They need reforming. Two chains, Thomson and Southam, run almost all our English dailies, and are busy buying up all the weeklies and stuffing them with ad flyers. In Sweden, the state, of all things, subsidizes community weeklies to keep them alive and discussing, and with lively political debate on their pages. And all parties support the subsidies.

In short: competitive flows of information. Pluralities of news outlets. But our political discourse as just another unregulated market-activity? Democracy can't afford that price.

The demand for political truth, patient Reader, exceeds the supply. Shouldn't it be the other way round?

CHAPTER 4

Alex tipples while Maz fiddles. Moosehead goes down better than Maz's budget does in Moosomin (Saskatchewan) or Moosonee (Ontario). The Moose and the author engage in a lively exchange, leaving uncertain which has the better head.

"Sit," Jim Fulton tells me.

For heaven's sake, gentle Reader – to his dog he shouldn't talk like that.

"Sit!" he repeats. "Here in my office. In front of the television. You watch the budget speech here while I listen to it in the House."

It is February 25, 1992, and I take off my rubbers and sit, obedient and polite to a fault.

Fulton fulminates further. "If you've watched one Conservative budget, you've seen them all. In fact, you will get a glimpse of *every* Canadian budget that's ever to come, as long as we have this go-for-it economy. And you'll have something to tell your grandsons about how their country is keeping house."

Thank goodness he didn't make me go to the House and sit in the gallery. I doubt if I could take this budget live. But here, it will be all right – especially with Jim pointing to the fridge and saying, "There's Moosehead there. Help yourself in the event the budget disagrees with you."

So here I am, in an office stacked and strewn with books,

papers, reports, memorabilia, and articles of clothing. Like a windstorm had struck. I have to make a clearing on his desk for my scribbling pad.

By the way, Jim's head used to be as shaggy as his office. But now — have you caught him recently on TV? He looks awful. He has shaved off his bushy moustache. He did this, he says, at the insistence of his infant daughter, who wanted to see what her father looked like. Shaving revealed a perfect rhetorician's face — perfect for radio, that is. I told him that words out of the mouths of babes and sucklings should be taken with a grain of salt.

"Have you forgotten, Jim, that politics is optical illusion? Look at your great grandfathers, the ones you're so proud of, hanging on the wall. Both shaggy! One a Mitchell, premier of New Brunswick, a Father of Confederation. The other a Stewart, premier of Prince Edward Island. Not barefaced, either one of them, are they? And don't listen either to those spin doctors — 'to merchandise a candidate, first shave off the moustache.'"

Jim was silent.

On the TV screen I see MPs trickling in. Budget Day. Lights, cameras. Ah, this amber brew has a pleasant taste. You have a better head on you, Moose, than most I see on this screen. As good a head on you as the Conservative house leader, Harvie André, with his pit-bull good looks. He's up now, arguing a point of order — some errant MP has made "improper and unparliamentary remarks about 'the other place'" (i.e., the senate — and about time too).

No way, Moose, can anyone call Harvie homely. In fact, it is no longer correct to call anyone homely. "Facially challenged"? Yes, you can still say that. But not of André. His face, mouth curling down at the corners, is one people remember long after he has left the room.

Now well-coifed Marcel Prudhomme enters. He is a lifer, having already served six consecutive terms. As he moves slowly to his desk, he throws quick, surreptitious glances toward the public galleries. "Am I noticed?" Ah, the pol's ache for recognition. How I miss it!

Meanwhile – look! There's the finance minister himself, Don Mazankowski. He sits at his desk, papers spread out, quietly minding other people's business. He can't deliver his budget speech until the speculators finish flipping on the stock exchanges. Any time now. (I take a precautionary sip of the Moose. Any minute now, this man will be taking important steps in the wrong direction.)

Now – oh, oh! A buzz and flutter in the chamber. Prime Minister Brian Mulroney makes has entrance. His smile betrays an infinite capacity for taking praise. His followers smile back – at least those who obey the 11th Commandment: "Thou shalt not even *think* ill of your leader."

I sit and ponder. What will I be able to tell my grandsons about this budget when they grow some? That it gives them more control over their destinies, or less? I can't pretend that it's easy these days for nations to direct their own fortunes. Three forces are sweeping this old world, tossing nations on their waves: more openness to trade; money sloshing across national boundaries; multinational corporations growing in power and wealth.

But does this mean we must say goodbye to the dream of national good housekeeping? No. Pick up and use, O Mighty Maz, the tools we still have to make democracy effective!

This brew I quaff – from our sudsy Maritimes – are you a vanishing Canadian species, O Moosehead? My heart goes out to you. I peer into your future, and see, yes, a definite need for some life support. I see dangers.

I see a Prairie farmer driving a truckload of barley to market. His truckload can fill a million bottles of beer. But this farmer is getting for it a go-broke, sell-the-farm $6,000.

I see, south of the line, a big vat company, Anheuser-Busch, with already 42 per cent of the American beer market. Multiple brews. Sly sales forces. Slick ads. (Is Miller Time catching up? They had an ad budget of $100 million last year. And, though a blind-taster can't tell one brand from the other, he can read the ads.)

They are watching you warily, Moose, the big beer conglomerates. Discounted prices for a while, to make you see reason ... Then, an offer you can't refuse? A few conglomerates can souse the whole western world, plus Africa; their consoles automating workers out of work.

And I see an off-the-wall, well fee'd, Harvard business "expert" – just listen to him! "Lower the GATT! Free up trade! Get mean and lean!" (Even as your competition gets leaner and meaner, eh?) As if, idiot, production was still the problem! Distribution is the problem, and people having the wherewithal to buy.

Seriously now, you so-called "experts," what is the purpose of economics in these days of over-capacity? Not profits, surely. The purpose should be people working, and growing things, for fair returns. Along with satisfied stomachs, of course.

So, Moose, what can I say for you? Some national economic management, please. To let Canadians brew some, and import some. There's nothing all that wrong with you, Moose! Why, in the British House of Commons, what did a British Labour MP reply to Lady Astor when that lady was on a temperance kick, saying beer would ruin your stomach? Tipsily he replied, "I've been drinking beer for 45 years, and I'll put my stomach against yours any old time."

Ah, the camera picks up Jim Fulton taking his seat. He gives Mr. Speaker a polite bow, and gets a nod back. Nice. Not long ago, the speaker put Jim in Coventry for calling the PM a sycophant and refusing to withdraw. Was that so bad? Jim told me later that sycophant simply means toady, a servile flatterer – or, in ancient Greece, a fig shower-offer. Nevertheless, I admonished Jim with the words of Confucius: "He who throws mud loses ground." And I added my own warning: "When you tell the truth about someone in parliament, they may get really annoyed." Anyway, now, Jim and the Speaker can't say enough about each other.

Jim sits beside "the Honourable" Lorne Nystrom, MP, the NDP's constitutional critic. Lorne tracked the PM's constitutional spoor for so long that Brian turned around and made him a member of the Queen's Privy Council. Now Lorne is the only plain MP to be called "Honourable". And he will never look the same again.

At last. The stock markets are down – and the Maz is up. He's a picture in Tory blue – blue telegenic suit, tie, shirt. Michael Wilson sits at his right, once finance minister, now clutching the trade portfolio. Now I'm wondering – is Maz wearing one of Michael's old suits? Will Maz reach down to pull up his stocks, the way Michael did? Will Maz use Michael's words? *That* I can bet on!

Maz and Michael are straight arrows in a government where a score of ministers have had to hire lawyers. Maz was a Vegreville used-car dealer 25 years ago, but you can see that his hands aren't blackened from turning back odometers. Or even from taking them right out. As I say, a straight arrow.

Now he begins this speech with something about "tightly controlled spending." Already this man is afraid that money will find its way into the wrong hands. And "free competition," as if *that's* what the big boys really want.

I'm calling some time out, Reader. How much of this "stiff competition" is good for your tender ears? How much of this "get the jump on whomever" is too much? Budgets reflect and impart attitudes. Where in this budget are the other values – cooperation, concern? And where are the proposals to advance those saving values?

Oh no! Can it be? Even our Maz is having trouble swallowing some of his own "free market" stuff. Well, take a look at his face – never mind his words. For years he was minister of farms. This poor fellow has to support free markets and marketing boards at the same time! No wonder I can't tell if he's smiling or scowling. He's like a man in an acute bout of schizophrenia.

Hey, Maz! Stop listening to Michael! Take this Wilson guy aside and tell him little Norway subsidizes marginal farming and fishing communities to keep them going. Ask him if he really thinks that means those farms are "inefficient." Tell him it's a darn sight more "efficient" *not* to let those farms go under; with Mom and Pop Farmer drifting to some city, maybe on to welfare, breaking up the family...

And Maz, tell Wilson that when Norwegians decide themselves the fate of their communities – instead of leaving their fate to blind, unpredictable forces – they feel better about being Norwegians. While in Canada – what do my sad eyes see, Moose? They see weakening public powers to decide; governments "retaining but a quantity of power, which bleeds away, even as a form of wax resolveth from its figure 'gainst the fire." I borrowed that from King John.

What's that, penny-wise Reader? Marketing boards bother you? You can go twenty miles across the border where milk costs a third less? All right. Agreed. Our boards need consumer reps on them to strike a fair balance between producers and consumers. But *please* don't interrupt me like this... I can't go into that now.

I'm still talking to you, Maz! Tell Wilson to leave his "free trade" luggage at home when he travels – to GATT conferences, free-trade confabulations, World Bank meetings, and so on. Those bodies are run by bankers and tycoons who naturally want a world order that suits their interests. I mean, is there only one way to trade? Does Wilson think "supply management" can't work between countries? What nonsense!

Try selling rice to Japan. She'll be the No. 1 economic

powerhouse in five to ten years, and not by practising "free trade." It practises – well, what would you call it? Capitalistic socialism? Which is definitely the worst kind of socialism. While Canada, unless it wakes up, soon won't be milling any of its grain into flour.

Oops. Maz has skipped ahead of me. Never mind; dull stuff anyway. Who says it's better to be dull than dotty? Certainly not me, Moose. But hang on – listen to this! Maz is talking:

"We will provide $100 million to the provinces to cover increased drug prices in Pharmacare and medical plans."

My goodness! Those hiked drug prices'll cost provincial health and hospital plans a cool $500 million next year! Yet clapping greets this from all the Conservative members. "To cover increased drug prices." What *are* you saying, Maz? Your own government, just last year, helped the big drug companies to increase those prices. And what are you saying now? Is it something in the water?

I will remind you. They came to Ottawa, the international drug conspiracy, demanding longer monopoly protection for their patented brand-name drugs. They wanted to drive out of the market the cheaper generic substitutes that work quite as well. Why, Mr. Maz, did you not just say "no" to *these* drug pushers?

If you look south of the border, you'll see there the big pharmaceutical companies really have government on the run. They have patent protection there for twenty years. (In Japan, they have no patent protection.) So, no surprise, Americans pay a third to half more for their drugs than the average world price. One, a sedative I sometimes employ, Xanax – a sedative that works better than your speech, Maz m'boy – well, the Upjohn Corp. charges $37.50 or so for 50 Xanax tablets in the U.S., while it costs $16.50 elsewhere. Why, Maz, didn't you say "up" to Upjohn, and "fie" to Pfizer?

Oh, I know your so-called defence. When the drug lobbyists swarmed in Ottawa last year demanding seventeen-year protection, your government only upped it to ten years. This year, they demanded twenty and you only gave them seventeen. For shame! I find you guilty! Guilty of committing a typical Canadian compromise. Read the Good Book, for heaven's sake: "Because thou art neither hot nor cold," saith the Lord, "will I spew thee from my mouth."

And guilty, too, Mazzy, on another count. Why did you let your government put our pride and joy, our Connaught Biosciences Laboratories, like a slave on the auction block, to be sold to the international drug cartel? This University of Toronto lab, which gave the world insulin as well as vaccines against polio, rabies and the flu. A money-making business, in the black, solid! Sold to Institut Merieux of France, its HQ moved from 55 University Avenue, Toronto, to somewhere in the Netherlands, its scientists terminated. Come to think of it, that Institut Merieux is controlled by the French state. Can the French be smarter than Canadians?

Suddenly, I hear the Moose clearing his throat. You have something to add, Moose? "Yes, indeed," he harrumphs. "Just tell your pals that half of what you pay those private drug pushers goes for 'selling costs' — like taking my vet to a spa, or running ads that'd land anyone else in jail for consumer fraud."

"Where'd you hear that, Moose?" I ask. "Have you been drinking? You're not supposed to horn in like this." But the Moose has clammed up, so I turn back to the budget.

Now Maz is telling us that "the cause of this recession was a build-up of inflation." He's right, Moose. This Maz is obviously off the drugs now. True, he doesn't quite say, "I *have* to use unemployment to fight inflation." That would be too blunt. But he comes close.

How will I ever be able to explain his economic mum-

bo-jumbo to my growing grand-boys? Economists make their
black art complicated so they can make a living by pretending to understand it! It's simply rules made by the strong
to have and to hold their privileges. It's just a stick to use
– and to be put to much better use than it is now.

Again the Moose butts in. "I once heard John Crosbie
say, in Dildo, Nfld., on October 3, 1990, that a man without
a stick is even bitten by a sheep. Canada has sticks. So
why don't we use 'em?"

I ignore this presumptuous statement, which seems off the
point anyway. I decide to put Maz's economic theories to my
grandsons like this. "We're on a merry-go-round, boys, that
we can't seem to get off. Round and round we go . . . "

○ First, unemployment rises to well over one million.
   That's too high even for employers who don't like
   full employment because secure workers demand
   living wages. And so . . .
○ The Bank of Canada lowers interest rates. As a result
   of which . . .
○ Foreign capital flees! The dollar falls! Foreign capital
   buys more of Canada with cheaper dollars (with
   Canada now paying to foreign owners some $3 mil-
   lion an hour in dividends, interest, and fees)! Canada
   exports more (although for less). Employment rises,
   and so do prices. Back to the medicine cabinet . . .
○ The Bank of Canada raises interest rates to fight
   inflation with recession and unemployment – until .
   . .
○ We go back to the beginning and start again.

How do we get off this carousel? There is only one way.
The path to full employment without inflation is impossible
without a firm incomes policy, consensual or statutory, set-

ting income and price guidelines and coming down hard on rapacious rip-offs.

Moose, do you have something to say? "Yes!" The beast is practically shouting. "You can't have jobs for all while the lucky, the smart and the shady pull in whatever they can get away with. What fools those bipeds be, if they don't understand that!"

"Well, Moose," I say. I feel I have to defend my species. "Lots of us aren't keen on workand income-sharing."

"So what!" comes the reply. "You can't make an omelette without ruffling feathers."

But back to the business at hand. On the tube, our Maz is talking about more "spending cuts." And he's saying this budget of his will be a "painful" one. Not to the well-off, it won't be.

The word "painful" startles John Crosbie out of his reverie. He seems to be in some pain himself, as if he were passing Hibernian gas. I know why. He is thinking of the budget he delivered in 1979. He called that budget one of "short-term pain for long-term gain." And it did bring a painful end to Joe Clark's short-term government, which only lasted eight months. "Too short," John says. "It gave us time to conceive but not to deliver."

Take it easy, John! Slip back into your reverie. You have "pain for gain" Maggie Thatcher on your side. In fact, Maggie proclaims that "if it's not hurting, it's not working." Maybe she has something there.

But what's the "pain" Maz's into? (We'll have to start calling him Maz the Maz-ochist.) Hey, listen to this! Cuts in housing — of all things. What *is* in that glass he's sipping from? What? He's saying that "the 15-per-cent reduction for social housing will have to be continued."

Oh, yes, he "regrets" this cut, the Maz does, and I believe him. I can tell when a politician is sincere. His body language falls into sync with what he's saying. Maz does know that housing cuts undermine the "family values" he holds so dear. He asks himself (and so do I), what chance do children have to pick up good civic virtues growing up in homes where half the income goes to meet the rent? Homes waiting for eviction notices? A healthy society must provide healthy, affordable homes.

And it's true, Mr. Mazankowski – as you say, your financial cupboard is bare. Your debt grows by $57,000 a minute.

Sometimes a sneaking admiration for Michael Wilson comes over me. It's his gumption. Didn't this man stand in the ditch defending the ghastly Goods and Services Tax against slings and arrows from all directions? He even said this tax would be "revenue neutral," manfully lying for his country – like a diplomat. No social democracy can support decent social programs without a value-added tax. None. And if the guy who buys a Jaguar pays ten times more tax than someone who buys a used Datsun, who am I to quarrel with that?

But where was I? Oh, yes. There is something really wrong when a society increasingly prices young families out of a home of their own. When young families are less well-off than their elders; when their real incomes slip by 18 per cent in the past twenty years.

Part of the trouble began . . . Well, listen to this. An old friend of mine, Leviticus he was called, saw this house price spiral coming. He warned the ancient Israelites to hang onto their land – lease it out, even for lifetimes, if they had to – but sell it off, never. "The land shalt not be sold forever," saith the Lord, "for the land is mine."

Well, sorry old boy – it has been sold off. Though there's still quite a lot we can do about it.

Another by-the-way – well, it is about housing, a point Leviticus missed. This free flow of capital is for the birds! To illustrate:

The Maz (and Michael too) has this loadsa-money Tory

pal, Frank Stronach, of Magna International, auto parts. Frank has just invested $55 million of Magna's capital in a ski slope in Colorado, a rich and famous playland of condos and townhouses that go for $2 to $3 million apiece and come complete with servant's quarters. What I want to know is – whose capital was it? Management helped create it, I agree. Government did too, what with grants, write-offs, etc. The community helped, with various public services. Workers, too, some investing twenty years, never far from a pink slip. So, Frank, I'm saying that was "social capital," and the rest of us should have some right to see that it goes where it will do the most good.

Uh-oh, what's bugging the Moose? He's snorting, "Play-pens, for a fortunate few... Don't these guys know by now that capitalism supplies things in the wrong order?"

I try to settle him down, saying, "Oh, well, nothing like a dry speech to raise a thirst, Moose. Aye, I'll taste some barley bree."

But all of a sudden, I snap to attention. What! Oh, my, now my man Maz has fallen into boasting. "The privatization of Petro-Canada will proceed." This to loud Tory applause and, off-stage, applause too from the Imperial Government of Oil. But no heckles from opposition members – strange. It's bad form to heckle during budgets, when something really holy – like money – is being discussed. And parliaments soon seduce new members into their old ways.

Maz, his chest puffed out, continues: "This government has privatized or dissolved twenty crown corporations with 80,000 employees." Even a man on screech wouldn't crow about that! Feel some shame, Maz, old fellow. You have sold off my share in Air Canada that I was leaving to my grandsons. "To reduce government waste," you say? When you're on the tennis courts, then you can say you're reducing government waist... Oh, Maz! You're driving me to make awful puns!

So you are privatizing and deregulating the skies, are

you? The Moose knows where that goes. Air Canada bought
by some big air carrier – to become, I'd guess, a branch
line of U.S. Air. And the poor Frequent Flyer – passing
through the gate of one of the few surviving carriers – will
no longer fly as the crow flies. He'll fly into a "hub" and
out on a "spoke." Going to Toronto, eh? Chances are, you'll
lose your bag in Minneapolis. Bargain rates? That was yesterday. My God, will I fly some day from Vancouver to Chilli-
wack on Korean Airlines – via Denver?

This man Maz keeps giving public ownership a bad name.
What kind of values is he promoting? A public company is
more apt to make decisions based on moral incentives than
a private company is. I'm getting sick of so much of this
other "value": that is, make money; make more money with
more money; make lots of money with lots of money. I
need relief, Moose, which luckily is at hand.

And besides – I should send Maz a note on this via a
page – *publicly owned* French trains throttle along at 125 miles
per hour, slick and comfy. That takes some beating.

And, Maz, keep an eye on that crazy Scot sitting beside
you. The Honourable John McDermid, the minister of privatization. He's had a rush of right-wing ideology to his head.
He smiles as you speak. That Scot will privatize the parliament buildings if you don't watch out. Sell them to a Japanese millionaire and lease 'em back. He'll privatize your own
prime minister before the people get a chance to do it
themselves.

And I wish that MP there – I think he's from Alberta –
wouldn't clap every time he hears the word "privatization."
Has he finished his lines? He threw a racial slur a while
back and Mr. Speaker ordered him to do 100 lines. What
did Chairman Mao say, in his Little Red Book? "It doesn't
matter if a cat is white or black, as long as it catches mice."

Here the Moose pipes up, with yet another thoughtful
comment. "That man can clap, but he should not talk. He's

an MP who should remain silent and appear wise, rather than open his mouth and remove all doubt."

As for privatization – don't these Conservatives know that private conglomerates are privatizing Canadian industry in their own way every day? And making off quickly enough across the border with bits and pieces of it, without the government lending a hand?

Item: Can't you just hear those Gillette corporate potentates musing: "Hmm – if Canada is open for business, why make razors, creams and foams in Canada? We can make as much or more manufacturing them down here and shipping them north. So let's shut down Gillette Canada."

But – those same potentates: "Those Russian communists won't let us give them a close shave, unless we open a co-ownership branch in Moscow. Hmm – figure we can't uproot a branch where the locals have equity. Smart Bullsheviks! But, yes, we'll do their deal."

(By the by, Reader, a Germanic friend of mine just bought a razor made by the Braun company, only to find that German Braun had been bought out by Gillette. And the darn razor was made in Chile!)

Item: Amoco of Chicago buys Canada's bankrupt Dome Petroleum. Amoco is attracted by the "buried treasure" in Dome's books. How's that? Yes, attracted by Dome's losses that it can deduct against other profits. But whose "tax losses" were they, anyhow? Why, they really belong to Canadian taxpayers, who gave Dome tax breaks, outsize depletion allowances, exploration grants . . .

(Incidentally, a Scottish import, one Howard Macdonald, sold Dome to Amoco. Hey, McDermid, why didn't you see this Scot coming? For running Dome into the red and selling it, this Mac flew back to Scotland with a good-bye golden handshake of $5.3 million! Stop these hold-ups! Call 911, McDermid!)

Item: Goodyear (U.S.) Inc. retires its Ontario tire factory, throwing 2,000 out of work. Meanwhile, Michelin (France) is buying Goodyear; Continental (Germany) is buying General Tire; and Bridgetown (Japan) is buying Firestone (on the way to buying them all?).

Tell them, please, Maz! – would you listen to me for one minute? – tell them a country that burns tires might just want to decide for itself whether to make some, even if they do cost a bit more. After all, Canada has an Auto Pact, which still provides that Canadians make three-quarters of the cars they drive. Why not other pacts – sector by sector – planned trade? Surely we have the bargaining strength to make fair arrangements with countries that badly want to sell in our market.

The Moose, clearly not paying attention, sticks his oar in. "All wealth comes from labour. Milling barley, tuning a violin. Those who can contribute to the production of real wealth, and do not, are thieves."

"Hush, Moose," I mutter. "You've gone too far now."

Meanwhile, back in the House . . . What's this? Maz says "freeze." Zero raise this year for the public service. The word "freeze" makes an MP from Northern Québec sit up. It may remind him of home. He claps – other Tories join in, puzzled. I suspect this Québec MP simply wants to be noticed. He's just back from an Inter-Parliamentary Conference of the Francophone Countries. This conference was supposed to be in Kinshasa, but was moved to Paris owing to human-rights abuses in Zaire, which is a recipient of Canadian aid, I might add. Why didn't they stick with Zaire, where the human-rights flag needs raising? Why Paris? Why not Harare? I feel sorry for this MP – my, he looks tired. And horizontally challenged.

The Maz is freezing, all right. He's frozen the tax-free $6,000 for hotels and meals that MPs have just awarded themselves. He's frozen the single parent at the bottom of the salary scale as fast as he's frozen the mandarins at the very top of the scale. Our Maz argues that union strength can't be allowed to set government's social priorities. He has a point there, but if I were his speech-writer (who writes his stuff, anyway?), I'd have him talking like this:

Minister of Finance: "Honourable Members of all sorts. We must *thaw* privilege and wealth! [Applause.] Canada has three classes, two too many. We have the 'haves,' the 'have-nots' and the 'have-lots.' One should be sufficient." [Cries of "two too many!"]

"What's more, this country must see the break of a new day in labour relations. Who benefits from the internecine warfare between capital and working people? Not the common weal. The strongest do too well and the weakest line up at the food banks. There should be a third presence at our bargaining tables, to advance union security for all, and the shared national objectives of social equality, as well as productivity. A stool should have three legs! [Stormy claps. Cries of 'Three legs!'] Why, I ask you, should a senior law partner in Toronto make 75 times more than the janitor who vacuums his carpet?" [Cry from an Hon. Toronto Tory: "Why? Tell us why?"]

"A little bird tells me that the two heads of Massey-Ferguson made $4.7 million (U.S.) a year for changing its name to Varity Co. and its country to the U.S.A. Why is it a crime in Ontario to reveal executives' incomes? It should be a crime to *conceal* them." [Cries of "Let the punishment fit the crime!"]

"My country, for thee, I will apply the GST . . . to stockbrokers' commissions! [Light applause, some consternation.] And take the GST off words! Eyes drink from printed pages!

"A Bronfman complains that, while it is hard to make $100 into $110, it is too easy to make $100 million into $110 million. We must speed to his relief, Honourable Members. What? Shall a Bronfman bottle and cap the Moose?" [Cries of "No! No!" Great indignation.] (The Moose, muttering: "Those cats never met a mouse they didn't like.")

"Must rich estates be frittered away on their heirs? Must

rich men trudge toll-free through the Pearly Gates without mentioning Canada in their wills?" [Cries of "Lighten their loads!"]

The minister sips and sits. Tumultuous applause. Cries of "Author! Author!" I stand and, smiling, bow graciously.

Later that day I called on Senator Philippe Gigantes. He had offered to give me a copy of his senate committee's report, *Only Work Works*. You should read it, Reader. This report is social dynamite. It sets out one practical way to make jobs available for all who can work. And *that* should be the first priority of any good society. (The Moose hinted at this, back in Fulton's office.)

Philippe Gigantes is an ethnic Greek, and a philosopher who can argue with the best of them that the table disappears when you turn your back on it. He is also an author of notable books, in English and French. (It is simply a rumour, and should not be repeated, that Philippe got a free French translation of his last book by reading it aloud during a senate filibuster.) All in all, Philippe remains a useful citizen, in spite of his appointment to the Canadian senate.

He courteously seats me by the fireplace in his office, points out the models of ships of all ages that decorate his shelves, and gives me a copy of *Only Work Works*. He tells me the report shows that, taking into account lost taxes, it costs governments as much to look after the unemployed with UIC, welfare and so on, as it would to create useful jobs at a fair wage.

He gives an example. A single parent with two children on welfare in Ontario receives $18,500 a year, plus the GST low-income credit. This money could create a tax-paying job at $12 an hour!

To this I reply: "True enough, Philippe. But this is subversive stuff. I've come to the sad conclusion that this economic system of ours depends upon a large pool of unemployed, rising and falling. Without that pool, inflation would soar. What you'll be into – and you can't stop just with full employment – are price, profit and income guidelines. In other words, social democratic planning. And that, Philippe, coming from a senator, is distinctly subversive."

The old fellow pretends not to hear me. "And I have not," he continues, "when I said no extra cost to governments, included what governments would save – the hidden costs of involuntary idleness that show up in hospital budgets, prisons, stress, depression. Nor have I included the humanitarian savings from creating jobs – savings that can't be measured in dollars, savings of personal self-esteem. Most people can't feel happy if they aren't useful, contributing to society."

This calls to my mind one of my legal cases. The parole people had taken a chance and let a hardened youngish con – guns, drugs, gangs – out of prison in Agassiz to look after a disabled child, a foster-home child, one the con had never seen before. When the child, a small freckled 9-year-old with cerebral palsy, pulled himself across the floor to greet this con – well, the con experienced some rehabilitation. I didn't think he'd hurt anyone again.

Philippe is still talking, getting downright socialistic. Now he's on to what our common store of wealth loses when idle people can't make things or render services. "Unmet social needs, we'll always have them," he's saying. "Parks to tend, trees to plant, pollution to clean up, even illiteracy to eradicate. Why not a civilian Conservation Corps, something like the Peace Corps?" Finally, the old fellow comes to his climax. "Your point, Alex, about inflation – yes, the social partners must get together. Governments, labour, management – they must cooperate to lay out fair guidelines, spreading work and incomes fairly."

My goodness, Reader. I've uncovered some sort of radical in the Canadian senate! Perhaps even a socialist mole, burrowing from within. And one who doesn't keep his head down – not like the hairless rat-mole that always stays underground.

He even remembers my speech on the constitution. Good on the whole, he says, although he thinks I missed some good stopping points. "One thing I especially agree on," he tells me, "is that we have to have national laws on the big things that affect all Canadians. But local traditions and customs should do the administering. That'll help keep the country together. Of course, bureaucracies will resist that, as you said. They grow inwardly and outwardly, as you know."

I try to hide my pleasure at these compliments. "Private bureaucracies grow too, when they can get away with it," I say.

He continues, ignoring me. "Take the Canadian army. In World War II, there were twelve privates for every officer. Now there are two officers for every private." Sounds like the British navy, where every time a ship went down, they appointed a new admiral.

Unless incomes and work are spread pretty evenly – the way you manure your lawn, Reader – this economy of ours seizes up.

CHAPTER 5

Alex, suffering exquisitely, does a London pub crawl,
wondering which way Canada, drift or steer? He plays
referee and declares the late Bea a knockout winner
over the Blessed Maggie.

You will have noticed, percipient Reader (at least, if you're
old enough), the radical right revolution of our times. In the
past forty-odd years, persons of wealth and influence have
captured the political centre and carried it far to the right.
My God, they've hauled centre plate into right field, leaving
me, with my liberal-socialist ideas, stranded like a beached
beluga, babbling quaintly in an archaic tongue.

Bear with me, and I'll take you tripping to the very birth-
place of the revolt of the right. With the help of some levity,
I want to shift the political centre back where it belongs,
and reinstate social democracy's durable goals.

It is June 1992, and Dorothy and I pitch up in Thatcherland. (As I passed through customs, an officer asked me if
I'd anything to declare. Said I, "I declare I'm against Star
Wars," and was waved through like an honoured guest. Just
proves that most customs officers are socialists.)

Thanks to Dorothy's connections (she's come to attend
the Royal Commonwealth Society's annual meeting), we stay
at the society's clubby digs near Trafalgar Square. One of
its delights is the magnificent British breakfast – kippers,

back bacon and blood pudding – eaten in the club's dining room among masticating RCS members of a certain age and political stripe, their faces buried in the London *Telegraph*'s righteous pages.

On our first London morning, Dorothy rushes off to her meeting. Wimbledon's on, but I've more serious matters on my mind, and I head for the parliament buildings at Westminster.

Walking down Whitehall, I catch a whiff of the battle of ideas raging in Britain. The tenets of this ideological melee have become the nation's chief export. From Addis Ababa to Toronto, these concepts flourish, not only challenging the way we think, but how we dress and eat and behave.

Like rival tennis players, proponents of these two beliefs face each other across the net. On one side of the court is Beatrice Webb, that hoary old 19th-century socialist and south-paw, backed up by others of her ilk: G.B. Shaw, R.H. Tawney, Jennie Lee, Harold Laski. Bea and her pals wanted, as she said in 1906, "To give mankind an ever-increasing control of the forces amid which it lives – away from anarchic profit-making."

Lately, Webb's principles have taken an awful drubbing, losing six-love in every game. But she and her cohorts have rallied bravely, racquets in hand, ready for the counter-attack.

On the other side of the court, Margaret Thatcher crouches, ready to slam back anything her opponents send her. Also known as "Herself" and "the Iron Lady," Maggie was recently deposed as prime minister – "bundled out," as she put it, by "Iscariots" in her own party. But she remains very much in the game, active and combative. Yes, she's out of office – and No. 10 Downing – but she's not out of politics. Far from it: at Conservative Party conferences, she still receives the longest standing ovations. She remains the Blessed Maggie to true believers; she, not the upstart brevet major who ousted her.

Yes, Maggie may have been elevated to the House of Lords as Baroness Kesteven. But she still talks like the grocer's daughter she is. Blunt. Mincing no words.

To say Maggie has little use for Bea's ideas is an understatement. Why should people cooperate and look after each other's well-being as if they were big happy families? Maggie can't see it.

She wants governments to keep out of the welfare and happiness business, and stand on the sidelines at the economic struggle. In her view, governments should leave people alone to get and spend as they jolly well please, and get as rich as they can in a splendidly unregulated marketplace. The market will pick the winners, and that, thinks Maggie, is the way it should be.

Of course, you know who I'm rooting for – Bea and her buddies. But I am not, I hope, underestimating dear Maggie's contribution. Mrs. Thatcher has some hard lessons to teach socialists – how to have both efficiency *and* social justice, for one.

Yes, we've got to adopt, or adapt, some of Maggie's ideas about competition, so that people work hard and well enough to produce plenty for all. *Managed* competition may sound like a contradiction in terms, but it's the ticket to a prosperous future.

And who has the intestinal fortitude to take on powerful interest groups, blind to the public interest? Maggie, that's who. Socialists must take a leaf from her book (a weighty one indeed), or Maggie and her ideas will pound Bea's team into the clay, leaving her and her pals broken like so many old racquets.

Well, I've finally reached the Palace of Westminster, the scene of earlier ideological battles. Here the notion of parliamentary democracy took hold and spread.

Yes, in 1649, under the arching oaken hammer beams of ancient Westminster Hall, carved in the reign of Richard the Second, another king rose from his seat on the dais – King Charles the First – to present his defence. He had been arraigned for high treason by Cromwell's parliamentarians. He spoke with quiet dignity, careless of life. "It is not for people," said the king, "to have a share in governments, sirs; that is not pertaining to them. A Subject and a Sovereign are clear different things."

Charles paid for his words under the executioner's axe.

Britain had manufactured, and then exported, the principles that in a truly "responsible" government, kings and cabinets must give way to the wishes of elected parliaments. (Long after that, our very own John Crosbie would declaim that "the election of Jean Chretien would be the end of responsible government.")

Then, to these parliamentary precincts, in 1892, came another idea. In this entrance hall, Kier Hardie once strode, wearing his cloth cap. He had been elected, the first socialist, to speak for the poor of Glasgow. He wanted them to have a share in the economic decisions that enhanced or ravaged their lives.

Hardie delivered his maiden speech in a barely intelligible Scottish brogue. But he spoke with fiery indignation. His speech met with jeers and derision from other members of the august House. Stung, he rounded on them and spat, "Ye well-fed beasts."

I sure feel at home in the Great Hall, which leads to the Commons and the Lords. I'll have to face it – I'm badly addicted to politics; just can't swear off the stuff. That hall echoes with the forced gaiety of MPs pumping the hands of constituents. They preen themselves, reminding me of something Oscar Wilde once said: The only thing worse than being talked about is not being talked about.

Here, too, Clement Attlee began his stint as Labour prime minister in 1945. He was a modest, unassuming man, but a leader for all that. He could sense consensus among his socialist colleagues, and together they transformed post-war Britain into a modern welfare state, bringing great industries (coal, for one) under public ownership, to serve the public good over the shareholders' interests.

Later, in 1953, in a small Vancouver living room, I had the privilege of an evening with Clem Attlee. Never one to push himself forward, he sat quietly in a corner, smoking his pipe. But Churchill had Clem wrong when he jibed, "An empty cab drew up and Attlee stepped out." No, to me, in the days of my youth, Attlee stood for a socialist future, rosy and assured.

He had soon begun to carry out the conclusions of Lord Beveridge's famous 1942 report to Britons, setting out stepping stones to a future free of "the five dragons" of want, disease, ignorance, squalor and idleness.

I still believe that people can slay those dragons. With science, good housekeeping, work and cooperation, more than enough can be produced to feed, clothe and house the human family, with ample leisure left over at the end of the day to enjoy recreation – the arts, sports, or just roaming the pristine wilderness and breathing clean air.

Alas, that we should still see societies in which many don't want to live, but seek escape in drugs, alcohol, gambling, television . . . In which women may not walk alone in cities by moonlight without fear . . .

I knew, back in '53, that there would be setbacks on the road to a rosy future. But I believed we would follow Lenin's dictum, "Two steps forward, one step back." I can still hardly believe that it's been more like "one step forward, two steps back."

In Britain, the 1979 "winter of discontent" – strikes, falling markets, a plummeting pound – saw the Labour government go down. Will it ever rise again? Maggie scooped up Labour votes and declared Britain a failure – and in many ways, it was. Too many workers were work-shy; management feathered their own nests. Maggie said it was laziness, and called it "the British disease." She was a rare bird in politics, sticking to her promises and refusing to trim her principles.

And did she, you may ask, instill pride in women as leaders? I should say so! She declared Britain to be the "United Queendom," and allowed that "though the cocks may crow, it's the hens that lay the eggs."

She made many political foes. She, who called male cabinet colleagues who flinched at the application of true market principles "soggy, not crunchy," and ditched 'em. But she lacked the drollery and sunny disposition that let a Ronald Reagan get away with murder, and her enemies finally did her in.

A Vancouver friend of mine, Jack Munro, a labour boss with the International Woodworkers of America, met Maggie when he was in London some time ago. Union Jack spotted her coming out of a private dining room in the spiffy Goring Hotel.

Jack, who was in high spirits, called out, "Mrs. Prime Minister, would you like to meet some Canadians?" Over she came, with her big set smile. "Oh, Canadians, how nice. And you have that nice prime minister, Brian . . . ?"

But Jack piped up, "We're socialists, Mum." Her face fell, though the smile stayed put. She bade him a curt "good night," and took off. That lady has no time to waste on up-to-no-good do-gooders.

Ah, what does she really think of our Brian? Who knows? Once, in an unguarded moment, she was heard to say of her right-wing pal Ronnie Reagan, "Poor dear, he has nothing between his ears."

Yet she's our Brian's political godmother, no doubt about that. That whirligig we're into in Canada – privatize, deregulate, free trade 'til the pips squeak – she started it.

Oh dear. I've been lallygagging around her, thinking about history, and I've gone and missed question period. Now the Iron Lady would never have permitted that. How she

used to work over, and work up, the Labour MPs, repri-
manding them like naughty schoolchildren.

Once, after cutting young school-leavers off their social
benefits, she got the MPs going by declaring that "com-
passion is a private virtue that cannot be legislated." They
howled like banshees – and looked bad on the telly later.

But with or without Maggie, the British parliament is not
about to drown in its own dignity. That's just as well. Parliaments are democracy's theatre, and who pays attention to
poor theatre? Of course, you can't directly call a minister
a fool in parliament. But one Labour MP, looking hard at
the minister in charge of culture, gave out this report:

"Mr. Speaker, someone in Russia has called the minister
of culture a fool. He got six months for libel and twelve
years for revealing a state secret."

Nor can you impugn the reputation of an honourable
member. But an ingenious Irish MP rose in his place to ask:

"Mr. Speaker, may I, under the Rules of Parliament, refer
to honourable members opposite as sewer rats? No? Well,
thank you, Mr. Speaker. The sewer rats of Dublin will be
most grateful for your ruling."

I leave Westminster on a hopeful note. Have you heard
that Glenda Jackson recently won a Labour seat in parliament? She has forsaken stardom on stage and screen to
become an accomplice of Bea Webb's. Yes, our Glenda
longs to put an end to "the obscene, unstoppable rise in
poverty."

As I pass the book stall on my way out of Westminster,
I overhear a man in spats insisting on a receipt for the
booklet he's bought. "What do you want a receipt for, guv?"
demands the spunky Cockney woman behind the stall. "Pay
your taxes like I do – your dues to society."

Soon it will be noon. I begin a walk-about in this city of
raging ideas. I stroll down the Strand, and decide to breach
the defences of the exclusive Savoy Hotel. I'll try my "so
well-heeled I don't have to make a point of showing it" act.

A ramrod doorman, his uniform festooned with gold braid, eyes my sandals with haughty disdain – but slowly swings the door open. I descend to a marble loo with gold-plated taps and bestow my matitudinal. (I have similarly honoured some of the best Hiltons.)

Coming out, hand in pocket, the Big Spender, I say to the doorman: "A Rolls like that one – set one back quite a bit?"

The doorman, playing along: "About 137,000 pounds, sir."

"Umm, let me see. $270,000 Canadian, give or take..."

"There's a waiting list, sir, six months for delivery."

"Ah, six months – and quite a few votes to cast."

"Sir?"

"In the free market. One pound, one vote."

I decide to fly my red flag. So I pull a Fabian Socialist pamphlet from my pocket old stuff, written in 1894, when Bea was a Fabian and read to him: "'The competitive system, which leaves each to struggle against each, and enables a few to appropriate the wealth of the community...'"

My switch-about astonishes him. "That's good stuff, squire. Where'd you get it?" he asks me. I tell him, and wonder: Was this doorman, beneath his braid, a partisan in the war of ideas?

I make my way to the Hall of the Royal Courts of Justice. Nineteenth-century gothic; stone faces look me over. I put on my lawyerly face and take a seat in a courtroom, where a wigged judge is soon to enter.

A barrister, waiting to try a custody case, drawls "Hullo. So you are a Canadian lawyer. Jolly good!"

"No," I say, "I *was* a Canadian lawyer. Now I am a reformed character, though still a Queen's Counsel."

Barrister: "Were you a bencher?"

Me: "No, I was a son of a bencher."

After a pause, the barrister tells me he's there on a custody case. Then he asks me a question.

"I say, old chap, can solicitors present cases in court in Canada as if they were barristers? Mrs. T. wants to give solicitors rights of audience in court. She really does. The barristers are upset – silly old girl, she'll lower the quality of justice."

Me: "As well as the fees? About time, I'd say, old boy. Of course, in Canada, any lawyer can go to court. She's right on, I'd say – de-reg, stiff competition and all that. Doesn't like the little man priced out of justice.

"Justice should be open to all. Just like the Savoy Hotel, wouldn't you say?"

The barrister, after a long pause: "De-reg. Umm. But English barristers regulate themselves."

I think, but don't say – was it Voltaire? "I was ruined only twice, once when I lost a lawsuit and once when I won one."

My learned friend, gathering his briefs for court: "Well, Mrs. T's party won't get my vote – even her attorney-general threatened to resign . . . "

Me, to myself: "I have to hand it to you, Maggie. What other politician would take on a group as vocal and as powerful as these barristers? And don't worry, this fellow will vote Conservative anyway. His property instincts have been honed over the past 500 years by rules such as, 'Who bulleth my cow, the calf is mine.' "

We shake hands and part. I try to jolly him with some kindly advice on his custody case.

"Keep your argument simple, old boy. Remember the barrister who mixed up the jury so much, they brought in a verdict giving custody of the judge to the defendant." My friend didn't take this too well.

As I head toward the Embankment, men are taking the morning sun, sitting on the sidewalk outside their cardboard-box homes. They are reading scraps of papers scavenged from trash cans. The disenfranchised. No pounds, no votes.

One, a beaten-down soul with the dignified mien of a judge and twinkling eyes, accosts me. "Sir, good morning, sir. I'm a Digger," says he.

"A what?" I ask.

"A Digger," he repeats. "We believe in common ownership of the land, that's what. Diggers walked on to empty land in 1649, they did, at Camden. With sticks, to till the soil, grow food. Hanged for it, they were, for trespass. Had the right idea . . . "

"A good idea whose time is past?"

"Past? Young families priced out of a home of their own – parasitical speculators flipping land for the fast-rail right-of-way to the channel tunnel? An extra billion or two that'll cost the taxpayer . . . "

"I wish you were a taxpayer."

"Thank you kindly, sir. Do you have a class system in Canada, sir?"

"Oh, no, not a class system. The rich are always ready to move over and make room for one more."

Good heavens, it's warm. I look at my watch, and decide it's time to rest my hot feet, and partake of a Cornish pasty and a Scotch egg.

Entering a pub, I take a stool beside a tweedy lady with a cane and a leash – no dog.

I tell her I've been to Westminster, and she snorts. "Politicians! You can't pin those creatures down."

"Yes," I say, "I used to be a politician – but I've been going straight for several years."

She has little use for politicians. She raises dogs for export; wants a law to dock dogs' tails while they're pups. Hurts less then. She phoned her Tory MP before the last election, quizzing him: "What's your position on docking dogs' tails?"

"I'm glad you brought that up," the fellow answers. "Capital idea! But we mustn't be dogmatic, must we."

She tells me that she'll never vote for that wishy-washy Tory — but she likes Mrs. T. "That woman," she announces, "will be prime minister again, mark my words."

I say I don't doubt it. "But Mrs. T's voice? Rather shrill, isn't it? Upsetting to people, puppies?"

"She's taking voice lessons — her husband, Denis, is paying for them."

I wander on, enjoying the sunshine and the good eye contact I get from Londoners. The English have a high happiness quotient — higher than their incomes. Political scientists don't know what makes happiness.

Suddenly I realize I'm lost in the West End. A friendly cabbie directs me to Canada House. I thank him, adding: "What do you think of Mrs. T?"

"Not my style, mate, I'm working class, socialist."

"So you vote the Labour Party ticket?"

"Blimey, not me. With Labour governments, the bums won't work. They just take it easy."

This cabbie has a point. How to bring out people's best efforts? Socialism *and* competition? Why not? When our Air Canada was publicly owned, it competed with the world's best, and beat the world's best.

A longing for a pint of bitter overtakes me, and I pull into the Red Lion. There I meet a broker, stripes, bowler, the obligatory rolled brolly (and not a cloud in the sky).

He has a complaint. Seems one Lady Porter, chairperson of the council in Camden, where he lives, has privatized the municipal cemetery.

"Sold it for one pound! Claims the inhabitants aren't paying their way. That they must be put under new management."

"I can imagine their ... murmurings."

"I'm on the waiting list. I'm planning to spend my retirement there."

"You should lead a tenants' strike."

Are you privatizing in Canada? he asks me. I say yes, $4.7 billion worth of public assets on the block so far. But not the army's privates; and not cemeteries – the slumber landlords have them already, anyway.

He tells me the Conservatives are going to privatize Britain's drinking water. He finds this hard to swallow, though he's a life-long Tory.

I find it hard to swallow too. "Beatrice Webb was in the fight for municipal ownership of water in 1902. Land and water – will they sell the air next?"

"Who knows? They just might. Maybe old Lord Tennyson knew something 100 years ago, lying in the grass on the Isle of Wight, when he wrote: 'The air of these downs is worth sixpence a pint.' "

It is mid-afternoon when I reach the Underground station at Marble Arch. I decide to treat my tootsies to a ride. The tube is on strike every Wednesday – but today, thank heaven, isn't Wednesday. A union man at the ticket office tells me the tube workers want an 8.8 per cent raise on a base of £105 a month.

He goes on to say that Maggie's friend, Lord King, has just given himself a raise of 116 per cent. He was the minister who privatized British Airways. Then he made himself chairman of its board, laid people off and put it in the black. He then thanked himself with a raise of 116 per cent on a salary of £335,000 plus perks. It's the old story, he says: "It's the rich what gets the gryvy; it's the poor what gets the blyme."

Did Maggie say anything?

"Sure – old Maggie hit the roof. But Lord King told her to mind her own business and not meddle with market matters. Besides, he claimed he needed more incentive."

"What!" I explode. "Was he going to lie around if he didn't get a whopping raise? My God, do judges need raises to give longer sentences? Would Lord Nelson have stayed a cabin boy but for the money?"

"You said it, old chap, not me." And he hands me a ticket.

Off I go, down the escalator to the train platform. As I squeeze through a train's automatic doors, a recorded voice booms: "Watch the gap. Watch the gap."

That's what the unions are doing, I say to myself – watching the gap. They watch the gap gaping wider between more than enough and less than enough. They see tax breaks at the top and more poor falling below the "official" poverty line. They hear zealots of the Tory right saying that governments should not help the poor by redistributing wealth. That, they say (the old refrain), is robbing Peter to pay Paul – sinful.

I rattle along in the train, lost in thought.

The Labour party won't beat those Tory zealots until their union allies agree to be part of incomes planning. Not until the trade unions sit down with government and management to set out broad guidelines – what's affordable in the coming year? What income disparities must be addressed? What communal needs, social and public services, need support – and how much? Priorities – putting first things first – that's the language of socialism.

Of course, those Tory zealots won't invite Labour to the table. But Labour willing, the public will, sooner or later.

After our supper, Dorothy prepares for tomorrow's Commonwealth meeting. I feel restless, and walk to the proms concert in the Albert Hall. The vast crimson brick hall is sold out. But for £1.50, I can climb six flights to the Gods – a wide circular gallery tucked under the hall's dome. I step over young and old, lying prone on the gallery floor, hanging over the balustrade. All listening – there are 6,000 listeners in that oval on a hot summer night.

The music wafts up, every note. A horn concerto by Mozart, a Haydn symphony, Beethoven's Pastoral symphony – all crafted for excellence, not for money. The music speaks to inner selves. Lost in that music, "rancor and envy and spite sleep like the scullions in the fairy tale," as Edna St. Vincent Millay once wrote.

Back in 1786, young Mozart lavished care on a string quartet and sent it to Papa Haydn for his approval. The world-renowned Haydn, in his generosity of spirit, replied with a note to his young rival's father – knowing this youngster would soon take his crown.

"I tell you," Haydn wrote, "before God, as an honest man, your son Amadeus is the greatest musical genius the world has ever seen."

Good politics is about inculcating Haydn's values – generosity, respect, concern. About inculcating ethical beliefs in individuals that trickle down to seed mass cultures and influence private and public decisions.

Better values, better measures. Better measures, better values . . . In the end, I think, the socialist tortoise is not as fleet of foot as the free-market hare. But sure and steady has won the race before, and will again.

CHAPTER 6

Alex, in his guise as a mentally disturbed professor, discovers (wonderfully assisted by his students) that if a country doesn't know where it wants to go, chances are it won't get there; and offers tips to the nation's youth culled from the breadth of his own experience, which are sure to be received for what they are worth; and advises the Reader that he or she need not read all of this over-long chapter, but may savour nips here and there, rather in the manner in which a prudent person might tipple from a bottle of excellent wine.

Dear Reader,

One fine day, a world champion knocked on the door of my cubbyhole office at Simon Fraser University. Yes, it was Shawn Lakusta, a student in my course on what we still call "the Canadian constitution." Shawn wanted to discuss his term essay, but I managed to deflect him from this, at least for a while. I like to hear my students talk about what they're shooting for in life, to hear how they're doing, and to offer them a sage word of advice.

(I'm plain lucky, don't you agree, to have retired into this teaching job; with keen, curious young minds shaking mine up and keeping me, I hope, young at heart. At last, a chance to redeem a misspent life as a lawyer and politician. And I mean that. Tell me, if you can, what's more important than trying to help younglings to learn and to make learning a lifelong pursuit? What's more important than helping them to form their own worthwhile life goals? And community goals, too?)

However, as lucky as I am, this particular day I was suffering, sweltering in my airless SFU cubbyhole. You see, dear Reader, I'd lost my office curtains, and I was broiling in the brilliant morning sunshine pouring through my unprotected windows. How came I to lose my curtains? Well, I'll tell you – but not now. Later.

And so back to Shawn. Bulky he is, but trim, and always cheerful. He had just won (I got this via the student grapevine) the world junior power-weight championship in Luxembourg. Shawn is modest, with little right to be – but with a little gentle probing, I drew out of him that he had won drug-free all the way. Now this, Reader, *is* remarkable, even for junior events.

"Well, yes," admitted Shawn, looking at his toes, "No 'oids, no beans, none of the juice."

Shawn, I can tell, lives under an auspicious star – that of fitness, in body and in mind. The lad still works out regularly.

"Hey, Shawn," I said, "The word is out that you just won the best squat-and-bench-press at a competition in Gold's Gym!"

Shawn allowed that he had, adding that he just missed his last dead-weight lift of 200 kilograms. But he'll make it next time, he vows.

Then he warmed up. "But no more international competitions for me. I refuse to compete with all those hopped-up athletic junkies. Some of them look like Japanese sumo wrestlers, they've popped so many steroids. Too much big money to be made in sports these days – by owners, coaches, players – by winning, and by winning any old way."

"Well, Shawn," I said, "keep working out that body of yours. It's like a fine old Stradivarius that must be played. That's what Simon Streatfield, our eminent conductor, said of his 18th-century viola: 'If you don't use it, it'll lose its bouquet.' "

You'd enjoy meeting Shawn, dear Reader. Perhaps I should invite you to the class reunion I'm throwing at my place on May 31, 2010, at 8:30 in the evening. And, hey! It'll be a chance for you to meet me. (Not to worry, my doctor said recently, "You're fine Alex, you may live to be as old as you look.")

Eventually, Shawn butted in about his essay. He wanted to write about Section 7 of our Charter of Rights, the section that goes, "Everyone is entitled to life, liberty and security of the person."

I played picador to this young bull, aiming my arrows carefully. "What's the right to travel worth, Shawn, to someone who can't afford the ticket? Don't forget those Charter rights are worth a lot more to some than to others."

Shawn, of course, knew this, and I'm pleased to say he planned to include some of the history of the fight for rights – the unremitting popular fight bloodily waged in the street, and the mental strife to win rights in the courts.

I suggested he look up the Sommerset case. Sommerset was a black, a fugitive slave on the run in England in 1790. His owner dragged him into court seeking a writ to repossess his property. But the old judge, Lord Mansfield, making a solid precedent, said simply and memorably, "By the common law of England, no man can have property in another." Sommerset walked.

I couldn't leave the subject alone. "The fight against slavery, is it a done battle, Shawn? What about Wayne Gretzky, bought and sold to Los Angeles by Peter Pocklington?" (Wayne is so good that "enforcers" on other teams maim him with sticks and elbows, and apply shock treatment to his spinal cord. The owners wink at this "necessary roughness" because it's good box office. Why, those NHL owners won't even ban anabolic steroids!)

But Shawn was not at all sure I should compare Gretzky to a slave, considering the money he makes. However, he did tell me, sadly, about some of the young boxers he sees around the gyms – waiting to be bought, getting their brains pitched around in their skulls, each punch a tiny death. Some are mismatched to take a beating and raise their opponent's price – and get jeered at for their pains.

I told him I'd read where master speculator Murray Pezim is in the market for a boxer. Pezim makes his living playing right-inside for the Vancouver Stock Exchange. He's in a good mood these days, between marriages, with plenty of jingle after a big killing touting "the biggest gold find in history." Yes, Pezim told the papers he's going to buy the B.C. Lions, and "a couple of boxers" – the two-legged kind; he's no dog fancier.

Shawn and I talked of what should be up for sale, and what not, with buying power so unevenly spread. Bodies for sex? Votes? No, surely not votes. Jobs? Senate seats? Organs? I mention a poor Turkish farmer who sold one kidney so he could pay for his daughter's medical treatment. The freedom to buy and sell wouldn't need limits, I argued, if there was social equality and all could breathe the air of liberty.

Shawn couldn't get out the door without me taking a parting shot. Must be the heat had got me. "Tell me, Shawn, why doesn't our Charter say, 'Life, liberty and *the pursuit of happiness*'? I'll tell you why. Happiness is not an end in itself. Pigs and drunkards can achieve happiness.

"No, m'lad, the goal is to live richly, fully – so strike up friendships with people who create things that last. People long gone, as well as the living. Take the time and make the effort to get to know some of them well. Nothing like that to rid yourself of the empty, bored feelings that are all too common today."

Now! At last I will tell you how I lost my office curtains,

leaving me, that morning, almost blubber – almost blubbering like a child! I was taking the heat of a really bad idea, one that most Canadians feel nothing can be done about. Down the hall in Economics, they call this idea "public squalor in the midst of private affluence." It's a baddie that can do us all in.

What happened? My curtains didn't make it through the wash, that's what happened. They'd been hung and left hanging for 25 years. When the departmental budget finally let them go to the laundry, they self-destructed. So I sat there sizzling. Well, never mind, I got a tan that would have cost big bucks in a salon.

But we don't seem to have our priorities straight. We throw money at what makes money. At fancy fixings in shopping malls. Not at libraries and universities and child-care centres. No, those things don't turn quick cash. They have to get by on whatever money is left over. We put last things first – which is not exactly what the Good Book advises.

No, this is not a malfunction of our acquisitive society. This is the thing itself.

But please don't think I want to give up this job. Hey, I can stand a little heat! The money's good, for one thing. I figure that, what with the time I need to think about what I'm going to say, I'm making 69 cents an hour. And I'm getting a terrific education.

Well, I don't have to worry about Shawn's life goals. But Canada's? The trouble with Canada, observant Reader, is not that Canadians are steering by the *wrong* stars. Rather, we are drifting none too merrily down the stream to wherever economics takes us.

Why don't we heed what a Roman (not a Canadian) senator once said? That would be old Lucius Seneca, who said, in AD 49, well before my time (he was speaking of individuals, but the same applies to nations), "If a man does not know to what port he is steering, no wind is favourable to him."

So I try to get my classes thinking, "Hey, what's this part of the constitution promoting? What goals?" Constitutions and laws are only tools, I tell them.

Fortunately, I don't have to belabour this with my classy kids. They get right into the what-fors. Does this really promote democracy? Order? Fair shakes? The right to be left alone? They all chip in, and I can sit back and listen.

But one day, I couldn't sit back for long. Pretty soon, it was: "Come on, Alex. What are your ideals? Give us the goals you want Canada to shoot for. Your biases and all."

That got me up from my chair, with some jitters – this prof bit is new to me. I have to know what I'm talking about – I'm not in parliament now.

"Well," I said, playing for think time, "when you talk about goals, there are two poles of thought. Some stress individuality and how individuals should be left alone to make or mar their own lives. Others start with ideals that focus on the interests of the community first, 'the common good of all'."

This generality didn't satisfy Sally. She thought I hadn't answered the question and said so. This unbashful child doesn't want an octopus professor – you know, one who goes on about "on this hand, on that hand, on the other hand . . ."

I tried again, using a cigar as a pointer. (I don't smoke cigars, I just munch them. They're my soother. I told my students that my wife says smoking cigars will stunt my growth! But she does let me chew on them. As a matter of fact, that's the only thing she does let me chew on.) Giving it my best go, I said with a gulp:

"Students. I came by my values like this . . . I was sitting one warm day in Paris, it was the 4th of August, 1789 – well before your time.

"I sat on a bench in the constituent assembly. The French Revolution was heading into internal combustion. My seat was to the left of the president of the assembly. (Kindly make a note – that's where 'left-wing' and 'right-wing' come from.) Around me sat a rag-tag bunch of disorderly delegates – 'sans culottes' they were called, meaning 'without knickers.' Some were regicides.

"The assembly was hotly debating a Proclamation of the Rights of Man. It was a wild scene, with bare-footed, down-trodden Parisians in the spectators' gallery, some with pitchforks, hissing and applauding the speakers.

"Then a delegate down the bench from me (rightly named St. Just) moved that 'liberty, equality and fraternity' be the rights of man. (He should have added 'sorority' for the rights of woman.) His motion passed, although delegates across the way kept nattering about the 'duties' of man.

"Those are still my trinity of values. Today, tricked out in modern dress (fashions do change), they can very well walk abroad on the boulevards, with a cane and a flowery boutonniere."

My soliloquy, however, had made a cluster of young conservatives quite restless. Their looks seemed to suggest I was living in the past. Had they come out with this, I was going to reply: "No, the past is living in me!" But I never got a chance. Instead, Sally (a member of the conservative cluster) put this to me, to give the rest of them a moment to reflect:

"This 'left' and 'right.' What do they mean today? Don't we just need practical answers to practical problems?"

I parried this with, "Yes, those labels have lost a lot of their meaning. If I'm not careful at an NDP convention, I find myself sitting beside a leave-things-be conservative. And I don't doubt there are radicals at Conservative conventions who want to change the world. There are many cross-dressers these days, and political parties keep stealing each others' underwear."

I got no further, because Ted broke in. Now there's a fervid young Tory. "If Canada is to grow and prosper in this world, it must have up-to-date values – competitiveness, self-reliance, individualism, thrift, order, distrust of the state," he opined.

Ted knows how to get me ballistic. "Okay, Ted. Stop right there. I can't knock most of your values. But competition? I'd call that a means, not an end. A means that socialists must learn to use if people are to work well, or even work at all.

"But your ends! Don't overdo them!" (I was in lift-off now.) "You'll have Canadians climbing all over each other to get ahead – if they're not doing that already – in a knees-and-elbows scrum, in a wild free-for-all. I don't want Canadians falling down to worship the Great God Gain. The price of that is not only paid by those who are left behind – it's also paid in the corrosion of the core values of respect for others and the community."

I was in deep water. But Shawn Lakusta pulled me out. He surprised me. He sits close to the conservative cluster, and he has lots of go, and big shoulders to throw against the tough world out there. All Shawn said was, "The trouble with the rat-race is that, even if you win, you're still a rat." Shawn's comments allowed me to leave the field of battle with my dignity in one piece. In the hall, I told him, "You know, Shawn, you're the best student I ever studied under."

Sure, it's a good class. A mutual learning experience. I just wish my children were a true sample of young hearts and minds coming on. Sorry to say, three out of ten B.C. youngsters drop out of high school.

Another thing I like. I positively like students who *don't* share my ideas about acquisitive economics. I like them because they are radicals, like me. They want to change things – and they care – and they get incensed about what they see as wrong.

I miss Tim – he's graduated. We got on. He'd come in,

tall, lanky, Lincolnesque. He had a right tilt like the Leaning Tower of Pisa. He'd sit in class near some young conservatives, but thought they were goody-goodies, the kind Mrs. – now Dame – Thatcher calls "wets." Tim sees liberty in the freemasonry of dollars, obtained and spent any old way, with no kindly government interference. No, none at all, thank you.

One day in class we were debating jurisdiction over the care and harvesting of provincial forest lands. Tim listened quietly, and then let go.

"Everybody's property is nobody's property," said he. "If private companies were left alone to own and run the forests, they'd be looked after and efficiently restocked in the interests of their own shareholders."

This gave Graham a turn (he has a leftward limp). "But won't the companies cut and run for quick profits? And leave the clean-up and restocking to posterity?"

I took Graham's side, saying: "Yes, those companies might be guided by the wrong Marx – by Groucho Marx, who once exclaimed, 'Posterity? What's posterity ever done for me? Why should I care about posterity?' " (Karl was the better socialist.)

Then someone asked Tim if he'd privatize and deregulate the highways. He had no trouble with that. "Of course. Supply and demand are the best regulators of any scarce commodity. If there are traffic jams, the tolls go up and more roads are built."

Did he have a point? No! If the sum total of individual "demands" determines the number of cars polluting the air and the space devoted to highways... I had visions of a super highway to Seattle, with 44 lanes each way. Bargain lanes for the not-well-off. (Today's special. $4.95 to Seattle, lane 13!) Exclusive, expensive lanes where the well-off could parade their wealth. With little overpasses at intervals so fast executives could overtake slowpokes.

The Swedes have a better idea. You must buy a pass

every day you want to drive into downtown Stockholm. Public regulation curbs individuals' demands in the interests of all individuals.

I come to, and come up with a verse to lighten Tim's mood. It's from Dr. Sam:

> How small of all that human hearts endure,
> That part that Kings and Laws can cause or cure.

Later, when Tim called in my office to tell me he'd liked that verse and wanted me to write it out for him, he brought me a present. It was a booklet to assist with my conversion. We each play the Christian missionary to the other's heathen savage.

You wouldn't believe that booklet, dear Reader! It was written by one Frederic Bastiat in France in 1848. Bastiat was a landed scion who didn't like the aftershock French Revolution of that year one little bit. And that book of his is still in vogue in comfortable far-right circles. "1987, 14th printing, 25,000 copies."

Bastiat — I've got it right here. Boy, does he ever put the boots to socialism. See page 22. Plunder by the state, he calls it.

> Legal plunder can be committed in infinite ways: Tariffs,
> protection, benefits, subsidies, encouragements, progressive
> taxation, public schools, guaranteed jobs, minimum wages,
> a right to relief — and so on and so on. This is socialism.

This Bastiat makes me think the late Mr. Genghis Khan had a bad press.

Et tu, Tim! Wherever you are. Yes, you. I heard you say socialism was robbing Peter to pay Paul. What's wrong with that? You want jungle law? Listen to your old prof. I told you that seven families already control half the wealth on the Toronto Stock Exchange. In seven years, 70 families will pull the world's strings. Are you listening, Tim?

Another of my wonderful students was Dominique – I miss her. Sure hope she shows for the class reunion. Last semester (ah! each semester another ring on my tree-trunk) she came in to see me, breathless.

I told her, "Looking pert today, Dominique." (I have the seniority to say that.) Russian-French blood, she has. Not bad, eh? She twirled and tilted in her jeans and showed me way down where she said she was pricked by a buckle on her backpack. Did she give me the eye? Oh, to be 60 again! If only I looked better and felt worse.

Dominique wanted to be a social worker. She worked a 30-hour week in a heartbreak house for mentally disabled seniors. She brightened their lives, I'm sure, and brightened her own with a world jaunt every five years or so when she'd saved up some money.

Dominique spun off an outline of her essay on equality for women under the Charter of Rights. My mind trailed off – no matter, she wrote well. I fell into a sorrowful reverie. What were the life chances of young women nowadays for marriage and family? Less than they used to be, I suspect – though fewer, I suppose, may want that life.

How many young women are in job-training to prepare for divorce? And so many single mothers, a million in Canada now. With so many children in the homes of single working parents, wanting more love and care than they get...

A Grade 4 teacher in Surrey told me a rising one-third of his pupils are from single-parent homes. (Four of his pupils have special educational needs, six have severe learning disabilities.) And run-away-from-home abused children selling themselves on city streets. One is far too many. Children are a precious resource; their future is our future.

I pulled out of my reverie – things are never as bad as I think, gentle Reader. You know that. I interrupted Domi-

nique in full flight – she must have wondered where I'd
been, as I said:

"Great novelists, Dominique, such as Dickens and Conrad,
have been telling us something like this:

> Structural improvements are of limited value;
> what is required are changes in human hearts.

"For my part," I went on, "yes, changes in human hearts
– but I'd give the change a lift with some structural improve-
ments, the sooner the better. It takes two legs to climb a
ladder, but I'd put the leg of structural improvement up
first, to help the other leg to follow."

This took her aback a bit, so I went on to say that the
best pre-school centres for children were in France. Open
to all, these centres are rich in play, the arts, languages and
learning skills. Just a matter of priorities. That's where socialism comes in – socialism is the language of priorities.

Dominique got us back on the topic, saying there are
limits to what affirmative action can do for women. We
agreed that as long as there are gross disparities in income,
women would be left behind. Others, such as the one in
five who carry unlucky genes, who are not as smart or
quick, will also be left behind.

I quoted Aristotle the Greek (who dished up for minds
in his restaurant; he's out of business now). Aristotle said
when one receives more than three times the income of
another, that's obscene. In North America, some get hundreds of times more than others. How many hundreds, it's
hard to say, for polite society decrees it in bad taste to
reveal incomes unless they come from wages or welfare.

Dominique got up, saying she was off to Europe after
her last exam – Reeboks, backpack, Eurail pass. I advised
her to take in the Van Gogh exhibit in Amsterdam. "Make
Vincent one of your acquaintances," I told her. "See his
troubled visions just as he painted them – faces looking

right at you, the eyes darting questions; century-old paint breezily passing the test of time."

Unfortunately, Dominique won't see Van Gogh's portrait of his doctor, Dr. Gachet, sadly surveying his patient's ailments with wistful eyes, head resting in his hand, under an off-white, orange-trimmed beret. A Japanese industrialist picked that one up at auction with a fistful of $82.8 million U.S. Later, he said, "Well, yes, it was $33 million more than I expected to pay." Old Vincent never got a sou for that portrait. It was unwanted in a Paris art dealer's attic when he died. Says something, I'd say, of the status of the artist, then and now.

As a parting gift, I gave Dominique a high-flown recital from the Bard: "Within be rich, without be rich no more." That young woman really cheered me up. She threw me a nice farewell in her fluent French, poking fun at mine. I have to admit, I learned my French between the covers – the covers of a book.

I sat in my cubbyhole, musing. Are those millions we read about real? How many meals-on-wheels would one million buy? It doesn't help me to say that prices – for paintings, whatever – are set by the iron law of supply and demand. Some law, that. The "demand" of a hungry child is strong enough, God knows, but counts for nothing if its mother is poor.

Some of my students also take criminology classes. There's a subject that spotlights just how well we're living up to the ideal of fair sharing. To measure the health of our society, take its cell count. Jail-cell count, that is.

In Holland, they have proportionately half the people doing jail time as they have in Britain. In Canada, we have twice as many as Britain. And in the United States – ah, there jail-building is a growth industry – already one million behind bars. And where do you suppose you're most likely to get mugged? You got it!

These musings remind me of another student, Ed, who

recently came in to ask if he could miss a couple of classes. He looked a bit tired – has to work to pay his way here (although he's not as tired as Mike, with two jobs, one delivering papers from midnight to 5 a.m., six days a week).

University fees have shot up 189 per cent in the last ten years, and the jobs available for students are often part-time, and always low-paying. I pass the job board downstairs. It's always services wanted, from nannying to sales. Alas, there are fewer young fingers – the young breed less (no, it's not late TV, they're tired!). And demand for young fingers increases as the marketplace restlessly turns desires into necessities.

You know, I was glad that in our class discussion of ideals, no one equated a high gross national product with happiness. The market is a subtle thief of youth. It won't quit. Who needs the 146 new pet-food products that hit the shelves last year? And do I really *need* an "aural lap-top amplifier" to pick up intimate whispers? For just $19.95 I can have one, so my TV says, by phoning in my credit card number. But what I'd hear would only upset me at my age.

Back to Ed. He was going to a friend's funeral, and would have to miss a couple of classes. His friend, a part-time electrician, about 30 years old, had left a Coquitlam bar too full for his own good. He got beaten up and stomped in the parking lot. He picked himself up, took a shotgun from the trunk of his car and killed one of his assailants. He got life. And three days after being taken to Kent penitentiary, he was himself killed in the exercise yard with a kitchen knife.

Hardened inmates at Kent, with little to do, are heavily into head games. The death toll there is three or four a year. Some are contract killings, a friend of a victim paying for revenge. Some are just too slow to join the games.

Shaken, I asked Ed whether the criminal was the cause of the crime, or whether both criminal and crime are the effects of other things. Of course, there's more to it than that, but there's an eerie sameness to a country's murder count and its distribution of income and wealth. Inequity saps fraternity – which is just people getting along with each other. They sap what the old Romans called "civitas" and we call "civility" – mutual respect.

Later on this particular morning, Hardev Gill burst jovially in. He's a new Canadian – well, fairly new, anyway, just 21 years old. Hardev's wearing white sneakers, red shorts and a blue turban. He's big for his size, and stars on our university football team.

Hardev wants to do his essay on the Sikhs in British Columbia. I ask him what that's got to do with my course on the constitution. He explains: If the Québecois are distinct from the English, then the Sikhs are distinct from just about everybody. And, he avers, the English and French are not that distinct anyway. They've been entwined in making either love or war for more than a thousand years. He then brings up a constitutional conference where no less a statesman than former premier William Vander Zalm said that every province should be called distinct in the constitution. "You are distinct – I am distinct – everyone's dis-stinked," said the Zalm.

I chuckled. "Go ahead with your essay, Hardev, and get your father to help you."

Hardev hangs around with a Socred wheel called Whistling Bernie Smith. The Whistler got this tag when he was a copper on the Gastown beat. He ran against me in 1979 for MLA in Vancouver East. I beat him because I got more votes. Nevertheless, I assured Hardev, I hold no grudge against the Whistler for licking him.

Hardev comes easily to Social Credit. I don't know, but suspect, that his father holds a chicken quota in the Fraser Valley from the B.C. Egg Marketing Board. You can sell a quota for more than it cost you to buy the farm. I did ask

Hardev once why chicken raisers didn't let hens run out on
the grass. He replied that free-ranging hens cost more to
feed because of the exercise they get.

In case this young Socred thought that socialists preferred
caged chickens, I gave him the Swedes. They love liberty
so much, I told Hardev, that they passed a law against teth-
ering pigs. They firmly believe that untethered porkers make
tastier chops.

Hardev loves Canada for the rich variety of its peoples
and cultures, and he adds his own bit of individuality. He
does this by playing a part – himself. My trouble is, after
so long in politics, that to play myself I'd have to take acting
lessons.

The lad had no fear of taking a run at my ideas, using
his pal, Bernie Smith, as a cover.

He put this to me. "Bernie says that socialism destroys
individuality – everyone begins to think alike and look alike
and stays in line, and everyone gets bored."

"Tell the Whistler," I replied, "that nothing makes individuals more conformist, and irons out their wrinkles faster,
than working for a corporation and wondering if they'll be
fired or get a promotion. People let themselves go when
they have sure social entitlements – health care and so on,
and some security of employment and control over their
work. Then you get odder odd-balls.

"And tell the Whistler this, too! Ah, progress! Ah, evolution! From Neanderthal Man to Cro-Magnon Man to Tasmanian Man to Los Angeles Man and now to – cock of
the walk! – Market Man. Market Man restlessly scanning
prices through his trifocals with a pocket calculator in his
hot hand – always buying to sell. Tell the Whistler I'd rather
party with a Tasmanian Man!"

Hardev (trying a new play, going for a touchdown): "Bernie
Smith says that the free market is the most efficient supplier

and distributor of goods the world has ever seen." (Does the Whistler really talk that way? All those polysyllables?)

"Efficient? Whistling Smith says efficient? Hardev, what a god we make of that elusive quality. Efficient to do what? Ants are efficient.

"Listen to this. Another Smith once heard from his boss: 'Nice going, Smith. You've finally got this operation running efficiently. You're fired!'

"Sunday shopping, which comes from market forces, not from the courts, is efficient. It gets people working longer for less – as if they were riding a bicycle and had to keep pumping away or the darn thing would wobble. You know, Hardev, an inefficient general can be a lot safer than an efficient one.

"Besides, give the Whistler this, too: the so-called free market makes a few too rich and many more too poor, with bad fraternity between them."

Hardev: "There's nothing wrong with being rich."

Me: "Not if you're rich."

I don't know what I'd do without Hardev. He keeps me fast awake in class. He saves me from being like a friend of mine at the University of British Columbia, who claims he is the only professor in the province who sleeps through his own lectures. Not me, not with the likes of Hardev.

If Hardev runs for the Socreds, I also have students who'll run for the Liberals one day: Angela and Kevin. One day, they turned up sporting big Jean Chrétien buttons. Monsieur Jean was then running for Liberal leadership. His politics are not mine, but we do need leaders who stick up for One Canada, a Canada that's more than the sum of its parts. So I cleared my throat and said, "I want to see you two after class."

Well, class over, everyone bunched around to take it all in. I sat writing a cheque for $75 to the Jean Chrétien campaign. And I was stage-whispering, "This mustn't get out – it's strictly between the three of us – no tax receipt to my house, please. If my wife finds out – or my political friends, almost the only kind of friends I have ... " (I am telling you this, gentle Reader, in the strictest confidence. The strictest.)

Well, those two ardent young Liberals took off by bus right after the exam that year to see and save Canada. They said they might have to mail their final essays from Moose Jaw, or some such place. This was okay with me, since I didn't think Moose Jaw was named after any of Canada's prime ministers ... though it well could be.

I almost urged these two to get married. But I caught myself, even though statistics show that married people live longer (correction! married *men* live longer), and wedded pairs have more children. Dear Reader, I am rapidly approaching the years of discretion. I even held back from telling them of a wedding toast I once proposed, speaking on Blue Nun, to two young friends. These newlyweds had come back from a vacation in Hawaii in time for the ceremony. I told their wedding guests the happy couple had enjoyed their honeymoon so much, they'd decided to get married.

Quite a few of my goslings want to go to law school. I try to help. The law, the best side of it, has been a lifelong love object of mine. I just wish our affair had been better consummated. Oh, to follow truth and reason, wherever they may lead. Yes, a good life value. To pare the evidence down to clean white bones; to welcome uncomfortable ideas. A country needs a good helping of this, especially in this emotional age. Too often today, passions, prejudices and feelings pass for thought.

I have to grade my goslings and the grades count a lot in their futures. That's something I really dislike. Does facility in passing exams, say, make the lawyer you can trust? The one who thinks deeply, if slowly? I try to stick up for slow thinkers, slow talkers, slow walkers. I'm one myself.

In order to put the law in a good light, I give my students the case of Murphy, a Toronto lawyer, who puts slow-talking to good use.

Murphy was a criminal lawyer with a good record. He began his career by auditioning for clients at the Don jail. Recently, he represented an accused up for sentencing. His client had been caught in the act of robbery and had a long-playing record that ran two pages. Murphy shuffled into court, late; couldn't find his glasses; lost his notes; got the accused's name wrong; and mumbled unintelligibly. The old judge cut him off, out of sheer pity, with: "Sentence suspended. Next case."

But in case this left the wrong impression, I quickly gave the class three classy Vancouver lawyers. The three unexpectedly left the courts and turned up at the gate of St. Peter's court. Peter put his usual question, "Have you led honest lives?" Two of them smartly turned on their heels and walked off. Peter, frantically phoning upstairs, asks, "What do I do with the deaf one?"

Seriously, if I can hone my students' ability to think, they'll be wanted, whatever the business. The busy world wants more than information stored in silicon chips. It wants know-how stored in brains. My job here shouldn't be filling half-empty vessels with facts. It's the significance of those facts, putting them together . . .

Hey! One of my students, who never took a commerce course, is being picked up for a Vancouver job by a big Hong Kong development company. They spotted in him a problem-solver, whatever the problem.

Ron is another of my students, one I want to keep in touch with. He's a likable young rascal who parlayed his way into my course just by turning up and taking part. He's not even a political science major. But his persistence paid off. He's on the list now. Ron's keen on politics; is he ever!

I always speak well of my students, but I'd be remiss not to tell you that this young fellow is an out-and-out Socred.

He could be premier some day. What's that you say? "We could look farther and do worse, and probably will." Oh, well.

Ron is wearing an impish half-smile, so I say, "Ron! Did you catch that radio flash? Terrorists have seized Parliament Hill and threaten to release Brian Mulroney and his whole cabinet, unless their demands are met."

I figure one way to unsettle his mind is to ask him to do his essay on election financing. Ron's all for it, and supposes I'll want him to include the National Citizens Coalition case. In that case, some pointy-headed Alberta judge held that special interest groups could spend any old amount during election campaigns to push what's good for them. "Free speech," he held, overrode the limit on party spending in the Federal Election Expenses Act. I'd say it's a licence to buy parliament. But enough Conservative types like the decision, and it stands.

I'm just glad that judge didn't hear the anti-metric lobby case. He'd have quoted in his reasons, "If Jesus wanted us to metricate, he'd have had ten disciples and not twelve."

Ron and I would talk politics. He was looking for pointers from an old hand. Brimming with his own idealism, he'd ask, "How can you win in today's politics and keep your principles?"

I spar for time – ask, "How come, Ron, when we talked ideals in class, none of us brought up 'sacrifice' as a public virtue? We can't keep on using and spending as we please – even the earth can't stand it. How much is it, 25 billion tonnes of carbon monoxide humans have hurled into the atmosphere already?"

Ron says he knows many young people who are being drawn into politics by environmental issues. "They know we must have 'sacrifice,' sacrifice of some kinds of jobs, of profits, of easy living, if there's to be a world worth living in."

"Yes," I say, "and they'll be drawn, and a good thing too,

into considering where the public interest must prevail over private gratification. And more people will be drawn, I think and I certainly hope, into rejecting our politics of attending only to the demands of advocacy groups. They'll demand, too, politics of substance, not ten-second sound bites and mindless banalities.

"As to your question," I continue, "winning with principled beliefs? You could do that in times past. CCF-style socialists won elections, even formed a government, with their principles hanging out. In times to come – maybe sooner than later – voters will go for candidates who stand for what they really believe. They'll find that refreshing as well as necessary.

"And another thing, Ron. When, not if, you run, remember this is an age of instant communication, of information glut. You'll have to express yourself compactly. What it took John A. Macdonald an hour and four tumblers to say, you'll have to say in four minutes. No fleshing out bare-bones ideas in fancy words, Ron! Not in your essay, either, or I'll ding you."

Ron doesn't seem to mind my ramblings, and I can't find a good stopping point.

"Tune in to the good comics, Ron. They're economical. Fr'instance:

> *Indignant diner, to waiter: 'What's this fly doing in my*
> *soup?'*
> *Waiter, peering: 'The back stroke, I believe, sir.'*

"And Ron, read poetry, especially some of Thomas Hardy's. You've got to startle, swing, almost sing. And good novels – they mirror their times and all times. Fill yourself in. They'll want many-sided politicians – ones who have sunk deep roots.

"Get to like all the arts. Don't be 'the man who pushed his chair back from the banquet table, laden with the choicest morsels prepared by master chefs, to stay his stomach by snatching and eating flies." (That's H.L. Mencken, as near as I can get it.)

We talked of political leadership – what makes it. I spun off into the sagas of the Vikings – two gnomes who became leaders. One led by capturing and sharing booty with his followers, the other by capturing their respect, admiration and trust.

Ron: "And Premier Vander Zalm – which is he? Both?"

Me: "Vander Zalm told a meeting, 'Vote for me and good government.' But a fellow in the audience misunderstood. 'What? I've got two votes?' "

A fog is creeping on little cat feet through these halls of learning, as through most Canadian universities. It blurs what universities should be – centres for the pursuit of truth without regard to its vocational utility.

Angela (she of the Chrétien button) alerted me. She kindly let me read an essay she had written on the "privatization of universities." She even enclosed in its fold a cigar, decently wrapped, I must add, in cellophane. (Safe eating?)

As public financing of universities falls off, private donors step in. They endow buildings, rooms. They want, naturally enough, well-trained recruits to fill future corporate slots; and the more pliant, the better. And some want, too, the baubles that gladden a giver's heart – a brass plaque with the donor's name, an honourary degree (*honoris causa*), a tax deduction . . .

Does it matter if one-third of the cost of the Fisheries Chair at UBC comes from the fish-packing companies? Angela thinks so. She fears that fisheries research will be primarily validated by its practical utility in improving company balance sheets.

Private money creeping into universities is persuasive. Almost unknowingly, the range of debate is limited. Almost unconsciously, serious challenges to things as they are tend to be avoided.

I hope you'll meet Angela, dear Reader, at the class reunion. (And Shawn, and Ron, and Hardev, and Dominique.) At a Christmas party, Angela was the one who asked my wife Dorothy, "Is Alex really as ornery as he seems?" My wife, in the babble of voices, thought Angela had said "horny," and replied, "You have nothing to worry about, my dear, nothing at all."

Paying a visit to my old tennis partner, Pat Nowlan, whom they call
Serve-and-Smash. 'Will you be taking lunch, Pat?'

Oh, my, the company I keep! My debating partner, Jean Chrétien,
and I share a laugh with (at?) . . .

Jim Fulton, MP. 'Nothing like a dry budget speech to raise a thirst!'

. . . John Crosbie, the Codfather, who's just called his own partner, Ray Hnatyshyn, a spelling mistake.

Which one's the real senator?
Alex, looking every inch a
senator himself, discovers a
socialist mole in Philippe
Gigantes.

In Thatcherland visiting with
my niece Mollie. Even
socialists can learn some
valuable lessons from
Dame Maggie.

It has been reliably estimated that 1.56 per cent of the world's
70,000 parliamentarians are airborne at any given moment. I
myself was invited along to Greece (above) and Cyprus (below). The
lessons I learned on these voyages of discovery I pass on to you, dear
Reader, elsewhere in this volume.

How did the Zalm get into my class? As a mature student?

'Grandpa, what are your views on the notwithstanding clause?'

In Rio for the Earth Summit, where Dorothy and I meet some new
Amazonian friends.

Rio had been 'cleaned up' for our visit, and we had a good view of
both the beach and the street cleaners from our hotel room.

CHAPTER 7

*Old Alex just won't hold his tongue, and — quite out
of step with his times, as usual — listens to a dead
judge who saluted "free speech for the thought we hate,"
and decides we should not even scissor Rambo.*

Dear Reader,

My blood pressure is up. Veins are probably bulging on
my forehead — and all because of a letter that arrived in
this morning's mail from my niece Mollie.

Well, to be quite honest, it wasn't the letter that sent me
ballistic. It was an article she enclosed, written by one of
her instructors at Carleton University, a Marvin Glass. Mollie
should have put a warning sticker on that article: "Dangerous. Handle with Care."

Imagine that instructor of hers claiming that people like
him can shout down the speech of someone else because
they think it's not good to let the rest of us hear it. And
he makes this sound so-o-o high-minded! "The moral permis-
sibility, on some occasions, of denying certain individuals
the opportunity to speak . . . "

Have we ever got prissy busybodies running around these
days. *They* want to decide what *we* can see and hear, and,
by extension, what *we* can think and believe.

They're too busy for my liking. I prefer the free-speech
ideas of old guys like Chief Justice Holmes of the U.S.
Supreme Court. Holmes thought we were better off allowing
bad things to be said, even if they hurt our feelings — at

least up to the point where someone is actually going to get hurt. That without free speech, we get less out of our lives – corruptions go undetected – hypocrisies and pomposities go unpricked – social change slows to a crawl – art gets tongue-tied – and on it goes.

Fortunately, Mollie's letter brought my temperature down again. I can't afford to stay mad long at my age. My clever niece's letter shows she wasn't taken in by this stuff. I just hope she gave that teacher of hers some critical counterblast. Like the old chestnut from Voltaire: "I do not agree with what you say, but I will defend to the death your right to say it." And defend, dear prof, your right to say it to a university class, where learning depends on the free market of ideas.

So I'll tell Mollie not to give up on that teacher of hers. He's teachable, even if he comes across in his article as "I'm so right, I've been born anew and now I am a Marxist." Well, if he is, great. Good chemistry: my Catholic niece studying under a self-proclaimed Marxist. That's got to be a fine blow-off of mental bubbles and gases.

Ah, but is he a real Marxist? "De omnibus dubitandum," my old friend Karl Marx used to say at parties (I was told this on Karl's 188th birthday, I did not hear him say it): "You should doubt everything."

That makes me wonder sometimes if I'm a real Marxist myself. Even Groucho must have wondered, when he said he couldn't bring himself to join any club that would accept him as a member. In my case, read "party" for "club."

Getting back to what that teacher wrote – I give him low Marx for this: "We ought to stand, morally, against the free speech of some individuals, for instance, racists." Uh-oh. Or, for instance, Marxists? There are people with deep pockets who jump at any excuse to stand against the free speech of Marxists.

And I give him no Marx for this, either: "We should not be lumped with those who threaten lives. One can prevent a speaker from speaking simply by shouting him down, or playing transistor radios at full volume during his talk, or blocking the entrance to the podium."

Oh no? Why shouldn't he be lumped with those who threaten lives? After all, it's only a thin line to cross from his morality to that of the Ayatollah Khomeini, who ordered the execution of Salman Rushdie for writing a book that would offend many Muslims, if they had a chance to read it.

What would Oliver Wendell Holmes have thought of that death threat? He's the one who held fast for free expression, even for the thoughts we hate. But he wouldn't tolerate threats of violence, no sir!

Of course, where there's a serious threat, a charge should be laid. Even verbal face-to-face taunting can be a criminal assault. Sure, there are limits in the ordinary laws I grew up with. Yes, gentle Reader, I'm with the old judge – at least, I'm with him on my good days.

On my bad days, I have my doubts. I look around this old world and see rising tides of hate and prejudice. And I say to myself, maybe we do need more than ordinary laws to curb hateful speech. I say to myself, if our human race is to go down, it won't be from a nuclear blow or some plague. Hatreds will do us in, the bottom falling out of values – such as civility.

Yet, on good days, I know shutting people up doesn't eliminate their prejudices. They fester, and they will out. Let me give you some examples of prejudices I've run into recently, and you tell me, sagacious Reader, how we should deal with them.

○ One of my students takes army training. He told me about being on training exercises recently behind Stave Lake in the mountains near Vancouver. He saw a group of neo-Nazis strutting around in black shirts, shooting at targets hung on trees. They had gun permits, and although the RCMP kept an eye on them, they were within the law. They are like the skinheads you sometimes see in cities – anti-Semitic, right-wing know-nothings. Though they are few in number, they can be dangerous – like cockroaches in the kitchen.

O My policeman son-in-law, Adrian, tells me that ethnic gang warfare is on the rise in Vancouver. The gangs are made up of sullen, bored young adults, drop-outs from the peer pressures of school, with poor job prospects. They have knives, some guns. They fight other gangs for turf, drugs.

O A construction worker is bringing up a family with three children in East Vancouver. He pays $1,200 a month rent to an absentee owner who bought the house as a ticket to immigrate to Canada. He makes $25 an hour on the job, though his wages are less certain than his rent. Yes, his racial attitudes are affected – even though, as I tell him, what we need are humane housing policies.

O A student tells me that a few rock singers and stand-up comics are sprinkling their acts with racial and sexual slurs. They seem to think prejudice has become hip, with lines like: "Immigrants and faggots, they make no sense to me." They are, I'm assured, vastly outnumbered by those who use rock and gags to pull the human family together. Still, it's ugly stuff.

So what to do, Reader? Can we still rely on the lofty dicta of freedom lovers of times past? Do we need more fines and jails, not only for what people do, but for what they say?

I looked up another dead U.S. judge, Louis Brandeis. He was a colleague of Holmes, and he wrote, "The right of free expression – to expose falsehoods and fallacies – to avert their evils by education – the remedy is more speech, not less."

Brandeis understood, 60 years ago, that laws can't root out the underlying causes of prejudice. He's still right, even though prejudices are on the rise again. Their causes are increasing poverty, social injustice and ignorance. Show me a society with glaring social inequalities and I'll show you a society where groups declare unofficial war on other groups. Better we declare war on these causes.

Restricting free speech rarely prevents harm and usually does more harm than good. Let me give you more modern instances (I'm full of them):

"We will not accept material that is racist, sexist, homo- phobic or otherwise degrading." This is from the masthead of the *Peak*, the Simon Fraser University student paper.

Now, what I think is that those youthful editors should be boasting that their paper *will* print any news. Instead they boast of what they *won't* print, floating a vague censor- ship rule that can mean anything or nothing. And censors always get carried away.

It was under this rule that the editors rejected an ad for a meeting of an anti-abortion club. The club, they opined, stood for sexism and something "degrading to women." Well, really! I happen to think letting pro-lifers talk makes them less, not more, apt to harass some troubled young woman.

Another instance. One day, I found my friend Elvidia sadly lugging books to the back racks of the Britannia library. Some righteous group had complained to the library board. So there she was, stashing away from public view such offending books as Shakespeare's *Merchant of Venice* (racist), *Cinderella* (sexist), and Mark Twain's *Huckleberry Finn* (racist again, because the word "nigger," part of common speech in Twain's day, appears). Elvidia cheekily told me she'd have had to stash Sophocles' *Oedipus Rex* if Rex had been a dog.

Ah, me, the censors' work is never done. In the 19th century, they snipped out sex. Now they snip out sexism – a more subtle evil, and trickier to spot. How can we find our path to the future without the strange visions and insights of authors past and present?

Here's another instance of the foolishness of attempts to censor. One morning, I had a Ukrainian breakfast of garlic sausage, scrambled eggs and perogies at "Hunky Bill's," a restaurant in Vancouver's West End. And there was Hunky Bill himself, Mr. William Konyk to you.

He was still harping on the $10,000 he was out in legal costs to defend his trade name (which does sound suspiciously like "bohunk"). Some high-minded fellow Ukrainians had hauled him in front of the B.C. Human Rights tribunal, and he had to appeal to the B.C. Supreme Court to lift his conviction.

These tribunals trivialize real wrongs when they chase words instead of just redressing acts of discrimination. Fortunately, they can't yet get at our thoughts, for, as a judge name of Baron Cockfield once said, "The thought of man is not triable; For the devil himself knows not the thought of man."

Besides, if making fun of someone is an offence, half the Scottish race would be in jail. The Scots even enjoy a joke at their own expense! As a matter of fact, that's the only thing they do enjoy at their own expense.

Who was it, clever Reader, who said humans would be humourous only if they stopped killing each other? He should have added that they'll only stop killing when they are humourous.

Fortunately, my students aren't prickly about letting others speak their minds. We've discussed in class some of the creeps whose speech we hate.

First, that really mixed-up Alberta school teacher, Jim Keegstra, who should have been fired by his school board years ago for misleading kids about "Zionist plots." Second, Ernst Zundel, a more dangerous Hitler apologist.

Both relished the coast-to-coast publicity their trials gave to their anti-Semitic ravings. When *acts* followed such mouthings, Reader, as they usually do, punish the actors – do not prosecute the words.

Although I have to admit, I'd be tempted to charge the religious right, who took over the California Republican party and passed a resolution to "re-take the Panama Canal." What, again?

My students are intolerant only of intolerance. And they are more optimistic about a tolerant Canada coming on than I feel in my old bones. What a mix it will be. Races, creeds, cultures – all there are. A fine mulligatawny soup. No other country can boast such richness.

But it's not going to be easy for Canadians to get along with each other. It won't happen without political changes that will make the comfortable feel less comfortable.

One student, Helga, told me she thinks too many Canadians get single-issue bugs in their heads and become awfully intolerant. We talked about the anti-abortionists, the far fringe of them. They say, "I obey God's law," and clog courts and jails for harassing young women who are trying to put their lives together by not having an unwanted child. And we mentioned the skinheads, sporting swastikas – and gun-nuts who talk with rising hysteria about their need for weapons.

So I tried for an up-note.

I told her of some Scottish fanatics who do good, even though they do it accidentally. I gave her Lord MacKay of Clashfern, the Lord Chancellor of Great Britain, no less. However, his Free Presbyterian church (no candles, no incense and hard pews) put him on trial and expelled him.

They charged him with consorting with Catholics – and dead ones, at that. He had, not once but twice, attended funerals of Catholic judicial colleagues. The good news is that Lord MacKay then started a sect of the Wee-Frees that may, God willing, be more tolerant of human needs. Helga (a Viking!) goes to an Anglican church. She proudly told me that the English Anglicans have ordained a black, polygamous arch-bishop – allowing him to keep his seven wives but on no account to take another.

I remember my friend Glen How, a lawyer for the Jeho-vah's Witnesses. He's a fanatic, if ever there was one. He truly believes that I am damned. I met him first 40 years ago in the Supreme Court of Canada. He was fighting for the free speech of Jehovah's Witnesses, who were then on the streets of Québec, deeply Catholic in those days, with pamphlets calling the Pope "the Whore of Babylon." The Pope had enough troubles without that. But Glen How's case marked an important advance for free expression in Canada.

Helga, and all my students – they'll bring some fun as well as tolerance into the Canada-to-be. As for me – well, you know me. I try to slip in a message – that tolerance comes naturally in a society where people are on a roughly equal footing, money-wise. Bigots don't try put-down slurs on their social equals. If they do, they get back a "Knock it off, creep. Get lost."

Meanwhile – yes, Canadians have quite a way to go, dear Reader, to that social equality. And on the way, prejudices, ethnic and religious, will flow and ebb. Lots of strife before we can say, "We have no black looks, or angry words, for our neighbour – if he enjoys himself in his own way."

Know who said that? The Athenian statesman Pericles, some

430 years before Christ, spoke those words over the Athenian dead when Greece was riven by bitter war between Athens and Sparta.

About fifteen years before those Peloponnesian Wars, Pericles had asked his friend Phidias, the sculptor, to oversee the building of a temple on an Athens hilltop dedicated to the virgin goddess Athena. It became the Parthenon.

I visited that temple on my way back from Cyprus a few years ago. One morning, our party clambered up the hill to gaze on the old Athenian dreams of Truth and Beauty, carved in white marble.

Of course, the Parthenon is a standing ruin now. The best of the carved marbles are gone, made off with by the English Lord Elgin in 1816. You can see them today in the British Museum.

Still, what remains is wonderful. Columns and friezes daring the skies, mute reminders of a society's high aspirations, expressed in sculpture and architecture.

That day, I remember feeling I'd been steeped in the best and the worst, the highest aspirations and the lowest, from the Parthenon to the big-buck, world-wide entertainment industry. I'd decided to spend the afternoon wandering around by myself, and caught a crammed bus to the old port of Piraeus.

It was raining, and I was pushed on board by the crowd behind me. My bus careered through the traffic, old cars darting around it. There were jarring stops and goes, squealing brakes, blaring horns. A courtly Greek, pitying my age, rose to offer me his seat. I almost plowed him one.

You wouldn't believe who I ran into in Piraeus. Why, it was Mr. Rambo of Hollywood, California. There he was, on a poster outside an old warehouse-turned-picture-palace. The poster advertised two movies in English with Greek subtitles, *Rambo* II and *Sex Kittens on the Prowl* – something like that. Mars, the God of War, and Venus, the Goddess of Love, back to back! For a couple of drachmas, yet. I know a bargain when I see one. I went in out of the drizzle. I sat on a straight-backed chair and peered at my fellow film buffs in the flickering gloom. Most of them looked like seamen on shore-leave. Underpaid labour from the Third World, ebony blacks, olives, tawny browns – far, far from homes and families. I think I was the only pink in the place.

They were all strangely silent, eyes glued to the screen, intent upon the goings on. Not a giggle nor an "ah" escaped them. Rambo had gone to Vietnam to rescue American prisoners taken in that most forgettable of wars. He seemed out of sorts, if not downright surly. Otherwise, he cut a fine figure. His bare torso bulged with anabolic muscle; he wore a Lillian Vander Zalm headband. Soon after I sat down, he had to shoot down an armed helicopter gunship with what looked like a medieval crossbow. Maybe that was what made him cross. No, he was still cross, blazing away with an Uzi assault automatic.

Anyway, he sure gave 'em what-for. The gooks, I mean – slinkers, with shifty slit-eyes. I took them to be Commies.

The gooks got Rambo for a while. They tied him to a tree and made him watch while they performed atrocities on an American POW hanging head-down from another tree. This would make anyone testy. Especially as some sprucely uniformed officers were standing by watching the eviscerations and buffing their nails. Their heavy Slavic features gave them away – Russians!

Free at last, Rambo soon had blood spurting in all directions. He'd freed himself single-handed – except for one Asiatic sympathizer, a white-haired, gnarled Philosopher who puffed away on his water pipe (opium?), who regarded Rambo with undisguised admiration. No Commie he!

Rambo had a funny way of talking through his clenched teeth. He didn't say much, but what he said was right to the point.

"Good guys," he grunted, "can't win if they play by the rules." Then, a hefty sigh. "We put them away and the judges let them out."

Later, suiting action to words, he drenched a wounded Vietnamese with gasoline. "You have a right to remain silent," he advised as he tossed a lighted match.

You'd have to fault Rambo's manners, but not his patriotism. As the film ended, a clean-cut, boyish American colonel asked, "What do you want, Rambo?"

"For our country to love us as we love it," Rambo replied, quite overcome.

I stole a glance at my companions. Yes, by now we'd supped full on horrors. We were ready for a different kind of warfare. Navel engagements. Venus at last! And, sure enough, the Kittens came on. The entertainment industry was going to play another game with our heads – or would it be with our libidos?

Clothes were coming off. This was better, I thought. No one without clothes on ever killed anyone.

Alas! The heroine was attacked with a friendly weapon in the second reel. All those undulations, and me without my sea-sick pills. I retreated into the drizzle.

On the late bus back to Athens, I talked to a grizzled Greek sage. "It's a long way," I said, "from what I saw at the Parthenon."

"Oh, those movies." His eyes flashed. "They're just a ruse to make money."

"Then the industry gives people what they want?" I asked.

"Gives them what they want them to want," he said. Sounded like some kind of socialist.

"But what does it do to the people who line up for tickets – all that gory violence?"

"They take it for what it is – fantasy, escape," said the old fellow. "But deep down inside, they come to take brutality for granted."

"As if," say I, borrowing William Blake's words, "'They become what they behold'? Can that be good?"

"Not good at all," he said, tapping his walking stick for emphasis. "Wars begin in the minds of men."

Later, back in the hotel, I looked out of the window to where the ancient Athenians sat in a circle on stone benches under the open skies to see a play by Sophocles. *Oedipus Rex* — now there was a violent ending. King Oedipus had unwittingly killed his father and married his mother. When he realized the enormity of his sins, he gouged out his eyes:

> *King Oedipus, reeling, blinded, from the palace doorway,*
> *Red tears pouring from the torn pits*
> *Under the forehead . . .*

His fate was ordained by the Blind Furies that punish human transgressions. That's how Sophocles saw it. He wanted to get to the truth of the human condition; the violence was an essential part of the play.

That was not the mindless entertainment we see so much of today. Have you ever seen in it the mourning family of one of the killed, dear Reader? No, it wouldn't be good box-office. Instead, you find what's true and false, what's real and unreal, all mixed up. No discomfiting thoughts.

The bracing community theatre of ancient Greece gives way today to global entertainment conglomerates. Mergers, buy-outs. A shrinking few produce the movies and videos, own the movie theatres, TV outlets and satellite transmitters, control the production and distribution of magazines, books, newspapers. They're interested in only one thing . . . and they give us pap. Alas, we're surrendering control of our culture.

But let's not cut Rambo. Censorship won't work, anyway, in this high-tech age of ours. A whole smuggled movie can fit on a pocket-sized cassette. Better we give a helping hand to the good arts in all their variety. And you needn't ask

me what the "good" is – you know it's what people like to
keep coming back to, for more meaning, more beauty.

A while ago, I listened on CBC-FM to a Mozart Singers'
competition from the Tannenbaum Centre in Toronto. A
hundred young competitors. Nightingales! The prize money
was $400, kindly split between two winners. Less than the
cost of Rambo's crossbow.

The trick for us is to deploy the resources and devise
the social devices so the bad doesn't drive out the good.
Ought to be the other way round.

Well, dear Reader, I'm spent! But I can't let you go without
this. I'm going to ask Mollie to tell her instructor about the
time I ran into the most pervasive kind of censorship. This
he'll appreciate.

It was when I went to a performance of *King Lear*, put
on by a repertory company in San Francisco. The Geary
Theatre is in a posh part of the city. But a few blocks away,
in the old Tenderloin district, innumerable shadowy figures
slouched or slept on the sidewalks. And you know what?
In this version Lear, the mad king, somehow neglected to
give these memorable lines:

> *Take physic, pomp;*
> *Expose thyself to feel what wretches feel,*
> *That thou mayest shake the superflux to them,*
> *And show the Heavens more just.*

Was even this spirited theatre troupe (never mind the TV
networks) mindful of the corporate grants it needed to survive? Enough! Too much! But what I'm saying is important:
When people are not ill-fed, ill-housed or ill-educated, they'll
not speak ill of each other.

CHAPTER 8

*The author visits villas in the California desert to sow
socialist seeds, but finds winter-sun fans prefer con-
spicuous consumption to socialist verities; later, loose
on day parole, he forms a red cell with a friendly
unmoneyed American.*

Dear Reader,

We are, my wife and I, ensconced in a low-slung bungalow
on the edge of a golf course. The bungalow lies within the
guarded walls of a country club near Palm Springs. We are
among . . . hey! these are glitzier richies altogether than those
who boost the neo-conservative cause in London, England.
They haven't had to work their heads to acquire their right-
wing views. No, they inherited them painlessly in their dad-
dies' wills. Their heroes are Ronnie Reagan, who always has
a good word for people of means, and Ron's female counter-
part, Maggie Thatcher, if only because a friend of Ronnie's
is a friend indeed.

Here I can take my ease in an easy chair on the grass
in the shade of a grapefruit tree, with a book of verse and
a cup of wine, hearing the whack of golf balls (and ready
to duck), the piping of birds, wifely kitchen noises (will it
ever be lunch time?), and Dorothy's ever-solicitous voice:
"Alex, will you do me a favour? Comb your hair."

I could get used to this life, I really could. No matter
that underground sprinklers spurt without warning, making
me take cover. And never mind that I have trouble finding

121

my wife in the king-sized bed. But I have to say I don't like that dog – that ceramic life-sized mottled collie on the lamb-white carpet. Are there any real dogs within the ramparts of this villa in the declining American Empire? I see none. How come? Fear of excrement, no doubt.

And yet ... I am strangely restless here. Why is that? Why can't I relax and enjoy all the pleasures of the damned? The other day I was quite overcome with an urge to search for signs of intelligent life in this part of the universe. I applied for a day pass (Dorothy had tennis) and Toyota'd south on Highway 111 – to Indio, where I had heard common people lived. At Indio, I saw a road-side mini-mart, gas pumps and a familiar sign – a 7-Eleven, open 24 hours.

As I beheld the vision, into my wandering mind came a flash of knowledge. Hey! Isn't that the company Sam Belzberg tried to take over? I know Sam from my home town. I've played tennis with the man! Sure he's getting on, but he floats like a butterfly and stings like a bee – on the courts, anyway. And he is *always* a gentleman (do gentlemen prefer junk bonds?). I decide to patronize the business Sam wanted so badly to own, and pull in next to a van. The bumper sticker reads, "Getting away with it."

Inside, customers are helping themselves as two smocked employees hop and skip about, restocking shelves, tending the gas pumps and making the cash register jingle.

At a plastic table sits a 40-ish man. He wears sandals and a baseball cap; a copper chain encircles his neck, which doesn't look too red, at least not from this distance. He is drinking coffee. He's lean and lanky, with the kind of friendly face you'd want on your jury.

His body language invites me to join him. Could this be a sighting of intelligent life? He has sincere eyes, with just a hint of the hunted look.

"Haven't I seen you some place?" he says.

"No," I reply. "I've never been there."

"So where're you from?"

I confess to being a Canadian abroad, wandering and wondering. A virtual Alex in Wonderland. He leans across the table, emitting a grunt of pain.

"My blasted hernia. Is it true you have medicare in Canada? I'm one of the 37 million Americans with no medical coverage at all – not even a private insurance policy shot through with holes."

Yes, I say, we have medicare in Canada. I tell him it gets awfully cold north of the 49th parallel, and Canadians are better (though not much) than Americans at sticking together and doing things for each other. But I also tell him that, what with all the evangelical preachers and me-firsters down here – and lately, up there, too – hot-gospelling about free competition and free trade until every worker's hand is turned against every other's . . . well, Canadians will be lucky to keep the social programs we have now.

He listens intently. Me, a kindred soul? His eyes light up, and he leans over the table, his voice low and conspiratorial.

"You talk like a socialist! Boy, am I glad to meet you! I'm a socialist myself. There are only five of us in the whole of this valley, and one has a fatal disease."

I'm stunned. "An American socialist? May your tribe increase . . . Whaddo I do? I teach children at a university – or they teach me. And you?"

Again he leans forward. "I'm a university student myself," he says proudly. And then, apologetically: "I also do dishes, until I find something better." And then, brightly: "I've been taking courses at universities all over the southwest. Right now, I'm studying medieval French literature."

"You remind me of a friend who was also a mature student," I tell him. "He liked the university life so much that he kept on taking courses until he was 47. By then, he had taken everything except theology. So he suddenly took early retirement. He had independent means. His mother had left him an apartment block. You – I guess you don't have a legacy to stand on?"

This set him off. This man turned out to be a Facts Machine, delighted to have a captive audience.

"Legacies?" he began. Suddenly, the fellow started rattling off statistics like an automaton – clickety-click, clackety-clack.

"Each one of the richest one per cent of Americans inherits an average of $3.6 million. Three point three per cent of Americans own 28.5 per cent of all the nation's wealth. In the last four years, the number of millionaires has doubled."

"But," I butt in, to calm him a bit, "I hear you have a mere 71 billionaires down here – and that's counting Ross Perot, who made a bid to buy the White House with his own money a while back. A nice twist..."

My friend shakes his head. "What must a Canadian socialist think of these United States?" says he, leaning back in his chair. Then, clickety-clack – it was the Facts Machine again.

"Four companies control the towel market." (Had I pushed the wrong button?) "Five companies control the bed-linen market. One American dies of a heart attack every 45 seconds." Click. Pause.

"What would Thomas Jefferson, who wrote our Declaration of Rights, think of America today? He warned against concentrations of wealth."

I jump in. "You mustn't be so down on your own country, old fellow. America is the mother of bustle and invention. She is the mother of every promise, as well as every perversity. She is multitudes – and contradictions. She'll be promises again." Here I'm putting Archibald MacLeish's words in my own mouth.

He seems to like this, saying only: "We're sure in sticky times."

"And they'll get stickier before they get better," I tell him. "Anyway, I still like what Brendan Behan said: 'The man who hates you, America, hates the human race.'"

"Hey, you're more up on America than I am. Yet I suppose you were born in Canada?"

Now it's my turn to declaim. "My grandfather was born in a farmhouse bed in Huron County, Upper Canada, in the British Empire. My father was born in that same bed, in Ontario, Canada. I was born on the second floor of a hospital in British Columbia, a province of the American Empire!"

"The American Empire?"

"Yes. We're pretty well borderless now, what with the free flow of capital, goods, and services – and someday, bodies, too. The same dollar."

I'm just getting warmed up. "Gone, old boy, gone are the days when my father could give a fine speech on your Fourth of July at the Peace Arch on the border, starting, 'The 49th parallel, the longest undefended frontier in the world between two sovereign states . . .'

"Those two sovereign states – well, one of them is no longer so damn sovereign."

"So," says he, "that makes you and me sort of allies, doesn't it?"

"You got it, comrade. You and I have become housemates."

"Housemates, you say! And we're living in the same bloc, too – in one of the world's three richest blocs."

Uh oh. Here was the Facts Machine again. Clickety-click. "The Americans, the Europeans and the Japanese – one billion people in all – one fifth of the world's population, but consuming, nonetheless, four-fifths of the world's total output of goods and services . . .

"Say," he continues, "that Free Trade Agreement with Canada – whaddya think of it?"

"Free trade," I say, "is for the birds. Now, *planned* trade, industry by industry, I'm for that, and lots of it. It should be governed by international institutions, so people can enjoy other countries' products with reasonable prices and wages – along with their arts, literature, scientific advances.

"But this free trade/free markets stuff – it leaves Canada prey to the greed of conglomerates. Now they're spreading it to Mexico – then all Latin America."

I'm sipping at my coffee, looking at two big pots of the stuff over yonder. "What do the coffee-bean pickers get out of what we pay for this stuff?" I ask him. "Nothing but longer hours, shorter pay, fewer safety regulations. They're just grist in a corporate mill."

He, sadly: "Nothing like free markets to separate the creators of wealth from those who enjoy it."

Then he starts in again about how exciting it is to meet a Canadian socialist, how we share the same grievances and hopes – and I'm saying I want American liberal democrats to do their own best things, and Canadian socialists to do our own best things, with the best of both catching on, spreading over the border. Fellow conspirators, working in our different cells.

"Fellow conspirators – I like that," he says. "Just like the savvy Greek slaves in the Roman Empire. Slowly civilizing the vulgar Romans; finally running their empire for them."

"Until it fell! Okay – but we mustn't be smug, old friend. Got to watch out for the sin of self-righteousness. One of the deadly seven, isn't it?"

I'm noticing how slowly he nibbles on his burger. Fear of pesticides? Or just anxious to prolong its life? My glance apparently stokes up the Facts Machine again, and he's off.

"In the U.S., agribusinesses use 2,500 gallons of water to produce one pound of meat. With only 25 gallons, you can raise a pound of grain or vegetables. Americans' house cats eat more meat than the average Guatemalan. If Americans cut their own intake of meat by just 10 per cent, enough grain would be saved to feed 60 million human beings. Sixty million human beings die of starvation every year. A child dies of malnutrition every four seconds."

"Right, steady on, old boy," I say. "You are hardly a vegetarian, hey?"

"Almost," he replies. "Who can afford meat? Buckwheat pancakes for breakfast – stuffed cabbage leaves for dinner. Yeah, a hamburger once in a while – for animal protein." A pause and he's off again, clickety-clack. "If the big ranches didn't browbeat governments for subsidized water, hamburger would cost $35 a pound."

He takes a breath, and I ask: "What's that sound? Can it be? Yes, it is! Mozart – coming from the parking lot."

"Yes, they play it to drive away loafing kids with time to spend but no money. The kids think Mozart's uncool. Prefer junk sound, junk food..."

"And Mozart drives them away? Like Raid drives off mosquitoes? Hey, that reminds me. Know who almost ended up owning this place? Someone from my home town! He made a raid on the Southland Corporation, put its stock in play. Belzberg is his name..."

"And green-mailing is his game? Really? I'm surprised," says my friend. "I've heard Canadians are – well, great, but slow."

"Nothing slow about the Belzbergs, old buddy. They are children of the times, and know a good buck is a fast buck. Learned that from your very own T. Boone Pickens, a big-time green-mailer.

"Why, the Belzbergs took a run at Southland Corporation. Forced Southland to sell off assets so it could buy enough of its own stock to prevent the takeover. All that buying drove up the Southlands stock, so although the Belzbergs didn't get it they sold shares they'd run up in value for a nice capital gain – $65 million, I think it was – enough, anyway, to more than cover their incidentals."

"And they got away with it?"

"Oh, sure. Though in another one of their raids, on Ashland Oil, the Belzbergs got fined by your securities commission. A $400,000 fine, for a parking offence!"

"A parking offence?"

"Yes. They parked shares with a friendly broker – shares way over the number they're allowed to hold before they send the company the ransom note. You can buy cheaper before you send the note."

"Fined! I'll bet that ruined their social reputation."

"Not at all. Have you forgotten old Seneca, who said that successful and lucky crime is counted a virtue?"

"I don't think I know Seneca."

"How could you. He was a Roman senator. Says nothing now."

"Takeovers," he muses. "'We create nothing. We take what's there' – that's the game, huh?"

"Know what Sam Belzberg would say to that? He'd say he does good by imposing on target companies the discipline of debt. Look around you. See those two employees? How they're skipping about? They're working away to help retire Southland's raid debt. Somebody's got to do it."

"There used to be three employees here," he tells me. "One was fired. Now two do what three did, for the minimum wage, $3.90 an hour. They tell me they never know till the last minute when they'll have two days off in a row, so they can plan something with their kids."

I've finished my coffee, and decide to drive on. After a "farewell, old mole," I take off in the Toyota, deep in thought. The bond is cracking, dear Reader, between doing good and doing well – between services rendered and rewards received. A bad signal going out, these days, to our young, that says what pays big is not honest, useful endeavour.

My mood is lower than a snake's belly. But then, driving north, a spiritual lift! All at once I see a crowd of golden jo-jo bushes, their leaves fluttering and dancing in the breeze. These shrubs yield, I'm told, an oil as fine as the whale's.

And that starts me thinking: hey, old *Homo sapiens*, more break-throughs like this and there'll be no need for Robbie Burns to say:

I'm truly sorry, man's dominion
Has broken nature's social union.

A look at my map tells me it's not far to Indian Wells, home of the Hyatt of Champions – a stately pleasure dome, swathed with greenery and bright with sinuous rills, foaming fountains, exotic wild fowl. I decide to pay a visit.

Around this chi-chi hotel stand Caesarean busts with oak-leaf headbands, statuesque discus throwers. Swimming pools with mother-of-pearl linings. But no nymphs that I can see.

This pleasure palace was conceived in corruption and born in money politics. A scam, gentle Reader. Oh, the scams change, but they'll flourish as long as money buys politics.

At the pleasure palace's entrance I come upon six young valet parkers, standing silently amid Greek columns. They wear crewcuts, white slacks and beige jackets. Six brisk, fond lackeys to park and fetch. There is nothing bogus in their smiles, although they betray, on this occasion, some amusement at an approaching stranger. They may have mistaken me for a fusty old professor.

Few cars are seen. This is Sunday morning; church has beckoned.

One valet, tanned and fit, shows his brilliant smile as he swings open the door for me.

"Good morning, sir. A guest, sir?"

"Yes, a paying guest. I'm going in to buy a paper and use the bathroom."

The lad lets me pass. When I emerge, refreshed by a courtesy glass of Chandon champagne laid out in the lobby around a fountain of block ice and flowers, I am intercepted once more by the car jockeys.

Jockey No. 1: "Our employer, sir, will appreciate your patronage, sir."

"And pray, who may he be?"

"Charles H. Keating, Jr., sir, of Lincoln Savings and Loan."

"Why, I know that name. He is a rogue. He has been in the papers. Every man should have a little larceny in his heart, but this man has lakes. Have you met him?"

Jockey No. 2: "I have met him, sir. He has a glad manner when his lips are not pursed in disapproval of sin."

I allow myself an audible aside: "Why, oh why, do sinners' ways prosper? Dear Jeremiah, I wish I could answer your question."

Jockey No. 3: "Mr. Keating, sir, got his start by forming a group to raise donations against pornography. He gave speeches in Washington against filthy materials. He even spoke to high-school students; a friend of mine heard him. He illustrated his talk to the students with passages from a book called *Lesbian Lust*. He told them pornography arouses sexual appetites which then seek satisfaction."

Me: "Like greed, I suppose. Greed, too, must out. And does Mr. Keating claim to be porn again?"

Jockey No. 4: "Born again? Oh, yes, sir! Raised a lot of money and didn't fritter it all away on anti-pornography. He used enough of it to collect powerful friends on Capitol Hill."

Jockey No. 5: "Yeah. He even collected the head of the Congressional Banking Committee, Wilbur Mills, with a fat donation. They became pals. Then Wilbur fell into the Potomac River with a stripper called Fanny Fox."

Jockey No. 6: "Well, Mr. Keating's congressional friends were friends indeed – they helped him get his licence to acquire the Lincoln Bank – in spite of a miscarriage of justice in his past, a conviction for stock fraud."

Me: "Ah, I see. Mr. Keating must have heard that the best way to rob a bank is to own it."

Jockey No. 1: "Yes, indeed. Rake in the taxpayer-insured $100,000 deposits by promising high interest. Put together your kit – a corporate jet to fly politicians, a yacht to entertain regulators. Put together sweetheart deals – with yourself, of course. That's how he built this Taj Mahal in the desert..."

Me: "Tut, tut. The way you talk – will he be behind bars? Listening to you fellows, I'd have to say that your employer, of the seven deadly sins, has five? Maybe six?"

Jockey No. 2, with a laugh: "He is doing time now, in a country-club jail. Got himself in the papers too much – not lucky, like hundreds of others. Look at George Bush's son, Neil – joined the very same gold rush with a crew from the Silverado Company."

Jockey No. 3, who had been listening thoughtfully: "I read some Alexis de Tocqueville back in college – a French guy who travelled all over America more than 100 years ago. He wrote that too much individualism, over a period of time, leads to downright selfishness and corruption."

Jockey No. 4: "And to too many high rollers on the make and politicians on the take."

Me, showing off: "I, too, have done some reading. How about D.H. Lawrence, who travelled all over America 75 years ago, and wrote, 'America is pretty much what I expected. Shove or be shoved.' "

A car pulls up. Jockey No. 2 assists the passengers to alight. Jockey No. 6 drives the car away. On its bumper, a sticker: "My boss is a Jewish carpenter."

More cars. I leave the car jockeys with an Irish prayer: "May you live as long as you want to, and want to as long as you live."

The boys laugh. "See you, professor."

I have to hurry back for a tennis game. An acquaintance has kindly arranged a game of men's doubles. I'd heard that this fellow had been re-born – not once, but several times. I was to partner him.

After the game (we won, with God on our side, I guess),

I'm lounging on the club terrace, and he comes to my table
bearing two burgers and two Perriers. He's no youngster,
this Evangelical, but there's a spring in his walk. He has
what's best in Americans, a friendly look-you-in-the-eye
openness; no put-on airs.

"Hey, partner," I say. "Did we ever trash those two
used-car dealers from L.A. So good of you to bring a snack."

"Please don't mention it, partner," replies the Evangelical.
"And don't mention your letting me provide the balls; or
your letting me run back to retrieve their lobs. I've heard
it said that socialists are even willing to share rich people's
money."

"Anything for you, partner," I tell him. "I'll share my thirst
with you any old time, if you'll share your drink with me.
Share the wealth! I've got to start somewhere – and I've
heard your friends say, in hushed tones, that you are a
man of means."

"A man of means, yes. By any means? Is that what you're
thinking, partner? Well, if it makes you feel any better, my
second son is a tax-and-spend Democ-*rat*."

"Hmmm. At least your second son had the sense to pick
a rich father."

"In America," says the Evangelical, "education and hard
work are what make it, not family connections. Anyone who
works hard enough can make a fortune."

"What!" I expostulate. "You sound like Ronald Reagan.
He says he wants tax reform. He says the rich won't work
hard because they have too little, and the poor won't work
hard because they have too much."

The Evangelical, showing some heat, responds: "You're
talking about a friend of mine, partner. I've given fund-raising
dinners for Ronald Reagan, and for George Bush too. You
know what Reagan'd say to a socialist like you? He'd say
you don't understand incentive. Come to think of it, even
in our tennis match, it seemed at times like you didn't care
who won."

"I knew you'd take care of that," I tell him. "Hey, partner, I loved the way you lobbed balls up to those used-car dealers so they couldn't see them in the noon-day sun! They probably can't see straight yet."

But the fellow has a point, I have to admit. "Yes, maybe I did ease up some in the game," I continue, mollifying him. "If I'd hit my overheads full out, someone might've got hurt. I went for one once, and a grown man burst into tears."

"It was probably," says the Evangelical, "your partner."

Then he once more harks back to his pal, Ronnie Reagan – someone I'd just as soon forget. He's trying for a quick conversion, as in football, maundering on about how Reagan is for Free Enterprise because it gives everyone a chance. As for the poor – not much a government can do for them, he says. They just won't work hard – personality disorders, and so on.

I tell him that he was lucky his partner today hadn't come from a broken home and been raised on junk food. Otherwise, we'd never have beaten those used-car dealers.

He carries on. "I hope you aren't one of those who think Reagan has no conscience."

I hasten to reassure him. "No, I think Reagan has several consciences. Just won't let much rest on them. And," I add, "his free-enterprise beliefs help leave his consciences unscathed. Free enterprise doesn't ask if a thing's good or bad – it just asks, 'Does it make money?' "

By this time, the Evangelical concludes that his conversion has missed the bars. So he just says, smiling: "Did you get too much sun, partner? You really should wear a hat when you play in the heat."

He is glancing at his watch now, mumbling about some Super Bowl football game about to come on TV. But instead of leaving, he takes another dig at me, saying everything he's heard about Canada is great except the income taxes, which are astronomical.

I reassure him. "Oh," I say, "Canada has cut taxes in the

top brackets almost as much as your friend Reagan – down from 70 per cent on top income to 33 per cent. And besides – you'll love this – we have no death duties in B.C., none at all to dodge, as you'd have to here in California."

Then I add, merciless: "Ever thought of doing your dying in B.C., partner? No tolls, medicare, lovely climate – not all that bad, not in the hospitals, anyway."

This makes him glance again at his watch. "Time to go. The afternoon game will be on TV anytime now." (Is it the Tigers against the Penguins?) He has, he said, taped the morning game. (Was it the Broncos against the Dolphins?) Now he was going to watch the taped morning game on one TV and, at the same time, the live game on another. When I question him, he strongly denies he has placed any bets on point spreads.

"We fundamentalists don't bet," he says. "And, for that matter, we don't use any stimulants or other drugs."

"No drugs?" say I, pretending innocence. "Hasn't professional sport become an opiate of the people?"

He lets this go by. "Catch the game, partner. The Denver Broncos, you know, are owned by a Canadian – Pat Bowlen, a Calgary fellow."

My flush of national pride lasts all of two seconds, then I bid him adieu. "And thanks for doing the winning for us. You proved that the broadest backs should bear the greatest burdens."

This riles him. "You sound like a Godless commie! 'From everyone according to his means, to everyone according to his needs.' That's Karl Marx."

Me: "Yep. And he stole it off Jesus Christ."

He (quite hot): "All right, partner, tell you what – you give the lesson in my church next Sunday."

Me: "Fine. If I'm here. I'll do the Good Samaritan. How it's not about getting a clubhouse seat in heaven, or even one in the heavenly bleachers. It's about helping neighbours here and now."

He: "Say what you like."

Me: "Jesus, in his parable, was hitting the comfy priest and the Levite – the two who passed by on the other side, avoiding the stranger, who'd been beaten and stripped by robbers and left lying in the ditch. Those two were so wrapped up in gaining their own personal salvation that as far as Jesus was concerned, they'd never make it."

I'm getting wound up. "But Jesus was high on the Samaritan, the one who helped the stranger with medical care, accommodation, a hot meal, some change. Today, that comes out as medicare, a housing plan, income support. You can look on that parable as an accounting device – a way to reconcile your cheque book with the Good Book."

"Well," says the Evangelical, "if you can't be here next Sunday . . . we'll settle for tennis tomorrow."

Well, dear Reader? Did I behave myself? I was his guest. At least I didn't say, and it bothers me I didn't – well, here I am in America, where, if you believe the polls, 90 per cent believe in God and more than 40 per cent are church-goers. And yet, how much Christianity is really being practised?

And I didn't say: Hey, America! Remember your democratic roots! It's *not* "government of the rich, by the rich, for the rich."

Tonight, Dorothy and I are off to cavort with winter-tan people a cut above us in social status. The Rogers, friends from Vancouver, are taking us to a cocktail party where there'll be some of the Canadian sun-belt colony. With luck, I'll meet some who became millionaires in only two generations – maybe only in three. But am I to learn anything?

I do! I do! I learn that it takes money to make money (or did I know that already?). And I learn how I can own my very own off-shore bank. (*That* I didn't know.)

The Rogers pick us up in a Lincoln and I'm surprised to

hear Dorothy say that I've invited them to dinner after the party at the restaurant of their choice. I feel a sharp pain in my exchequer.

The party's at a condo in Vintage – *the* most exclusive enclave down here, Bill Rogers tells us. The waterfalls are higher, the lots are costlier (none less than $1 million), the building restrictions are tougher (you must spend at least $3 million on a house). Yet at Indian Wells, says Bill, an even more exclusive development is coming on line. It's tough on zillionaires, keeping ahead of the Joneses – all that moving.

In Vintage, we pass a monster home-away-from-home that sprawls all over a king-size lot. Six million bucks, that one, says Bill – owned by a John Bircher who has similar hide-aways in Florida and Colorado Springs.

How, I ask, does the Bircher come by his change? Oh, he has "honourary recourse," Bill says. Like, say a contractor wants to develop a $40-million subdivision, but the banks won't talk to him. This Bircher, with a few phone calls, raises the money. For this he gets 85 per cent of the profit – not bad, without putting up a penny of his own money.

This is how I relearned that big money makes bigger money.

We pass an 18-hole golf course, one of many in the area. Bill – a veritable fountain of information – says it takes one million gallons of water each day to keep one of these courses green. There are a hundred down here, he says. Beneath them, a huge snow-fed aquifer feeds the pumps. With demand like that, for how long, I wonder, will we Canadians be able to hold our water?

A little while later, after a glass of good California wine, I'm just starting to enjoy the party when disaster strikes. I am trapped in a corner by The Great American Bore. He wears a silly "I know something you don't" smirk. Asks how I am and responds to my question by saying he is "terribly well." Drones on about how the American medical system is superior to the Canadian one – better vasectomies, better transplants, better triple bypasses, better this, better that.

In self defense, I start talking, although he won't stop. We are a duet of the deaf. I try to penetrate his wall of sound.

"More people die in California of unnecessary heart operations than are saved in Canada by necessary ones," I tell him.

He ignores me, so I try again, with a true story from the Vancouver courthouse barristers' room.

"There's this lawyer," I tell him, "representing a Vancouver man who went to Seattle for a sex-change operation to become a woman – that operation not being covered by medicare. In Seattle, the operation is performed by a Dr. Miracle. [No, dear Reader, I'm not making this up.] But the doctor's knife slips and cuts the sphincter muscle. Now the patient is suing Dr. Miracle. Instead of becoming a woman, he is wearing a diaper."

But the bloke keeps blabbing – now he's on about how lucky Canada is to have free trade with the U.S.

"Yeah, great!" I shout at him. "Canada's like the patient with his feet up in the dentist's chair – with Uncle Sam, drill in hand, whispering, 'This won't hurt a bit. I'm only going to remove your gums.'"

My patience is at an end. I make a sudden break for the bar, where my luck returns. I meet Sylvia, a live one. She writes a chit-chat society column for the local paper, and takes me for a kindred soul who won't repeat – or remember – the tidbits she confides.

She's a mine of gossipy tidbits – so I dig right in. "Who's that?" I quiz her.

"A Canadian," she murmurs. "Flies in his own jet to play polo. Married to the one in go-go boots and fishnet stockings – his fourth. He's still well within his quota. Wife's a bit of a celebrity. She and her dog used to sing in a nightclub. But she's underprivileged, poor thing – only had two husbands."

"Seems like more than enough marriages to me," I say.

But Sylvia, sucking on her wine, differs. "Some of them marry for the divorce. She'll be all right. And he's a gentle sort. Tells his wives, 'I won't keep you long.' "

We stop to listen to some show-off telling Dorothy he's with Senator Herbert Kohl of Iowa. "Kohl," he's saying, "made $49 million last year and spent $6.1 million of it to win his Senate seat."

How refreshing, I think, a senator who has not been bought. He bought himself.

Sylvia keeps filling me in. "See the man in cowboy boots and the gold-studded Swiss watch? There's a son of a workaholic! His father left him a fortune, and left his work habits to someone else."

"Doesn't he look a little out of sorts?"

"Could be the junk-bond market," says Sylvia. "It's off a point or two. Or it could be his wife – she's started a rumour that she's going to give up modelling to spend more time with him."

I leave Sylvia, reluctantly, and circulate among people whose names I can't remember and whose faces I can't forget. One claims to be a Vancouver director of the B.C. Gas Company. This company got the gas when Premier Zalm privatized the gas division of B.C. Hydro. At once the new company bought a VIP jet, which lands in these parts for some directors' business meetings. This director starts to talk up privatization to me, but I tell him, "No need. I know its advantages."

I wander into the sun-room, and what do I hear? Music coming from one of those damn automatic pianos. The keys and pedals rise and fall as if touched by a ghost. Not even a man on the piano stool with a silly grin. Efficiency!

But, oh, what a god we make of that particular commodity.

Why not, for a few bucks, hire a budding Rubinstein to play a real baby grand? I can see why this place is a desert – a cultural desert.

We leave with the Rogers – but on the way out, an American paper-money man tries to sell me an off-shore bank in Montserrat. He takes me for a high roller – why else would I be at a party where it's not who you are but what you have?

"Hurry," this fellow whispers, "only six Montserrat bank charters left. Hurry – only $29,000 with a $20,000 discount. Strict anonymity. Political stability. Refuge from the tax man."

I speak in his ear. "Slutsky rates Western Samoa as one of the best tax havens. Keep in touch," I tell this no-goodnik, for whom too much is never enough.

Sylvia has been listening to our whispers. "What is the difference," she asks me mischievously, "between tax avoidance and tax evasion?"

"That I know," I tell her. "But it's not what you're thinking – it's not six months. It's more like six months out of Canada each year." Yes, six months away and you're a non-resident, with no taxes. A neat exchange of honour for money.

We drive off in the Lincoln and end up at a restaurant called Wally's. I can see at a glance that it's a place where you go in flush and come out flushed, with no doggy bag.

I can't read the menu prices in the candlelight, but I hear Bill order white truffles and a large sirloin. I order a mini-steak with a baked potato. I'm ready for the waiter when he comes to ask me how I found my steak. "Easy, I turned over my slice of tomato and there it was."

I can't help overhearing a man with a squeaky voice at the next table. In the gloom, he looks like a refugee from a fat farm. Did his last face lift fall? Too many nips and tucks?

"Got the best collection," he trills, "of Laker tapes. All their games for the last eleven years." He's a basketball voyeur.

Then, a small catastrophe – I sign for the dinner on my
Visa and fish in the candlelight for nine American one-dollar
bills for the tip. Only to find, much later, that I'd put down
my only $100 bill. I'd tipped $108! No wonder the waiter
had become so smiley, helping me up, murmuring what a
privilege it was to serve Canadians.

Back in our bungalow, I try to forget Wally's. Dorothy
turns in, but I slump in an easy chair and push the TV
remote-control – to drain my brain.

It's the sales channel. What delights are spread before
my eyes? Semi-precious jewelry at half-price; acrylic or fiber-
glass nails; a watch that tells humidity, with a genuine lizard
strap; an ivory-handled pistol, "the perfect gift for her." And
for him? "A non-surgical face-lift, look twenty years younger."
Plus a hair transplant (rugs are passé), only $1,700. Is it
true what some say about capitalism? That it provides things
in the wrong order?

How about a brain transplant? Good condition, never
been used? See no special on that. But pooch-perfume
Parisien, only $30 an ounce. Could use some, but sure don't
want a job as a dog-sitter, $10 an hour. No, I'm ready to
retire – to bed.

CHAPTER 9

Alex ventures into Los Angeles, a city that now appears to point the way to a future that Canadian cities want to avoid; and is told where to get off by the Cheshire Cat, the one who told Alice that where she wanted to go depended on where she hoped to get to.

'Twas the day after yesterday, and I decided to pay a visit to the City of Tomorrow. Correction: I revisited what was once proudly called the City of Tomorrow, but is called that now only with a shudder.

You, caring Reader, are perfectly welcome to come along. As a matter of fact, you *should* come along. True, you will witness some unpleasant scenes. And you will doubtless worry that this might be Toronto's future in twenty years, or Calgary's in thirty. But list thee to the immortal words of Thomas Hardy:

> *If way to the Better there be*
> *It exacts a full look at the Worst.*

We'll go to the city in style, in my rented Toy-auto, leaving this desert Eden where I languish to penetrate the San Bernardino mountains. I'll be thinking of my first visit to this City of Lost Angels, ah, so long ago, in the days of my youth.

That was in 1939, and the trip was a graduation present from my father. Four college chums in a Ford jalopy set off from Vancouver, to find...Yes! A humming city of gla-

mour, innovation, bustle; a confident city, pre-eminent in
public amenities, parks, fountains, galleries, people-go-a-
meeting places – a trail-blazer in science, in the arts.

And now, in this January of 1992, the sun stands fair in
the sky as my Toyota and I climb westward, up from the
desert floor through a defile in the coastal hills. Easily we
slide past trudging eighteen-wheelers, my Toy-auto humming
the song of the open road. I am four wheels and two arms.
We are both, the car and I, looking forward to seeing the
multifarious city. And to talks with perfect strangers, hard
as they are to come by.

An octogenarian in an old Buick, bent over his steering
wheel, passes in the curb lane. My Toyota can't help accel-
erating to keep pace. (Put this down to the impatience of
youth. "You are *not* to give chase," I tell her.)

9:15 a.m. I push radio buttons. The freeway report. A Mr.
Bynum (that's how it sounded) has just been shot dead on
the Santa Ana Freeway. What! Crime without intent to steal?
This is ridiculous! Bad karma.

Bynum was shot in the passenger seat, with his girlfriend
at the wheel. A driver behind, not yet apprehended, apparently became annoyed when Bynum's girlfriend did not pull
over quickly enough to let him pass.

What's that you call it, dear Reader? A drive-by shooting?
And some in Canada, too, you say. Pity! Oh, just one, a
teen in Surrey killed by a passing car. Oh, you just recalled
another? A bullet spraying of residential windows, also in
Surrey? What is the world coming to?

Back to Bynum. Why him? He wasn't even driving. No
explanation. Still, an analysis does come on air from a psychologist of the Los Angeles police department.

This fellow talks of a recent rash of drive-by freeway
shootings. He brings up the case of a Mr. Russell Primrose,
age 17. Primrose was shot last Friday after exiting too slowly.

Next, he tells us of a no-name pedestrian shot in the lower pelvis, but still alive, while "sauntering" across a pedestrian crosswalk.

This psychologist, I'm glad to hear, does not say that the victims "asked for it." Nor does he criticize them for not wearing bulletproof clothing, though this clothing is selling well. No, he puts the blame on "self-centred attitudes" and "a lowering of the respect for human life."

But why didn't he say what caused these attitudes? He knew, I'd guess, but he wasn't about to say it on the airways. He should have said the cause was an economic system that puts far too much emphasis on getting ahead by climbing over someone else. Greed, dear Reader, is having a dance with humanity – and is humanity ever getting its toes stepped on!

9:45 a.m., and I want a real breakfast. Grapefruit, even if it is practically free-falling from a tree by our sun-belt hide-away condo, is not manna. So we turn off at a Bob's for a ham and cheese omelet. Besides, the traffic is thickening, and I wonder how long the morning rush goes on in these parts.

I take a stool beside a couple of old guys nursing cups of coffee and jovially trading quips with each other. They appreciate me as an audience. One deplores the invention of chipless china; says he'll lose his hearing with the din the waitress is making, tossing dirty dishes into a tub. His pal, a retired salesman, teases him about his reluctance to accept *any* new-fangled inventions.

"Yes," replies his friend, "I'm against the glow-in-the-dark condoms you used to hawk to discount stores – though they won't impair *your* eye-sight any more. And I'm against that line of powered nasal-hair clippers you had . . ."

"You could make use of them right now," replies the salesman.

To my "How're things going?" they say, "Fine" – but then
get serious. Neither of them are looking forward to their
golden years in a nursing home, nor are their wives.

"If we're not cheated, our life savings will be gone with
the costs anyway, in a year or two."

I sense their fear of falling. They probably know someone
or other who fell, all the way down into the underclass.

Now the waitress chips in. She's single, pregnant, about
30 I'd guess, and is working twelve to thirteen hours a day
to save for the birth medicals.

I'm having a mood change. How come this incredibly
rich country has the lowest social spending of any developed
nation? How can the U.S. claim it has no classes? You don't
see class barriers on its TV or in its movies. Sure, they
show us the working girl at the bottom of the heap, ordered
around by the boss – but she always climbs up to become
a top dog who can sass the boss back. Class dismissed.
But in reality, the barriers are there.

The two old guys are asking me about Canada. How do
oldsters fare up there?

Better, I tell them, than down here. But with the dreaded
Free Trade Agreement pushing Canada and the U.S. ever
closer, our health care programs are shaky. Canada's just
a little guy sleeping with an elephant, I say. An elephant,
especially one with more problems than you have, is not
a partner of choice. We'll have to give it some behaviour
modification.

Bemused, they toddle off and leave me to my omelet
and the Los Angeles *Times*. What I read doesn't improve
my mood. They've had a "cold snap" in L.A., though they'd
call it spring in Winnipeg. Nevertheless, the paper says that
some shelterless souls died of it – "hypothermia" – in the
streets. Not many, seven or eight out of – it says – 35,000
homeless in Los Angeles.

The story is about a motion passed by the L.A. city

council with the votes of "liberals." (George Bush used to sneer at what he called "the L-word.") The motion threw open the council chambers to the homeless for the duration of the cold snap. The Chamber of Commerce didn't like it. Ah – but who came to sleep in that manger, there being no room at the inn? Maria – yes, Mary – with a baby wrapped in swaddling clothes. I see the picture; she's 15, Chicano, dark, wide-eyed.

What am I to think? "What you do to the least, to the weakest, you do to Me..."

I read on. A culprit has been apprehended. He's suspected of killing no fewer than ten of his fellow down-and-outers between September 4th and October 9th. And another drifter picked up for killing several other drifters. He tells police he "dislikes bums." Poverty is addling minds. The poor are preying on the poor like monsters of the deep.

11:00 a.m. Highway 10 is an unreal river of vehicles. I could be on Ontario's Queen Elizabeth highway. Rigs, RVs, bugs, a Tonto Safari with big tires and canvas flaps (I want to shout, "Africa's that-a-way!"). American cars built in transplants in Taiwan or somewhere, like my own Toyota. Slowly passing my driver's window is a yellow matchbox, pedal to the floor I'm sure, pretending to be a real car. Why do small yellow cars have this urge to speed? One of life's mysteries.

11:15 a.m. A rivulet of up-market cars trickles into the river. A Lincoln – I hear Lincolns have passed Caddies in the sales lane.

I see the affluent hamlet these cars come from, up in the hills. I've stayed in one – they're much alike – with my friends Mike and Inga. Curving avenues, arc lights, locked gates, man-made lake. Inga misses over-the-back-fence neighbourliness. Since both parents work to pay the mortgage (fear of foreclosure), commuting miles and miles, depositing any children in spiffy schools and day-care

centres, they get home late, tired. They don't see much of
the neighbours, apart from washing cars on Sundays. They
have to run hard to survive, toward the end of their lives.

(Why, gentle Reader, do people want to escape into lonely
isolation with their own kind? I will await your answer.)

My Toyota snorts annoyance. Snobbishly, she doesn't like
being passed by a smoking, unwashed black van with a
crumpled back fender. The driver sports a bandana and
ponytail. Then gives us both a raspberry look as he passes!
A "don't know where I'm going but at least I'm on my way"
look. Now I'm sticking *my* nose up at that fellow and his
van – a vehicle of surpassing ugliness. How could they hang
Tom Mooney and let that thing live?

11:30 a.m. Uh-oh. Just my luck. The radio flashes a smog
alert. This is awful! I might as well be back home in the
Fraser Valley when the westerlies force city fumes inland.
And me with no gas mask. Tail-pipe gasses and other
pollutants are mixing it up with sunlight over the city.

"Stay inside," says the radio voice, "if you can. Don't,
repeat *don't*, jog, jump, play, especially if you're old or if
you're young. Breathing may be dangerous to your health.
Watch out for tight chests. Rheumy eyes. Running noses."

Sure enough, I can see and smell yellowish brown fog,
as if the city were paying tribute to Crepitus, the Roman
god of air expelled through the bowels.

11:40 a.m. Never mind the radio, now I am seeing distinct
signs of criminal activity – like that missing stretch of freeway
fencing. I do not see the metal guard screening twisted, as
if hit by a car. I see it gone, stolen, by thieves. Probably
to feed their filthy drug habits.

I am still hearing crime reports on the radio, amidst
bursts of trip-hammer rock. Now it's a 52-year-old business-
man who gets it. He wouldn't turn over his $10,000 Rolex
watch to two muggers on Olive Street. They shot him. Did
his watch feel so good on his arm? Did he have to flaunt

his wealth on the streets? That is no longer advisable in big cities.

The radio says that the Rolex shooting and others have prompted the L.A. coroner to ask for a raise for himself. And for more staff. The coroner is complaining he had 387 bodies to sit on last year, and that bodies with lead in them are still dropping in at the rate of one a day. I can see his workload argument, but surely cases like the Rolex are open and shut – shouldn't take much time. If they find the shooter, and mostly they don't, it's surely: "You've rolled snake-eyes; go directly to jail – unless you own Park Place."

My thoughts trail off to a really involved murder I brought up a few years back in the B.C. legislature. Getting to the bottom of that case would justify a raise and more staff for any coroner.

The body in question is mouldering in its grave. Been there seven years now. Lies some 400 miles away, over my left shoulder, in Texas. It belongs, or did, to a Mr. Michael Opp. His killer got off on some technicality or other, but a deeper question remains. Was the shooter of Mr. Opp put up to it to prevent him from talking? To say yes or no to that, you have to follow a well-covered trail that leads all the way back to Howe Street, Vancouver, British Columbia. An inquiry into Mr. Opp's untimely end might very well go like this:

Coroner: "Gentlepersons of the jury, you have heard the evidence; that a Mr. Trujillo kicked in the door of the cheap apartment Opp rented in Phoenix, Arizona, marched Opp into his bedroom and put a bullet in his head.

"You have also heard what Trujillo's girlfriend was heard to say: that her boyfriend shot Opp simply to steal his $25 black-and-white TV set and a few smokes of marijuana. If she knew more, I must warn you, that evidence would be only hearsay, for that young woman has vanished, never to be heard of again.

"And, gentlepersons of the jury, I must warn you to treat

Opp's dead-say with caution. That is, the letter he left saying he 'feared for his life' because of his part in the salting of the Texas Oro Grande gold mine.

"Opp was, you have heard, an employee of Chemtex Laboratories. This 'assay lab' was set up by gentlemen from Howe Street to report on this mine. The gentlemen who set it up – here's a twist for you – were associated with the New Cinch Company that owned the mine. Chemtex Lab, you have heard, found spectacular deposits of gold in drill hole number 29. Did that evidence surprise you?

"Were you surprised that when news of hole number 29 leaked out, New Cinch shares shot up from $2.50 to $29.50? That New Cinchers in the know blew off their shares and made a killing?

"Well, the bogus assays hooked a big Toronto mining company, LAC, into putting $25.7 million into New Cinch shares – this surprised me. Boy, were the LAC fellows mad when word came that the mine had been salted – when New Cinch shares collapsed to 50 cents. So mad they sued New Cinch, its underwriters – even the Vancouver Stock Exchange. LAC got a settlement, and got back some of its lost $25 million. But the rest is silence. A term of settlement was that all court records were to be sealed – lips, too, were to be sealed. No one was to say anything.

"Even Opp. He's not saying anything – that's for damn sure.

"Gentlepersons: You will now retire to consider your verdict. Was Opp's death work-related or was it not?"

Opp (unlike the Rolex man) never got an inquiry into what led to his end. A mystery it remains. And King Lear? Oh, the king was at his wits' end when he shouted out:

> Plate sin with gold
> And the strong lance of Justice hurtless breaks;
> Arm it in rags,
> A pygmy's straw doth pierce it.

I tell my Toyota to stay within the speed limit so I can look around. Am getting a little cramped. A wonderful bird is my all-purpose Toyota – but not that much leg room. You don't hear of many Toyota babies.

12:15 p.m. There – way up – I see two white smoky trails in the blue yonder. Circles, climbs, dives. They must be from attack jets, though I can't see them. Jets from Vandenberg Air Force Base, F-16s, I'd guess.

An F-16 uses as much fuel in one hour – 3,400 litres – as you use, dear Reader, in two years of driving your car. Say, you must tell me sometime, why isn't the military under environmental regulations?

But right now, I'd better forget fighter jets and pay attention to this car racer I see in my rear-view mirror. He swooped down a freeway exchange in his low-slung super-charger of some kind, right onto my back bumper. Goggles, facial hair, fat tires. He flashes his brights. Feints to the right, then to the left, then zips past me. I get a blast of his big battery of stereo speakers. And then his tail fins disappear ahead in the shoal of cars.

What's the jig in his head? Got it! We're near Riverside, California, and its car-racing track. That guy thinks he's driving in a grand prix race. Has the wheels, and a rich dad.

Ever catch a look at the Riverside track on TV? Acres of campers on a weekend, their kids playing in the track's infield. On the track, grinding away – Indy racers, dragsters, stock, monster trucks . . . While the helmeted racers drone on, fans line the fence throwing down beer cans . . . waiting . . . will death never come? Some racer missing a hairpin turn and flying at 180 miles per hour into a pit stop? Or a tree? A fireball death? Or just multiple injuries, thanks to a designer seat belt?

Vancouver has its own Indy race now too, sponsored by that benevolent giant, Molson. And I have noticed more tailgating after an Indy. Drivers catching the Indy spirit! More drag racing, too. You may have heard – two going to work at 4:30 a.m. were killed by a drag-racing car not so long ago. Yes, Riverside is a Mecca of this so-called sport.

But maybe you think car-racing is not up to the blood sports of yore? Not up to slaves and Christians pushed among animals in the Roman Colosseum? (They had to wrap animal skins around the victims, or the animals would leave them alone.) No, car races are not up to picadors sticking bulls, or bear-baiting in Merry Olde England. Still, it compares favorably with hockey fights, or with 300-pound anabolic steroid-inflated linebackers crunching bones.

(By the way, Reader, that bear-baiting – the Puritans banned it, not for the pain it gave the bears, but for the pleasure it gave the spectators...)

We must be getting close. Trees and mountains are long gone. Now, if you see any scenery at all, it's billboards, litter, guard fences, graffiti, all along this concrete chute into the metropolis. A roar and reek of traffic. Sometimes a vista: box houses ringed by cars, discount waterbed stores, Midas muffler shops, malls surrounded by acres of parking.

Oh dear, where are the fountains of Rome, the plazas of Madrid, the pedestrian precincts of Amsterdam, the meeting places of Paris? History is felled here by the wrecker's ball. Demolished to make car parks or office towers. A shapeless blob, it seems to be, this city that money builds and continuously reassembles. A paradise lost.

12:45 p.m. Pomona, California. I'm on the brake as much as the pedal. My Toyota and I are both a bit disgruntled. I think I'm seeing the crime of the century. So I put this to her.

"This affair we're having – man and motorcar. You should have been parked and left in the desert. I should be coasting downtown in a comfy rapid-rail. I'd be there by now."

No reply.

"You, and your part in it, are surrounded by definite indications of a criminal conspiracy. Oh, a most respectable conspiracy, I'll grant you that. As respectable a conspiracy as the arms race. Yes, just oil, tire and car companies getting together and trashing street-cars – and buying politicians. Thank goodness, Toronto was able to keep its trams."

Hey! Another traffic stop. A black man, neat, a looker, gets out of the car ahead, casually opens the trunk, takes a package, returns to his seat and puts it in the glove compartment. What – smack? A gun? Is he up to no good? That's what the voices of my accursed education tell me. I shouldn't listen to them.

1:15 p.m. What a pickle! Traffic is so jammed up, I could be passed by a covered wagon! To avoid gridlock, I snake off the freeway onto a one-way street going the other way. A U-turn. Lights, a siren. An L.A. traffic cop swaggers toward me, sunglasses, cocked hat, hand over holster, a "hey, boy!" look, hitching his pants. Has this guy seen too much TV? I walk to meet him.

"Officer, am I glad to see you. Will I ever get to city hall? Where is it?"

He examines my licence. Canadian, eh? I chatter on. "Grandsons sired by a Vancouver policeman. Used to be his boss, back when I was attorney-general. Not a happy lot, is it, the policeman's?"

"Huh?" he says. "Well, we do our job. Illegal U-turns – and soon into something worse. Cal Code 2010."

"Not a happy lot," I push on. "Policemen have to clean up society's mistakes. Have to put bandages on boils, rashes – but the diseases are not being treated. Must get you down. And you don't get much thanks."

"Law and order – we are the front line . . . "

"Your governor here, what's his name, Deukmejian? I see in eight years he's appointed a hundred hard-gavel judges, built eight more penitentiaries, doubled-bunked them . . . But the crime spree?"

"We send them to jail and they come out to make room for someone else. The courts let them walk. Governor Deukmejian favours capital punishment."

"And does nothing about capitalist punishment... I hear you lock up black males at four times the rate they do in South Africa. Couldn't the money be better spent?"

"You – what are you? Some kind of liberal?"

"I am, I am."

"Well... Yes, it does get me down. I picked up the body of a young boy the other day. Hit by a stray bullet. Some gang's kids scattered out of sight – a turf war over drugs, angel dust, car thefts... Yes, I know bad conditions drive lots into drugs, alcohol, crime..."

"To escape the reality of despair in their lives. Is it easy for them to get guns?"

"Look. When someone plunks $800 in bills on a gun-store counter, nobody asks questions. They get machine pistols that spurt out fifteen rounds a second – with silencers. Police now have 65-shot automatic revolvers, just trying to keep up."

"Another arms race. You know what I'd like to see, officer? Even your Deukmejian might go for this. I'd like to see national service, in America, in Canada too. A couple of years when you're young doing useful community work, not military, some steady pay. Cleaning up toxic wastes, clearing forest paths, pushing wheelchair victims, making nice parks with fountains, building sports and recreation centres – conscription with a purpose! Making unwanted kids feel wanted, teaching them skills – good for the children of the idle rich, too. Kids suffering from a disinclination toward work of any kind – even if they could find jobs, and that's tough..."

"Yeah, I know one girl signed up for the Peace Corps, in Africa. We should have something like that here, too." He's putting his ticket book back in his pocket. "You can't miss city hall. Go down Alameda – big block with an antenna tower."

Phew. Last time I did a wrong-way street was in Mexico City. Luckily, I was with a friend who knew the local customs. He fished out a 1,000-peso note – worth maybe $2? – and the officer took his customary, and needed, income supple-ment and waved us on.

I have no intention of seeing city hall. They can take crime off the streets and into city hall without any help from me. I park under Pershing Square, the town centre — if this town has one.

1:45 p.m. As I come up the stairs to the sidewalk, I almost stumble on a tiny, wizened woman with a bony hand held out. She's selling coloured woven wristlets. In her lap I can just make out a baby in its wrappings. Or is it a doll? In Mexico City, you often can't tell. But this is a baby. I buy a 50-cent wristlet for a dollar and see her black saucer eyes widen.

Rising beside Pershing Square is the huge, opulent Ambassador Hotel I first saw in 1939. Now its opulence is fading, its baroque carvings sullied. When I saw it first, movie stars with dazzling smiles would leave this grand hotel to step into top-down Caddies. Waiting throngs would sigh and blow kisses. A natty bow-tied little man in spats would press forward with a bouquet. That's an old movie now.

What used to be grass in the square is concrete now, the "Keep off the grass" signs gone. Racks on the heavy bolted benches, so the winos and bums can't stretch out. Litter. Prone bodies on the concrete.

I watch an elderly, dignified lady. She trundles a luggage car with bulging plastic bags tied on to it. With a businesslike air and a three-foot stick, she deftly pries open the empty outlet of a garbage container, rummages, retrieves. The entrepreneurial spirit is alive in her.

It's also alive in a young black. He has a shopping cart full of cans and bottles. He makes, he tells me, from $10 to $15 a day. Ten cents a pound for pop cans and bottles — more for beer cans. When I toss in my drink can, a scroungy dog leashed to the cart looks up and growls. No way am I about to make a pass at this dog. "Nice black dog," I say.

"Jeff, I call him – after Thomas Jefferson, man! No slavery. Nobody owning nobody. Black? Yeah. We all come from the same black African mother."

I start down Fifth. A black dude. "You lost, man?" He's dapper, smiles, black suit, tie, fancy shoes. "Alligator, $315," he says. Beside him, a scruffy young white looks sheepishly down at his Nikes. "$35," he says. "All I had."

A woman gives me the finger. But it's the Jesus sign. "Bless," she says, as I give a bow.

I pass under the Golden Arches into a McDonald's and place my bet. Old moo-cow comes down the track and I take her to a formica table. A rumpled man at the next table makes out to be reading an old paper. He eyes me warily – he could be on the lam – and there's loneliness in his eyes. "Me? I'm from Michigan. Used to assemble Cats. Last hired, first fired, so I hitched out here.

"Where do I live? Under the underpass. Harbour Freeway. Keep my things there, a blanket, some cassettes, shaving stuff – it's home."

Does nothing change? A man who sleeps under a bridge! Brings to mind Anatole France, in Paris, a hundred years ago: "The law, in its majestic equality, forbids the rich, as well as the poor, to sleep under bridges, to beg in the streets, or to steal bread." In Vancouver, the city crops the bushes under the Georgia Viaduct, the easier to spot sleepers of all kinds.

"But you could be mugged, robbed?" I wonder.

"It's a hide-away – I make sure no one sees when I come out. I wash in a reservoir. Short walk downtown."

"Sure you're not wanted by the police?"

He, with a wink: "Why would the police want me? No one else does ... No – no food stamps. I can't even get a library card. They say I have no fixed place of abode."

"But there's a California court decision that says even a park bench is a residence when you register to vote."

"Rights! People are dying in the streets here with all their

legal rights intact ... A homeless shelter? No way. Bed bugs.
I'd be raped! I'd rather be my own man. Besides," – another
wink – "the rent's good."

"Rent-free?" I say. "Beats Burt Reynolds, I guess. I see
in the *Times* he lives mainly in Florida – big house and
ranch to keep up. And he rented another big house here
in Beverly Hills for his young son to use while he goes to
private school. $40,000 a month! Say, have you got a
girlfriend?"

"Well, sort of ... Yes. I see someone in the library – we
talk. She lost everything – home, kids – beat up. Lost all
but her car. She drove out here, won't take welfare or she'd
lose the car. She sleeps in it. Hotel maids help her. They
sometimes let her into a room when a guest checks out
early. She can wash up, get some bed-sleep."

As I leave – "See you," says a Mac girl, cute cap and
smock. (No pockets in her smock. Pockets might lead her
into temptation – to steal from the company, that is.) She's
minimum wage. In the last ten years, McDonald's executives
have gone from making 25 times what she does to making
88 times.

Still on Fifth. A rainbow group of teenagers pickets a
book store. On a placard, "Only a heel would wear an eel.
Only a flake would wear a snake."

A gangly young fellow hands me a flyer (not before taking
a quick glance at my shoes – old-fashioned cow leather).
"Trafficking," he explains, "in elephant hides, crocodile skins,
ostrich feathers – speaks to our basest commercial instincts."

"You getting anywhere?"

"Sure. Python skins can't be brought into the U.S. any-
more." Then he adds, "But ostrich skin, for shoes, belts,
from Thailand – they're still fair game."

His voice has become angry. These kids like their to-
getherness in a cause beyond any personal gain. But the
anger they share is edgy, close to breaking out into some

kind of vandalism. They see the killing of rare species as an absolute evil, to be fought at any cost.

Further down Fifth, young teenagers have made a parked car their private club. They lean on the fenders, sit on the hood. Lots of surface gaiety. They are pale, thin – the unwanted children of broken homes? Shunted from one foster home to another, abused when really young in more ways than one? They feel the sting of wanting and not having.

I'm looking at a gap-toothed girl, about 14 years old. "Her?" says a youngster with spiked hair. "Her old man beat her up." She grins.

Fifth and Main. The bus station. The eyes of missing children watch me from posters. I check out a young suited woman who does not fit in. A social worker, I'd say, on the look-out for runaways, off the bus and into the big city. She wants to catch them up with some caring services and advice before they sell their bodies on the streets.

My mind goes back to railway stations in London, a hundred years ago. Then it was Sally Ann workers trying to save youngsters coming off the trains. Fresh flesh to gratify the lusts of the rich – the younger the better. Then a memory intrudes. Me, waiting for the light at Drake and Seymour in Vancouver, a young male face at my car window giving me a hot come-on look that I couldn't handle.

Yes, prostitution is the last extremity of capitalism.

4 p.m. I stroll down Broadway. The movie palaces are dingy but brightly flash their wares. Neon proclaims that Die Hard II has hit the screen. I'll catch it. Without a word, the movie cashier punches me a senior discount ticket, upsetting me some.

I kind of miss old Rambo, gentle Reader. He, by the way, has gone back to Philadelphia, his home town. Must like it better than W.C. Fields did. When asked if he'd rather go to heaven or hell, Fields replied that, on the whole, he'd rather be in Philadelphia. Anyway, Rambo went back to

Philly after pulverizing the Russian mechanical hulk called
Diego. And what happened then to Rambo? His city fathers
cast him in an 800-pound bronze statue! And put him on
the museum patio, to the intense annoyance of the museum
directors.

What do I see on the screen? All right, I admit Art has
a hard time keeping up with Life these days. That severed
head, for instance, that turned up in a garbage pail somewhere in L.A. a while ago. Still, Art tries – as I'm sitting
down, the hero stabs someone in the eye with an icicle.
He does that – and doesn't quote from King Lear, either:
"Out, vile jelly, where is thy lustre now?"

Still, with an icicle? I sense a slippage in imagination. I
find it hard to keep up with the body count – hangings,
drownings, stompings, eviscerations, and so on. I lose track
at 78 when one man, I swear, is killed a second time. And
the rapid-fire images and thumping music make it difficult
to do simple addition.

Values. Say what you like, but Rambo always fought for
a cause. He'd be after some dirty Commie, or faggots in
the Pentagon, his eyes moist when he saw his flag. This *Die
Hard* hulk has nothing but a relentless commitment to car-
nage, for no reason whatsoever. Mindless, screwed up, no
human relationships. You can't even tell the good guys from
the bad in this picture. Everyone is trashed – the doctor is
a drunken sawbones; the teacher, ducking under his desk,
is a nincompoop.

I even lose track of the commercial plugs – Pepsi, Colgate,
Hilton, Alfa Romeo. And it doesn't help to have a man three
rows ahead muttering the whole time. I see only a penumbra
of matted hair and the duffel bag beside him. "Deal with
my gun, not me," he keeps saying, talking to himself – the
only one he has to talk to, I suppose. As for his gun, I
doubt if he has the money to buy one.

I'm wishing now they'd roll this reel backwards in slow motion, slow enough for me to see bullets winging back into gun barrels, the dead rising with fallen weapons returning to their hands, that eye reassembling its lustre...

I get up to leave. This movie will do well in Canada in Hollywood-owned theatre chains. Ah, Yeats! Where are you now, to remind humanity that

> *We have fed our hearts on fantasies;*
> *The heart's grown brutal on the fare.*

All-pervasive, ever-emulated American "culture." Alas, even the artful Czechs, liberated as they've been, are buying American sitcoms for their public TV channel because it's cheaper than putting their own artists to work. You want a culture with good creative juices flowing? We'll have it, we'll have it — *when* we summon up the will to put community resources into it.

Outside the theatre I pass a man with a sandwich board that reads "Kit-Kat Club." He hands flyers to likely males, but not to me. I've been unmanned! I'm not a live one? I go back and get one.

Back in the car, I start down Western Avenue to gas up. So I'm seeing too much of L.A.'s bad and not enough of the good, you say? True enough. So did President Roosevelt when he said, some 60 years ago, "I see one-third of a nation ill-housed, ill-clad, ill-nourished." Would that FDR could see it now — a nation of poor within a rich nation.

Well, next time, I promise, we'll see some of the good: the campuses, the parks and museums; the shops on Rodeo Drive where the clerks wait on the rich with reverence.

Up ahead on the right, I see the Accurate Gun Shop. Bet it's doing well. Half a million handguns were sold in L.A. this year — the "riots" were good for business.

Beside the gun shop is a tidy Korean grocery, where I stop for two cans of beer. There I see some good — a family making it, with Mom and Pop and a young daughter

– albeit with long, long hours and low returns. Part of the wave of Latin American and Asian immigrants whose hopes and varying values are propelling L.A. (not to mention Vancouver) into an unknown future. A welcome infusion of energy from new cultures.

But bad, too, I see in that store. I wait in a line-up as food stamps are traded for lottery tickets.

Later, at the gas-up, my Toyota drinks thirstily for a third of what it should cost her. Gasoline is cheaper than bottled water here in the U.S.

"And they fight wars," I tell her, "over the Tar Baby your drink comes from. You should have a battery in place of your gas tank, you know. State of the art, sodium-zinc or nickel-cadmium. When do you think the Tar Baby boys will let you run on one of those?

Passing the gas station inch by inch is a black, bent woman with match-stick legs. She walks without destination. What I see I have seen in pictures from Somalia.

6 p.m. Further down Western Avenue, in the parking lot of a Farm Fresh Supermarket, I see a sign, "Food Workers' Union." A table. Lists of names. Beige cards. I know this scene. The union wants enough cards signed to get bargaining rights.

As I approach, I notice that employees leaving work give the table a wide berth; their eyes down, they're pretending not to see the union organizers.

"How're you doing?" I ask at the table. A young woman answers, breathlessly. "I'm fired – and he [pointing to a passing employee] is scared. They have a new cashier doing my work." (When, oh when, dear Reader, will all Canadian provinces protect legally striking workers from being "replaced"?)

"Our lawyer is fighting it," says an organizer. Young, crew-cut, suit and tie – a college grad, I'd say.

The fired cashier is still talking. " ... $5.50 an hour and two kids to keep. Most of us are single mothers. If we got in a full week's work — but everyone works only in prime shopping times. I couldn't afford to pay into the health plan or the pension."

The organizer: "This is make-or-break for the Food Workers' Union. If we can't get union conditions in the Farm Fresh chain, they'll undercut the union supermarkets we have, and drive them out of business."

"Yes," I say. "A down-market drive against unions these days. In Canada, too. Once, 200 years ago, capital used the criminal law to prevent employees from bargaining with one voice. 'Criminal conspiracy,' they called it. Now capital is content to fight unions with the laws of economics. Free competition, so-called, is what the unions are up against."

Organizer: "Well, we're not giving up, no way."

Me: "You can't. But remember that unions have to fight on two fronts, not just at the work sites. Without guidelines for fair sharing of work and incomes, unions can only do so much."

6:30 p.m. Almost my bed-time. I find a ramp onto the freeway. I'm pining for the rich green pastures of Palm Desert. Cars crawl in slow columns like ants. It takes me one hour to do five miles.

Then — good tidings! An announcer on public radio tells us that somewhere afar, in Vermont, a socialist has been elected to Congress. He wants, the radio says, millionaires and multinationals to pay their share. He wants "production for use and not for profit." Oh my! How strangely old-fashioned, but curiously relevant, that sounds.

But this? "Flash! From Palomar Observatory [on a mountain to my left] our infra-red spectrophotometer has picked up a red dwarf heading directly toward Earth. It has escaped from a cloud of red dwarfs. It is 65 million light years away, travelling at one-tenth the speed of light." The voice then calculates its time of arrival at 500 years hence — lots of lead time, really, for that particular problem.

Another news bulletin. I like this. A young voice says,

"Come to the Great American Yard Sale in L.A. tomorrow, in aid of the homeless. Bring shoes, sweaters, crockery . . . " They'll gather, those who care and hope.

7 p.m. Some more good, this time a string quartet by Papa Haydn. Composed in 1786, when Papa sensed the breath of freedom in the air. So I listen as he gives each of his children – violin, second violin, cello – equal chances, each instrument made to feel wanted, belonging.

Why, I ask myself, do I continue to believe in progress, when the evidence is all the other way? Military build-ups; luxuries ceaselessly redefined as necessities; bloated expectations of over-abundance, even in the Third World; child-killer diseases we thought long banished returning to the cities – TB, mumps, whooping cough, rubella . . .

But believe in progress I do! I return, the fugitive day waning, with Shakespeare's one drooping and one auspicious eye; with a small wager on the second.

CHAPTER 10

The old doc treats a large country suffering from a fever for which there is no disease, by prescribing a truth serum to be taken as directed (not by the country but by its political leaders); and voyages to Québec, posing as a Western innocent, taking temperatures as he goes.

A word in your ear, dear Reader. Call on Parliament Hill between its attacks of constitutional delirium. Then MPs are more likely to heed when you tell them what really ails us.

I went, in November 1992, right after the referendum on the constitution collapsed in a hail of No votes. The country was in remission, and the Hill – the Hill was in shock. "How could they? The common people! *They* tell *us* we have a working constitution now, and it's not the problem!"

Meanwhile, you and I, dear Reader, can prepare for the next attack. How? One, by advocating patience. Two, by exercising good humour. Three, by employing plain speaking. Then we'll see, in twenty or thirty years (if you take care of yourself), if our old British-French feud has burned out. Our other tribalisms? They'll need our close attention.

So, here I am, about to make my pilgrimage up the Hill, first stopping for a coffee to steady myself. It is nine-ish in the morning, and the coffee shop is already thronged with public servants on their break. (No, naive Reader, it isn't true that the 35-minute coffee break was discovered in our own capital city, circa 1974.)

Then, bundled up, cigar afire, I step out into a lightly blowing snow. There's a soft "snup" sound, and I realize my cigar has frozen. I make my way up the Hill, knowing I'm on the right track when I pass a large Labrador with a senator on her leash, who gives me a friendly wag of her tail.

I cast a warm eye on the East Block, to my right, imagining it is 1867, when our first Fathers of Confederation holed up there, knowing strength in unity was our only chance to escape a ducking in the American melting pot.

Ah, she's looking good, the East Block, I must say. Her aged stones reflect back the snow-shine. Those stones — my Irish niece's dad told me this; his family memory goes way back in these parts — are sandstone from near Nepean. The government gave contracts to local farmers to quarry and sleigh the stones miles to the Hill. Paid by the ton and all too human, the farmers overloaded their sleighs, and many were grounded in the early thaw. Horses and carts had to be rounded up to finish the carrying.

The Fathers, in 1867, had to beget a "can-do" national government. Looking to the south, they saw the victorious northern armies who'd fought the American Civil War, marshalled in battle array. Twice already, American armies had struck. Then, to the west, the Fathers saw sparsely populated lands stretching to the far Pacific, up for grabs. They needed a ribbon of steel to bind in those lands. They needed a world credit-rating to support immigration and settlements. So they allotted specific powers over matters of local concern to the provinces, and for the centre they kept the residue, for "the Peace, Order and Good Government of Canada."

A good baby they begat in 1867, those Fathers (and with no Mothers of Confederation in sight, worse luck). They begat this country in short order, from conception to delivery, and without the assistance of schools of lawyers. But sad would those Fathers be today to see our politicians ready – twice, yet! – to fritter away essential national powers, especially "spending power."

That's the national power to launch social programs (remember medicare!) with enough leverage to set basic standards as well as to partly level up the costs of such programs wherever the services are delivered. I can't for one moment imagine the United States giving up *its* spending power.

I look forward to the day when a mother in Newfoundland or Québec has roughly the same day-care entitlements as a mom in B.C. or Ontario. Call that "brother's keeper" if you will. I call it a practical necessity of world-building – for no one person, and no one country, however rich, is an island.

Which interests want to crimp national social powers? Moneyed behind-the-scenes movers and shakers. Ask Wealth if scattering national power among the provinces is okay by it. "Sure, fine, provinces are easier to handle," will come the reply. "We can even play one off against the others."

Well, here I am at the senate entrance. I breeze through security. They take me for a cigar-waving senator dropping by to pick up his cheque. Even when my niece Mollie is with me, we breeze through – security is used to senators with pretty "nieces" in tow.

In the senate rotunda, I wander over for a look at Sir John A. Macdonald's portrait. This Father of Confederation always strikes me as a political pro through and through. He used politics to achieve the public purposes he held dear, and didn't let politics use him.

But, alas, Sir John is looking miffed. And I think I know why. The old fellow's upset at what he sees our leaders doing these days – all wrapped up in running for election instead of running an effective national government.

And what's Sir John got to say to me? (I recall Schopenhauer saying a face can often tell you more than the words

that issue from it.) "Och! A prime minister of Canada, gan-
tering around, saying Québec is oot of the constitution! And
the two opposition leaders chirping, 'Yes, oot!' All of them
protesting that votes are the furthest things from their
minds."

And I think you'd add, reader, if you were here: "Bet Sir
John doesn't think much of a prime minister who supported
the Charter in 1982, and now claims it was an awful thing
to do to Québec."

Sir John, by the way, said much the same the last time
I saw him. Mollie was with me then, and she, naughtily,
kept glancing from Sir John's bulbous nose to mine. "Say,
are you two Macdonalds related, by any chance?" she asked.
I put her off, saying "Only the nose knows, my dear," and
quickly drew her attention to the gentleman's hands, so
decorously clasped.

"Sir John," I told her, "was inordinately proud of his hands
– so proud that a yokel, so the story goes, once bested
him at a county fair. After the great man finished his speech,
the yokel came up with, 'Your hands, Sir John, so well-
tended, so soft, so white.' Pleased, Sir John replied, 'Yes, I
always sleep with them between my wife's thighs.' To which
the yokel replied, 'Och, Sir John, then hadn't you better try
that with your nose?' "

His speeches won the election that year, 1872. All right,
say it if you must – by a nose. And the CPR was pushed
to tidewater. The face that looks so miffed today always
shows determination. I'm musing that in his head still
sounds the war cry of Clan Macdonald, farmers on the
snowless Black Isle in the Highlands, leaving their plows to
beat the piratical Vikings back into their longboats; letting
go their Gaelic war cry, "Nie Sick Dam," never give up.

As I leave, I try to jolly Sir John out of his gloom. "I
asked my classy kids," I tell him, "*what* can't we do now
with our constitution as it is? W*hat*, including the language

and culture of Québec, isn't protected and should be?" They told me, "Nothing." Sir John gives me a wry smile, and I bid him adieu.

Yes, the last time I was here, with Mollie, we paid a visit to my old friend from CCF days, Eugene Forsey. We went up to the small office he'd been given, though no longer a senator, because he was Canada's Grand Old Man.

Sadly, Eugene died, last year, at the age of 87. I'll not forget how he took to Mollie, age and youth easily at ease. "A descendant you are, Mollie, of the great philosopher and statesman Edmund Burke!" he said. "'Ceremony, order, reason.' You must be proud of your lineage."

Eugene will no longer be firing fusillades for One Canada from that small office. He didn't join the NDP, by the way, because it came out for "deux nations" at its founding convention.

I liked Eugene for his capacity to feel anger. I don't mean a bad-tempered, kick-the-furniture splutter. I mean lasting indignation at seeing people treated meanly for no defensible reason – the indignation at what's unfair that comes with a longing to right wrongs.

Eugene once told me how he, a prickly character, came to be a senator. Seems Trudeau, his mental sparring partner from Montréal days, phoned him one day. "Eugene! Ambassador to the Vatican?" P.E.T. offers.

"What, Pierre, me, a Baptist, in Rome?"

Another call. "Indian Land Claims Commissioner?"

"Sounds a bit separatist to me, Pierre."

Finally, "How about senator?"

"Yes, but only if I'm my own man, not yours."

Eugene continues. "Three days after I was sworn in as senator – it was October 1970 – Trudeau sends the Canadian army into Québec and suspends civil liberties. It was theatrical overkill. But it cooled down hot young heads just beginning to flirt with violence. Saved some, I think, from long jail terms. Once ethnic violence gets going – well, look at Northern Ireland. Yes, it was overkill, but I supported Trudeau."

If you'd scratched Eugene, you'd have found a social democrat, after his own fashion. And a Canadian through and through. I can still recall some of his oratorical flourishes:

"I don't want a Canada that is just a splash on the map, with six letters scrawled across it. Better separation than that. I want a Canada that can *do* something – for Canadians, for the world's hungry, for a clean, livable planet."

The spark of indignation didn't die while Eugene lived.

This morning, I'm wondering: What would Eugene have thought of the Canada Clause, among those voted down in the referendum? Not much, I'd guess. He'd not like a constitution defining groups by race, gender, disabilities and so on. That, dear Reader, is the politics of differences. It may pay off in votes, but it results in Canadians being too little aware of what they have in common.

And the list of groups waiting to be called "disadvantaged minority" goes on and on. Over time, these separatisms exacerbate tensions, based on race, gender, language – even occupation. You know, Reader, this old fellow often gets along better, and shares more opinions with, an immigrant "woman of colour" than he does with some of the benighted "white Caucasians" he knows.

This day, as I mosey about the senate precincts, I feel the old euphoria. Nowhere, nowhere else, does one age more gracefully than in our Canadian senate. Why, senate wives have been heard to explain that their hubbies, on their appointments, hadn't looked so well since their honeymoons.

Then I see it! There! A dead give-away. Carved in the stone lintel of the hall leading to the speaker's chambers are the words of Senator Cicero: "Principum munis est resis-

tere levitas multitudinous." Must I translate for you, eager
Reader? "It is the duty of the nobles to oppose the fickleness
of the multitude."

Cicero has let the cat out of the bag. Our senate was,
and is – and could be, even if elected – the last redoubt
of privilege and wealth. Two thirds of the senators are corporate executives or their lawyers. The senate banking committee has more directorships than the Canadian navy. It
scans any laws that might menace the corporate citadels,
and can apply the brakes.

Whatever was Sir John thinking of when he gave us an
upper house? Oh, I know that Quebeckers were afraid of
being swamped in a lower house elected by rep-by-pop.
But that's not how it turned out. For 24 of the last 25 years,
Canada has had prime ministers from Québec.

No, there was more to it. Something stuck in Sir John's
craw. Was it the oatmeal? Just listen to him: "The rich must
be protected from the numerous, otherwise the numerous
might just help themselves to some of the rich's money."
(Which, come to think of it, is not that bad an idea – the
"numerous," after all, do the hard work.)

My theory is that Sir John sat up too late reading a Scottish philosopher called Anon., who wrote: "Democracy can
only work until the people find out how to raid the public
treasury."

I take a look into the Senate's Red Chamber – red, dear
Reader, not for its politics or its complexions, but for its
carpet. I gave my anti-Meech speech there, getting a good
reception from the senators, mostly Trudeau's Old-Timers.
They didn't like the way Meech would have bled national
powers. Anyway, they kept nodding their heads as I spoke,
without actually nodding off. Mollie, who was with me, said
she liked my speech – "especially the end."

I remember keeping an eye on one Trudeau Old-Timer

from Saskatchewan. Luckily, he kept silent. Even when he asks a simple question, he is apt to overheat – internal combustion takes place and he starts to revile anyone in sight.

Good thing I didn't tell the senators they should be history. I'd have lost my audience for sure. All I said was, Québec had the sense to get rid of its upper house.

Upper house, lower house – what's this odd propensity of Canadians to think that two of something is better than one? Much-taxed Reader, do you feel better with two departments of labour, one provincial, one federal? Two departments of agriculture? Two of forestry? A dual court system, what with our expanding federal courts? Costs you a bit, doesn't it, that duplication of administration? National laws and responsibilities are all well and good, in matters of national concern. But why not implement those laws at the provincial level? Québeckers, those who are not all-out separatists, want this kind of devolution.

And devolution can take place without changing a word in the constitution. It'd just take political will. Federal politicians telling the swelling bureaucracies what's to happen, instead of the other way around.

Will they? Our federal pols are set today to replace the senate with an elected upper house. The cost, another $100 million a year or so. Who needs another hurdle that any social legislation will have to jump? Not the Canadian people. Why not give the whole senate early retirement – as we can now, under our present constitution?

That evening, I crashed a senate party. Senator Ray Perrault had told me there was a reception for a retiring Nova Scotia senator. "Why not," Ray said with a wink, "just go."

Why not indeed? I go, heading straight for the canapés and wine. Mingle. Why, with a four-in-hand tie and a decent haircut, obtained in the cut-rate senate beauty parlour, I passed. (Sometimes I dream I've died and gone to the senate.)

I fall in with a silver senator who kindly introduces me to myself. And do I support property rights in the constitution?

"Great idea," I reply, "if it wouldn't get in the way of a redistribution of wealth. Might have to relieve the 30 families who double their holdings in our economy every ten years of some of their burden."

A strange look comes over his face. Too much free air? Then he blurts out that property rights and freedom of contract have to be inviolable under free enterprise. I seem to agree, saying: "Nothing like freedom of contract among unequals."

Listening to this exchange is a handsome young woman with a delightful Barbados lilt, Senator Anne Cools. I have a vague recollection – she's from Montréal? "No, I'm from Toronto," she says. Then it comes back – Montréal, Sir George Williams University, student riot, computers smashed, convictions entered, and Cools cools her heels in jail for four months. Still, I know a kindred soul when I see one, even if I don't share all her, uh, convictions. Sure enough, "I liked what you said," she tells me. If Canadians do ever opt for an elected senate, here's one senator who may not have to be pensioned off. She's electable.

The next day, I'm on the VIA to Québec City. I pass into our strongest culture – one that's 350 years old. I'll just give you some snapshots from my memory collection and sign off. And please don't butt in with tough questions. Like, "Will Québec make a break for it?" Just look at my pictures and make up your own mind.

From the train, I spot the Ottawa River, grey between white snow banks. It is spring break-up time, 1605. French-

Canadian boatmen are paddling their birch-bark canoes up-river from Montréal. They wear red toques and calico shirts, and carry knives, pots and pans to trade with the natives for furs. They are paddling into a vast unknown – the Red River, Detroit. They paddle in time with their boisterous voyageur songs, staking their claims in the west (long, long after the Native explorers). And I'm saying to myself, my land is theirs, too, and their land is mine.

On the VIA beyond Montréal, friendly eyes give the rumpled old doc with his Canada pin the once-over. I like my solicitous conductor with the twirled mustache. Now there's a distinctive Canadian. But aren't we all? He stows my bag for me, brings me a tray lunch, and gives me careful directions to a *bon marché* hotel, cliffside, in Québec City.

"What do you think," I ask him. "Should we uncouple Canada?"

He doesn't say. But I bet he knows of some passionate *affaires de coeur* between couples, each with their own living quarters. The voice of experience?

Say, Reader, tell me this. When will the Scots, having run England for close to 400 years, finally decide that the English are ready for self-government?

Across the aisle on the VIA, a French-Canadian family spreads a picnic lunch. *La mère* kindly passes me a cold chicken leg; a left one, at that. I employ my best French and we converse, with some breakdowns. You know, Reader, with three, maybe four, easy liaisons, I could be fluent *en français* . . .

Le père of this family is a school trustee from northern Lac St. Jean. To my surprise, he's unhappier than I am about the regulation that students can't be taught English until Grade 4. He wants his youngsters to be bilingual, the sooner the better, the better to get ahead in this world.

As for me? To me, expedients like that regulation, the sign laws and so on are props to help French survive in North America – little though laws can do about that. Our mellifluous English language, you know, is something of a killer. How many indigenous languages has it done in already? Here are 6 million francophones in a continental sea of 300 million anglophones. What life-belts there are, I'm for.

In Québec City, I find my cliffside hotel and then meander, crabwise, toward the Québec National Assembly. I pass the post office. Though it's closed for the day, it reminds me of a photo I took there back in June 1990, when the Meech deal was coming unstuck. The polls were preaching that Québec nationalism was reaching fever pitch. The tabloids were going crazy – to boost their circulations, I suppose.

It was then, outside this same post office, on the stoop, that I fell into conversation with five or six posties who were taking a smoke break. After salutations, I asked them: "When Meech goes down, will you march, demonstrate?" A pause. They looked at each other, until one replies (with a slight shrug): "Mais oui. We will march." And then, "Certaine-ment. Our union has asked us to take a day off work."

"Que pensez-vous de la souveraineté?" I asked the posties. Heads slowly bobbed and dipped; they allowed that "souveraineté" sounded pretty good to them – with, I sus-pected, no more idea of what it might entail than I had. But the anger, the fervour, of a French revolution? I didn't see that in them.

Still, when French-Canadians go to a meeting... Well, think of Lucien Bouchard speaking – the words spilling out, no smile, a dark forelock falling carefully and casually over his right eyebrow. He comes on with, "We [he means dyed-in-the-wool French-Canadians, the *pure laine*] founded Canada. Now we are only one of ten provinces." He finishes his speech with, "We have been *humilié* once again by the anglos."

Crowd-psychology fires nationalisms. Conversations de-
fuse them. Gather a crowd of well-paid doctors in a room,
listening to a militant at the mike, and they'll soon feel
financially challenged.

By sheer chance, I arrive at the Québec National Assembly
in time for dinner. I glide through security after a frisk and
a glance at my ex-MP pin. This building has a touch of the
baroque, with its blues, golds, whites. You feel you are stepping into a medieval tapestry. Twenty years have passed
since I was last here. Then I was introduced in the assembly
as the attorney-general of B.C. I wore my kilt and regalia
for that occasion, in honour of ethnicities of all sorts.

In the dining room, some Liberal members kindly ask me
to join their table. Nearby, a buffet laden with delicacies
and bright wines. Thirst is a dangerous thing.

We talk of many things. We agree that religious animo-
sities, God be praised, have pretty well disappeared in
Canada. It was different long ago, when Ontario Protestant
Orange Lodgers and Québec Catholic St. Jean-Baptisters
saw deviltries in each other.

In those days, a Protestant family wouldn't think of having
a baby born in a Catholic hospital, for fear the Sisters would
favour the life of the baby over that of the mother. At our
table, we count Canada lucky not to have religious bigotries
mixed with ethnic dissensions. That's as combustible a mix
as air and propane.

One Liberal member even illustrated the bad old days
with a story. Did he make it up? He told of a Mother Superior, 30 years ago, who paid a visit to her convent students
at St. Hyacinthe.

"And what will *you* be, little girl, when you grow up?" she
asked a pupil.

"A seamstress, Mother Superior."

"Oh, good," gushes the Mother Superior, with a head pat. "And you?"

"A nurse, Mother Superior."

"Good, good – and you, child?"

"A prostitute, Mother Superior."

"A *what*?!" Mother Superior swoons, coming to after smelling salts are applied. "*What* did the child say she'd be?" she asks.

"A prostitute, Mother Superior."

"Oh, thanks be to God," says Mother Superior, with a sigh of relief. "I thought she said a *Protestant*."

We part. I head for the Plains of Abraham, thinking of something I wished I said and didn't – that Canada needs hope, and a social agenda. Glad steps forward. Not this stagnation, this slippage. Then our dissensions, our messing about with the constitution, could take a nap.

Hope! I even notice among my students that those with hopes of success in life score better marks. And for all I know, score better with the opposite sex.

Out I walk onto the dark, haunted Plains of Abraham. Above, fateful stars; a night wind sighs. Below, across the gloom of the St. Lawrence, shine the lights of Lévis. Time rolls back. By what frail threads hang the fates of nations – and individuals, too, for that matter.

Just think. If a dissipated wencher of 55, King James II of England, had not in 1688 begot a male Catholic heir to his throne – thus dashing the hopes of the Whigs for a Protestant succession and prompting them to call over from Holland old William of Orange to mount the English throne – uniting for battle the fleets of Holland and England . . . Why then, but for that baby, King Louis XIV of France would not have had his fleet sunk off La Hogue in 1692 – and England would not have become mistress of the North Atlantic, able to pick off France's American colonies. And Canada? Well, you tell me.

And if a certain Captain Fraser, leading Wolfe's regiments

in the dark up the escarpment in 1759, to where I stand now, hadn't been able to speak a word of French, he would never have been able to assure the scouts patrolling above that his was just a French provisioning party. And General Wolfe, with winter nipping at his heels, wouldn't have got his troops arrayed in battle-line before the walls of Québec City.

And that September morning would not have seen on these plains two bodies: Wolfe's dead and the Maréchal de Montcalm's dying. Nor seen numberless other dead. Nor heard the savage victory yelps of Wolfe's Highlanders until their orders (in Gaelic, for they spoke no English) came to reform ranks.

Nor would that morn have seen French settlers, who had rushed to aid Montcalm with sniping from behind trees, returning heart-stricken to their homes. I stand here with strange feelings of kinship with both slayers and slain.

That battle left Canada with a deep wound. It still suppurates today. Only time will heal it. What a lot we Canadians have to remember – and forget. The French author Renan, not thinking of us, wrote that the essence of a nation is individuals having "beaucoup de choses en commun; et, aussi, aient oublies bien des choses" – having a lot in common, and also forgetting a lot of things.

But twenty years later, those French settlers who brought their muskets to help Montcalm stood by Canada when troops of the American revolution invaded Québec City. There, in Lower Town, on a cold December 31, 1775, the American general, Richard Montgomery fell. I've seen his stone bust in a niche on Lower Broadway in New York City.

And what became of the Scottish soldiers drafted into British regiments to fight in Canada? Well, most, their battles o'er, stayed on in this rude country. One was a James Macdonald – Thérèse Casgrain, a friend from long-ago CCF days, told me how young James came to be one of her great-grandparents. (Thérèse, later Senator Casgrain, has roots in Canada reaching back to ancestors who settled in Québec City in 1651.)

As Thérèse tells it, James Macdonald got cut off from his regiment in 1837, and was lost in the woods. I saw those woods from the VIA, on my trip back to Montréal, just after passing Trois Rivières. James was a soldier of the King with orders to put down the rebellion of the French habitants and Ontario farmers who were fighting for representative government. He was decked out in tartan, fur cap and chin strap. He spied a cabin in the woods and entreated a drink of water. A French lass, against her father's orders, opened the shutters and gave James a cup of water. Love at first gulp triumphs in the end. James marries this Archange Quevillon, blending Scots blood with French. James passes from his Gaelic tongue to French without ever learning English.

In 1943, when I first saw Montréal, I discovered a city of romance – one of the cities of the world I've never minded being lost in – a city with a past. A city with legends. The Lachine Rapids? Were they really so called because China lay somewhere in the far west where the river had its source? And was it true that Champlain in 1615 eagerly tasted the waters of Lake Huron, hoping to find they were an ocean's brine?

Montréalers have memories, dark and bright, floating close to consciousness.

In 1535, two branches of the human family rendezvous on Mont Réal after a separation of 10,000 years – cut off since the ice melted and the seas rose to cover the landbridge to Alaska. Jacques Cartier is received by the Iroquois chief at Hochelaga on the mountain. His party is feasted within the palisaded fort.

Settlers follow, occupying ancestral Native lands. Resistances. Sleeping settlers are attacked at Lachine by Iroquois warriors in an August rainstorm in 1660. French military reprisals. Time passes . . .

At Oka, masked armed Mohawks man barricades. A strong people. Some of them welded the high steel skyscrapers of Montréal's Place Ville-Marie. Natives take up the cry for self-government, perplexing separatists who want that just for one Québec.

Is Native self-government the way to redress historical wrongs? We should not, dear Reader, constitutionalize racial segregations. Homelands based on race marginalize their inhabitants. Forms of municipal status for Native communities? Of course, wherever feasible. Laws will not cut the rate of teen suicide (twenty times that of the Canadian average) on remote reserves. Social and economic opportunities will.

I used to be the lawyer for the Native workers in the sawmills at Kitwanga, far up the Skeena River in northwestern B.C. Those sawmills supported a Gitksan community rich in Native customs – until competition, and timber allocations, shut the mills down and put the Natives out of work.

Where was I? In Montréal, in 1943. I had a Montréal friend in those days, Michel Chartrand, a fiery young socialist. Together we denounced the oppression of French-Canadians by the Anglo-Westmount big-business establishment. Even in Ottawa, I had seen that French-Canadians were at the bottom of the economic ladder. If they were secretaries, they were at the bottom of the stenographic pool. If they were elevator operators, they disappeared at night into Ottawa's Lower Town. But since then – although Québec has had its Quiet Revolution – a curtain has fallen between me and Michel. Call that curtain nationalism, sovereignty – it hangs heavy between us.

I was with David Lewis in Montréal in 1943. We were at a CCF convention. David was the CCF's poorly paid secretary, later an MP and leader of the NDP. He'd come into Montréal's yeasty Jewish community as a young immigrant from a village in Tsarist Russia. We got along fine; he was my mentor. I used to tell him Israel was one of the lost tribes of Scotland, something you could say back then.

Today, I wonder what David would think of the present exodus from Montréal by so many Jewish artists and professionals – and businessmen like Steinberg, who are no longer stitching clothes there. I wonder what David would think of the law that changed the name of Victoria Hot Dogs to Chien Chaud Victoire? I can smile at that from where I sit. But David, with his Jewish heritage? I think a wistful look would come into his eyes, that he would catch a whiff of acrimony, intolerance.

That great Jewish sage, Albert Einstein, wrote, "Nationalism is a juvenile disorder, the measles of mankind." I don't go that far. To me, there are two kinds of nationalism hanging in the balance in Québec. One is a generous, inclusive aspiration to honour roots and history. The worser kind is surly, exclusive, insensitive, afraid. Which kind will win out, gentle Reader? My money's on the first.

Today, in Montréal, I have a meeting with some young *separatistes* of the Parti Québecois. It has been kindly arranged for me by Marie Bourgeois of the Francophone Alliance of B.C. It is 7:30 p.m. and I am sitting alone in the recreation room of a house in Outremont, chewing at a cigar. Enter the young Péquistes, in a body. Formal introductions. What are we to make of each other? At least, I could tell, they were pleased that a *sauvage* from the far west considered they were important, seemed to care...

Our match begins soberly – serious business, this. I suspect they had caucused first to select their designated spokespersons. We to and fro for two or three hours, getting to like each other.

We cover constitutional reform, to them a futile attempt

to distract Quebeckers from sovereignty. And free trade, espoused by their leader, Jacques Parizeau. It's all right with them; lessens Québec's dependence on Canada and makes separation easier. But me, I'm murmuring, "Nothing deculturizes like free trade," and thinking, "they don't seem all that sold on Jacques's separatist credentials."

(And I don't take Jacques as a dangerous separatist. He just can't help smirking when he thinks he's scored a debating point.)

They take shots at the Anglo-Westmount Establishment, and to this I say, "Have a care for what you trade it for — an American Business Establishment, perhaps?"

Later I try this on them. "Québec is changing, with immigrants and Natives rocking their cradles. Now it's their numbers that are growing faster than your own." For this, I get a shot from André: "B.C. will soon be Oriental." I return this with a cheerful, "Yes, a rich genetic soup." And I ask, "Will you desert the Francophones outside Québec?" "They are doomed, anyway, to assimilation," comes their response.

Around this time I call for the wine I had brought. As we partake, I relate to them the sad case of one Francophone outside Québec: a Catholic priest from Chicoutimi sent by his church into the wilds of northern B.C. Bears, trees, White Fang, the whole bit. Nothing is heard from him. At last, his bishop goes searching and finds the priest snowbound in a log cabin. "Bishop," moans the priest, "if it were not for my Rosarie and two martinis a day, I'd go crazy in this place. Would you care for a martini?" The bishop, quite distraught, allows that he will take one. "Hey, Rosarie," calls out the priest. "Bring the Bishop a martini."

My new friends are not sure how to handle this. Finally, Claude replies, "Just goes to show you what happens to Francophones outside Québec – absorption. Inside Québec, that priest would have called for wine."

We are pleasantly finding that we are all social democrats under the skin. Still, the curtain does not lift. Huegette sums up their feelings: "We want to be free to be what we want to be, not what you want us to be – to govern ourselves."

"Self-government?" say I, with a sip and a chew on my cigar. "I haven't had that since I married in 1944, and can't say I miss it. You'll find, Huegette, when you marry, that what you lose in freedom you more than make up for in responsibilities."

This puzzles her and she comes back with, "Say, are you writing a book? You sound like one. Will you send me a copy?" I assure her that I am well beyond such child-bearing – but if there should be a miraculous conception, why of course – if she'll just give me her address . . .

I think I kept my resolve, dear Reader, to say nothing to these young Péquistes that wasn't nice. I wanted to tell them, but didn't, not to feel so put-upon.

But I did tell them – and this does matter – that Quebeckers need other Canadians as much as we need Quebeckers. Canada's east-west axis is fragile, while the north-south pull is strong indeed. Either we stick together, or region by region we'll slide into the American melting pot.

After this chat, I take the metro downtown. No litter or graffiti in the ruddy-hued brick stations. But murals – a fine expression of community values. I get off on St. Catherine to wander in search of economical sleep in Old Montréal. The night streets are tense with lively activity. I walk past history: a sculpted crest, "Armoury of the Black Watch Royal Highlanders." I pass odd new history: a garish neon sign on a once-Catholic church warns passers-by that "La salaire des péchés est l'enfer." I pass Place des Arts, where the Montréal Symphony under Charles Dutoit "suspends Time in strange skies."

I don't quite make it as far as Old Montréal. A clerk beckons me into the Hôtel St.-Denis. He is of Moroccan origin and asks me in fluent French if I would like a room with a bed or with a bath. I choose the former and stretch out my weary limbs at last in Room 403. The bed palpitates

like the ones at the Holiday Inn, where you put a loonie
in to make your liver quiver. The whole room is trembling
to the monotonous thumping of rock music from a club in
the hotel basement.

Morpheus interruptus. I tune out the rock and play Handel
in my head. Handel asks, "Oh sleep, why dost thou leave
me?" I tell Handel it's because of that American barbarian
down below, beating on the gates of French culture.

In the morning, no longer shaking, I visit the campus of the
University of Québec at Montréal, only a stone's throw from
the hotel. Down in the university cafeteria – ah, students!
The future! – I walk the tables where they are genially
munching from brown bags. At one table, I ask: "Que pensez-vous de la séparatisme?" They put me on some, with
smiles, replying: "Une bonne question!"

I figure these students are too jovial to go far down the
road into the tribalisms of our times. They're not feeling so
sorry for themselves that they've little concern left over for
others.

Another student table, which seems to regard me with
some amusement, proclaims: "Mangeons le gâteau ensem-
ble!"

This lifts me up. If only all Canadians would take our
small share of the world's ethnic dissensions with such light
hearts, as these students seem to do. I wonder what Mother
Nature thinks now of this human critter of hers? She let us
go from invertebrates to vertebrates – to become the only
animals that can smile and shake hands at the same time.
But her humans became too clever by half, stealing all of
her secrets and taking themselves far too seriously.

So serious we are about our ethnic differences these
days. Nationalisms, to be sure, are tearing some countries
apart these days. They instill hatreds in good people, even

turn them into killers, "All pity chok'd in custom of fell deeds," as in the Bard's Rome.

But other revolutions of our days – in economics, technology, communications – are stealthily obliterating political borders, bringing people together. These centripetal revolutions will, I think, win in time over centrifugal nationalisms.

I repair to the Hotel Bonaventure for a drink at the bar before boarding the VIA for my trip back to Ottawa. I take the elevator up to the sixth-floor lobby and stroll toward the porters' stand. There are three Quebeckers of Chinese origin. They are alert, at attention, waiting to be of service. At once they know me. From my last visit. They remember my multi-zippered shoulder bag and my Scottish tip. I draw up on them with a flurry of Vancouver Cantonese phrases, inquiring into their healths. Then I slip into what Jean Chrétien calls "da Queen's French" to discuss the weather. Finally, in my mother tongue, I ask them: "This country – cleavages – have you noticed much?"

What I discover in these Quebeckers is three trilingual, multicultured, unhyphenated Canadians! No fissiparous tendencies in them whatsoever.

They check my bag. I order a glass of beer and sit sipping. Welsh Captain Fluellen, with a leek on his cap, serving under King Henry V, butts in with his question: "What is my nation?"

Were *you* to ask that, dear Reader, I would reply: "Canada is nations within a nation. Who could ask for anything more?"

CHAPTER 11

Alex, in Wonderworld, wants Canada to play a new role on the global stage (and not as straight man to any super-power), and calls on Earthlings to "support your local police."

I must report to you, dear Reader, that Canada's preparations to fight the last war are well under way. Orders are now being filled for the acquisition of state-of-the-art military hardware. Cost is no object – a pity, since, from inquiries I have been able to make, the Second World War will not be rescheduled for another performance. As for World War III, if it hits the stage, poof! It'll be over early in the first scene, almost before it's begun.

You know, getting ready to fight the Battle of Armageddon is really an awful waste of time and effort. Yet our old world is still spending $567,000 a minute for "defence" (read: "buying offensive weapons").

To be sure, Canada – modest as always – is only spending about $16,666 a minute for "defence." Still, when you add it all up, it's a lot of money indeed, money that could go a long way toward paying for the good things that make peoples *less* suspicious of one another.

It makes me think that *Homo sapiens* is being tickled mad by some demonic force. Our late, great novelist, Hugh Mac-Lennan, thought something of the sort. I heard him utter some spooky words once, when he was speaking at a Writers' Union banquet at Queen's University not long ago.

"This curious drive to self-destruction" was his phrase, and he let it go at that. Didn't spell it out. Did he have to? We see rising tides of bad feelings between peoples of different races and religions; more muggings on city streets; TV touting violence as entertainment until it actually becomes entertaining to millions; ugly words like "ethnic cleansing" slipping into our vocabulary, reminiscent of Adolf Hitler.

Then there are the little wars, so nasty that we wonder, when one is over, "How could *that* have happened? Are these harbingers of thermonuclear war? Of self-destruction?" We hope not, all the while thinking, "Is there something I can do?"

By the way, MacLennan's speech was witty as well as wise. He told of a boy of seven peering up at Hugh's 80-year-old frame and asking, "How does it feel to know you are going to die?" Which reminds me of my grandson Andrew, when he was little, peering at me and asking, "How long *have* you been on this earth, grandpapa?"

But what can Canadians do before some little war boils over into a big one? How can we halt terrorisms and brutalities? And do it before someone invents the nuclear suitcase bomb? Well, I have some suggestions – which will surprise you not one little bit!

First, let's call to order those idiots who say Canada is the right country, but in the wrong place. Let them buy woollies. This country couldn't be better placed. No foreign armies will appear on our horizons. If we are molested at all, our big, absurdly over-armed southern neighbour will be distinctly annoyed. Invaded by three-piece-suits with brief-cases? Yes. By little green men from Mars? Highly unlikely. By foreign troops? Not likely at all. One nuclear cannon would see them off.

Second, for heaven's sake, let's get onto the right path. There are two paths to one world, not one. The one we've started down, and should get away from, leads to One Big Market Bazaar, where everything is for sale. But in that market, money clusters restlessly, making more money by making people and whole states their supplicants – a prescription for conflicts of every kind.

The right path leads to cooperation, with countries forming international institutions, not only for safety's sake, but to promote social justice within and among nations – without which you can't have safety.

Third. It made me nervous, it really did, when our former defence minister, Marcel Masse, paid one of his rare visits to Ottawa. He'd announce, every time, more "military procurements." His last order was for 50 "next generation" anti-sub helicopters, to keep the sea lanes open, should World War II resume. For only $5.8 billion, plus God knows how much for frigates and refitted destroyers – the 'copters can't land on the sea! Does it make sense for Canada to spend five times as much on weapons to fight a war than it does on peacekeeping and foreign aid to prevent one? Hey, Kim! Do you hear me? This is ridiculous! As for you, dear Reader, kindly read the Talmud: "He who can protest, and does not, is an accomplice in the act." This Scot agrees wholeheartedly.

Fourth. Canada, as you know, has its own military-industrial complex, which must be treated, with or without psychiatric help. I used to think only the USA had such a complex. That's because I heard an American president, on leaving office in 1961, warn his fellow Americans about the power of their military-industrial establishment, with its spin doctors, political wire-pullers, etc.

Which president? Why, it was General Ike Eisenhower, himself a close relation of General Motors, General Dynamics, General Foods . . . If anyone knew what to watch out for, Ike did.

But Ike could have saved his breath. Since then, the huge American military-industrial complex, and our smaller one, have dug in deeper. Canada's largest department is defence, with 110,000 employees. We, too, have generals and defence bureaucrats retiring into six-figure jobs in defence industries. Whole communities rely on defence for employment...

Is it beyond our wits to provide useful, meaningful employment? A lunatic provides jobs – a keeper, a psychiatrist, someone to replace broken window panes. Does that mean we need more lunatics?

Fifth (and here endeth the lesson), let's stop being co-opted into the Pentagon's priorities. Such as...so proud are we that the U.S. Space Centre allows a Canadian to fly in the space shuttle *Discovery*. Dr. Roberta Bondar, the first Canadian woman in space! But Roberta couldn't go on the *Discovery*'s last mission. That mission was cloaked in tight military secrecy; its payload was a satellite to be launched as one step toward an orbiting space station, a space station able to spy out and rocket anything on Earth. Part of the Star Wars scenario. Oh, Reader! Could anything be more dangerous to your health? Or your finances?

The initial cost of this to Canada, we're told, will be only $1.2 billion. We can't be against probing the secrets of the universe. But why these billions? Why now? Would a careful mother go shopping for a pearl necklace with the food money?

I'd like a mom to phone our Canadian ambassador to the United Nations and tell her, "Espouse a treaty to demilitarize space before it's too late." Let's shout that until Uncle Sam says uncle.

Way back in 1960, a Canadian war correspondent, James F. Minifee, wrote a book. He called it *Canada: Peacemaker or Powder-monkey?* Powder monkeys were boys who fetched gunpowder for a battleship's cannons. Minifee didn't want Canadians playing that role.

But he agreed with Canada sending the first United Nations peacekeepers to Egypt, dispatched by Prime Minister Lester Pearson in 1956. Pearson got a Nobel Peace Prize for that initiative. Since then, we've sent UN peacekeepers in blue berets to Lebanon, the Congo, New Guinea, Bosnia (or is it Serbia?), Somalia – the list goes on. And to Cyprus, where our peacekeepers have helped patrol a scary truce. I was privileged to see them at work in Cyprus.

Four years ago, Dorothy and I went to Cyprus as guests of the Cypriot government. Exotic Cyprus! My last junket, and I loved every minute. And we went in classy company, with four members of parliament and their wives. Some of those members had fine futures ahead of them; some had fine futures behind them.

Our Olympic airliner drops down on this crossroads of world history as the sun is setting – the "hidden" sun, of which the poet James Elroy Flecker once said, "rings black Cyprus with a lake of fire." A so-official greeting! The speaker of the Cypriot parliament streaks across the tarmac in a black top hat. Black limousines draw up to take us to our hotel, and my wife darts to help load the baggage. No way! Not on this trip! Good help is hard to find, but they don't need hers here. The limos take off, motorcycle escorts, sirens, flashing lights, the works.

At the spiffy Nicosia Hilton, a maid trips in to turn down my bed. She wears a smile that seems to conceal some naughty secret. I am even assigned a personal bodyguard – although – two days later I am sitting in the hotel lobby when a short, good-looking man in a baggy suit sits down beside me. With a sigh, he says, "I'm security. For two days, I've been looking for an Alex Macdonald..." "Look no more," I tell him.

We walk the spic-and-span streets of Nicosia, not a beggar to be seen. Greek Cyprus is a beleaguered society, but strong, and everyone works. We pass Arabian sheiks in white burnouses, with wives in their wakes. We walk to have lunch with the mayor at the 17th-century restaurant Reijiotico – and arrive late. Jean Chrétien is the culprit. He attracts passersby like a magnet attracts steel filings. He glad-hands; there is a talking in tongues. Jean slipping from French to English in the same sentence; they babbling away at him in Greek until, once more, Bill Blaikie says, "Come along, Jean. These people vote *here*."

The next morning, the limos pick us up for a tour of the truce line dividing Greek and Turkish Cyprus.

We pass the Venetian Fortress. Its sloping outer walls of reddish brick were thrown up in desperate haste to meet an earlier Turkish invasion, in 1590. Thrown up in vain – that Turkish tide engulfed the whole island. Ah, perhaps it was in this fortress that the Venetian mercenary, Othello the Moor, "perplexed in the extreme," throttled his bride, the fair Desdemona. Those star-crossed lovers, made flesh by art.

In Nicosia, you see traces of its silent, vanished conquerors – in the architecture, the colours, even the dress and manners. A modern city, as old as time. Here once came the ancient Assyrians with their war chariots gleaming purple and gold; the Egyptian pharaoh's soldiers in white dresses; King Agamemnon's warriors in their Scottish kilts; tramping Roman legionnaires; St. Paul in sandals; Saracens with long, curving scimitars; marauding crusader knights in armour; and then those proud Venetians under the banner of the Lion of St. Mark – and their nemesis, the Ottoman Turks.

Then, in 1878, came Sir Garnet Wolseley with his British Grenadiers, to see off the Ottoman Turks. He brought in his baggage-train the Common Law of England and the sweet English tongue – that killer language that stings the others to death. English is still *lingua franca* in Cyprus.

And last came our own Canadian Princess Pat's Light Infantry Regiment, sporting the blue beret of the United Nations Peacekeeping Forces, the only troops who came to make love, not war.

We reach a rambling old house that has become the Princess Pat's headquarters. There we are cordially received by

Brigadier-General John MacInnis, resplendent in stripes, his roaming nose surmounting a broad smile. A lawfully begotten Scottish brigadier-general if ever there was one. Ah, that we all could be Scottish!

I clamber into the back of a jeep with cheerful Jean Chrétien. Our driver wears his blue beret with a cocky tilt. We reach the mouth of the Canadian section of the Green Line that straggles through old Ledra, now Nicosia.

Talk dies away as we start down the Green Line. Along this line, in ferocious fighting, Greek Cypriot soldiers and families stopped the onslaught of waves of Turkish troops from the mainland.

We bump past their makeshift defences. Gun slits in living-room walls, cement-filled oil drums, barbed wire, sand bags. Nothing can be moved or reinforced. That's part of the truce. I see shattered dishes on a table, relics of a meal never finished. Only the bodies of the dead have been removed.

I have never been so close to war. I feel as if I'd been part of the fighting. The chill of fear creeps up my spine. Lines of Dante Alighieri ramble in the empty spaces of my head, lines spoken by Odysseus as he picked his way through the smoke and glare of the Inferno:

> Green fear took hold of me,
> The Spirits of the Dead rising before me.

On our left, we pass the observation posts of young Turkish soldiers. They stare, rifles at the ready, looking through us with hardly a glimmer of acknowledgment. To the right of the narrow way, young Greek Cypriot soldiers cradle their guns. They're wary too, but more feckless, fun-loving. They smile and wave. The blood feud of Turks and Greeks reaches back through the mists of time to the abduction of Helen of Troy. When will it cease?

We stop for a briefing at what was once a luxury hotel.

It's shell-shattered now, bullet-pocked, windows blown out.
Nevertheless, it serves as a billet for our Canadian peacemakers – not to mention the roaches.

Major Martin Talbot gives the briefing. We gather round
him in the sun. Dorothy dabs my nose with a white sunburn
lotion, although I'd rather wear it red than white.

The major says Canadians lost two killed and many
wounded stitching together the uneasy truce. To the north,
out of sight, lies a battle-ready Turkish army of 34,000 men.
To the south, proud Cypriot Greeks pine for the well-tended
orchards and homes from which they were driven. They
have not seen them since.

Occasional shots are still fired in anger – bodies drop –
protest notes are exchanged. The peacemakers use their
own weapons: tact, good humour, steady nerves. A bad
incident, and the whole island could explode again in war.

Our Pats patrol the broken city section of the Green Line
– the narrowest part, crackling with tension. They do a
three-week stint of duty, then enjoy a week's leave. After
six months, they're posted home to Canada. On leave, they
party with other peacemakers – Finns and Austrians, Norwegians and Britons, Australians and Danes. To party with
Cypriot Greeks would be seen as taking sides.

Back at headquarters, we have a fine lunch with common
soldiers of all ranks. A smoky retsina wine proves to be a
mind-altering substance.

The soldiers have a better hang of what modern war is
all about than the folks back home. And a good hang of
the importance of what they're doing. One says, "Little wars,
like the one we're baby-sitting, can spread if they're not put
to sleep." Another says, "If nuclear missiles start flying –
and more countries have them all the time – the weather
forecast will be short and sweet: No weather tomorrow."

There was only one scrappy soldier at my table. He got
started on, "It's them or us," and "We gotta be ready for
the big one." The others just kidded him. "Never mind,

Rambo, if the big one comes, you'll be in the only safe place — the front lines."

Good hearts and heads, our soldiers. Later, I look up Dante — some lines he wouldn't have dreamed of applying to our peacemakers. They are in no way like the broken soldiers Dante described, shuffling around in his Inferno:

> Surely, I saw, and still before my eyes
> Goes on that Headless Trunk that bears for light
> Its own Head swinging, gripped by the dead hair,
> And, like a swinging lamp that says, "Ah, me,"
> I severed men, my head and heart,
> Ye see here severed, my life's counterpart.

(Ezra Pound helped me with the translation.)

Some 20,000 Canadian soldiers have served peace in Cyprus over the last twenty years. They have received training sorely in demand today, as the United Nations turns, as it must, from peacekeeping to peacemaking, in ever more dangerous hot spots — such as Yugoslavia, where old ethnic hatreds have stoked indescribable brutalities.

In Cyprus, Canada plays the part of the good cop, in UN blue. In Iraq? There, Canada has played the bad cop, thickly disguised in UN blue.

Jeff, one of my students, left class in January 1991 to join the military strike against Iraq. It was all over, thank God, by the time his naval vessel reached Naples — I had warned him about the dangerous pickpockets in that city.

Jeff got the call because he had trained in our army reserve. On army exercises once, he claimed to have seen the bunker dug for the New Brunswick cabinet, where they could sit out Armageddon; a deep steel and concrete cellar with stores of dried oats and other delicacies. I told Jeff that bunker should have a place for our Mendelsohn Joe. Joe is our all-Canadian who sighed, when he was abroad, that what he missed most about Canada was "the apathy."

As for me, I expect it'll be a long nuclear winter, and I'd as soon be frozen, cryogenically, to wait it out. Emerging, I could teach history as one who had lived through what he taught – and by then, who knows, I might even have tenure at my university.

After the Iraq strike was over, I caught Michael Wilson giving his budget on TV. All he said about the Iraq war was, "We have allocated another $600 million for national defence."

National defence? Really now. Anyway, Wilson passed quickly over this. Could it be that war left him with some internal bruises? I know I have them. I also have a sinking feeling that humanity slipped a rung on the evolution ladder.

Many have already forgotten that war. That smash hit has been off TV for quite a while now. But the Iraqi dead remember; and the still dying, including children maimed for life by malnutrition and disease. They will not forget.

Our House of Commons was used and neutered as that war unfolded. Oh, there was the big debate and the government vote, sure. But that came long after the powers-that-be had decided against UN sanctions and in favour of the military strike. And long after Canada's small naval and air contingents had been deployed in the war theatre.

I remember the feelings of uselessness I had when I argued, sometimes on radio, for a UN oil embargo. I feel no better now that – guess what? – we are back to using the oil embargo again – with, as we are now told, "devastating effects" on Iraq. I can't forget that interval of bombing.

People seem to have been caught up by uncontrollable forces. As if that rough beast of war, its gaze blank and pitiless, had an unstoppable momentum of its own.

Unstoppable, even though we could see that war coming. Other little wars had heralded its advance, their real causes unspoken. Grenada in 1983, for one. Suddenly the Marines landed, shooting. Few fatalities, fortunately. The spoken cause? To "save" medical students who were really only put in danger by the invasion.

Again, in 1989. Panama bombed and strafed. Fatalities in the thousands? We are not told how many. The spoken cause? The kidnapping of General Noriega, who was – no doubt – one of Central America's drug lords, just as he had been all those years the U.S. called him their great friend.

Then January, 1991. A coalition led by the technically advanced countries carpet-bombs, unmolested, a land where once grew the Garden of Eden. The fatalities? Who knows? High tech cannot, will not count its victims. The spoken cause? The restoration of the unsavoury shiekdom of Kuwait within its colonially drawn boundaries. But there would have been no military strike if Kuwait did not lie in an area containing 40 per cent of the world's oil reserves.

This biting confrontation with part of the Arab world will not be over any time soon. But did any good come of it?

Well, some good. That war moved the United Nations closer to centre stage. Oh, to be sure, it was co-opted and used for that war. But through that use, the UN was advanced a little toward the world forum it should be.

Or do you think I'm still too easily tricked by my own young hopes for a Parliament of Humanity? My young hopes. Back in 1949, I think it was, I met Dr. Brock Chisholm of Saanich, B.C., the first head of the World Health Organization. And I knew, as a friend, the late Dr. Hugh Keenleyside of Victoria, B.C., the first head of the UN's technical assistance department. And I remember, from 1941, the promise of the Roosevelt-Churchill conference on a battle cruiser in Placentia Bay, Newfoundland. There they called for a United Nations that would, among other things, "Give equal access to all nations to the trade and raw materials of the world."

Oh my. Today it's downright dangerous for anyone to put a hand on the oil life-lines of the oil-hog nations.

In New York once, I had a view of the United Nations as it is seen through the eyes of an African delegate. I managed to get up to the Ambassador's Dining Room in the UN headquarters building. Passing the security desk wasn't that hard. I kept producing and withdrawing some of my old cards in rapid succession: MP, MLA, AG, QC, etc. – they have no expiry dates. A perplexed guard soon pointed me toward the elevator.

In the dining room I met Samuel Alain Nguiffo Tene, a delegate from Cameroon. In private life Samuel, apparently moving in the best circles, is a "pasteur" of "le cercle de la création." He kindly asked me to sit. Steep prices on the menu! So I ordered a bagel. The waiter affected not to hear my order, and curtly ordered me to the buffet – $24.75 U.S.

Samuel saw the UN as an organization where the Western industrialized states call the shots. "A club for rich white boys," he exclaimed, "with their fags, their trade and aid dependents who supply them with votes." He went on to say that these states are blind to the biggest threat to the human family – soil depletion, deepening poverty in the developing world.

"In Cameroon," said Samuel, "the Sahara desert is advancing south at a speed of five kilometres a year. Think of the rows and rows of trees that could be planted for a tiny fraction of the cost of one Trident nuclear submarine."

"Yes," said I. "Those Tridents do seem somewhat superfluous – each with sixteen missile-launchers, each missile carrying twenty Hiroshimas."

Samuel continued. "The rich and poor worlds are rubbing against each other like tectonic plates, fault lines. There'll be earthquakes and civil disorder."

"But," I said, "the UN is trying to establish some sort of world rule of law – without that you can't have social progress."

"True enough," he agreed. "But your rule of law – can it stand up as long as the richest one billion people earn 75 times more than the poorest four billion people? Where do you think Islamic fundamentalism spreads fastest? Where there's poverty, exploitation. People without hopes turn to intolerant religions."

I replied that in Somalia, the UN was trying to get food to those who need it.

"Finally," Samuel said. "Armed food escorts should have started a year ago, but the big powers had no strategic interests in Somalia. Only when people's consciences everywhere were shocked by mass starvation, only then did they act." (No companies sniffing for oil there, Samuel? Yes, there are.)

"And then, what a military extravaganza! F-16 jets swooping over mud huts with roofs of galvanized tin. Marines at the ready pouring ashore in armoured vehicles, all under the glare of TV lights! Welcomed by urchins of 11 or 12 firing assault rifles into the sky. They must have thought they were in Chicago!"

"Well, the UN Secretary-General, Boutros Boutros-Ghali, wants to disarm Somalia, all its gunslingers and gang lords..."

"Then disarm Chicago too!" said Samuel. "But it's war, you know, in the arms business. When the Americans leave Somalia, they'll hold one of their garage sales of used armoured trucks, tanks and so on. Meanwhile, this big military exercise will make it easier for them to get their taxpayers to give them up-to-date replacements."

"Do you think, Samuel, that it's a mistake to make the arms business such a profitable money-spinner?"

"It's madness! Like making it profitable for a doctor to cut off your leg."

It was Samuel's belief that the UN, not the U.S., should command the UN Forces in Somalia. He even wanted the UN to have its own police force.

"Then *you* should have been elected, Samuel, by the

people of Cameroon. The UN assembly will have more moral authority when it truly represents the people of the world," I pointed out.

"Yes," he agreed. "That's the way to go, if humanity is to have what your poet Tennyson called 'the Parliament of Man, the Federation of the World.' "

I left, musing. Is humanity in a race with catastrophe? It took the British parliament centuries, to see off the kings and noblemen, to win legitimacy and acceptance. The UN doesn't have that much time.

CHAPTER 12

Snapshots from the UN Earth Summit in Rio.
Statespersons congregate in Rio Centrum, plain per-
sons gather in Flemengo Park, bent on a new green-
and-red world order. Alex robbed at last! Castro — not
one of the 'getting along by going along' crowd — spills
the beans.

Dear Reader,

We are on the Flemengo Park beach, beside the polluted waters of Guanabara Bay. Across the bay, you can see Sugar Loaf Mountain raised like a warning finger. But we aren't admiring the view. Part of an enormous crowd, we are watching a woman standing in front of a microphone on a platform erected on the sand. As she speaks, thousands strain to hear.

"Human and national inequalities are clearly the planet's main environmental problem," she states.

This is Madam Gro Haarlem Brundtland, Prime Minister of Norway. A combatant for clean air and land, grain and rain. Her jaw juts out as she speaks; no giver-upper she. Sadly, twenty years have passed since her environmental report, commissioned at the United Nations conference in Stockholm, put the world on red alert. And in those twenty years, degradation has advanced on every front.

"So little done yet," says Gro. "So much to do." And the crowd, with her all the way, hangs on her words.

These thousands rally under only one flag, the United

Nations blue. Each individual has scraped to get here, with
nary an expense account among them. They hail from every
clime and country, the young of all ages, of every sect and
skin colour. Even a Mongolian made it, and he kindly lets
me stand in his spacious shadow.

As I look around at my neighbours in the throng, I can't
help wishing I was a photographer. Foremost among them
would be that Senegalese woman, Chocolate she said her
name was, in lime-green *kente* cloth, a yellow *chall* on her
head, golden bracelets on her arms and silvery rings at her
ears. Or how about that Buddhist monk, swathed in orange
from shaved head to bare brown, white-soled feet. Or the
Indian swami, tugging his beard, clothed in white samite,
looking like a mystic with a scroll and a wicker fan.

And the T-shirts. "Arms are for hugging," cries one, worn
by a youngish man from San Francisco. He hangs out at
the HEMP (Help End Marijuana Prohibition) booth. I note
his Nikes, scruffy now. Some Third World woman stitched
them, earning 12 cents an hour for a six-day week. And
those sneakers retail for at least $80 U.S., enough to pay
for oodles of hype and still rake in the profits. Why is the
hardest, dirtiest work paid the *least*? I've asked myself that
question many a time – and have been radicalized in the
process.

Gro's words about inequality are quite appropriate here
in Brazil. Along with dazzling natural beauty and bounteous
resources, Brazil boasts its share of poor. A tiny minority
of Brazilians – 2.5 per cent – own 43 per cent of the country's wealth; 2 per cent own 60 per cent of the arable land.
And to think, recently *Forbes* magazine counted five – yes,
five! – Brazilian billionaires.

Who feels the bite when the price of Brazil's coffee beans
dips on the world market – a market that is not as free as
some would like us to believe? Alas, there is a statistical
correlation between the price of coffee and infant mortality:
one falls as the other rises, in the same proportion.

From this beach, I can see one of Rio's *favelas* up there on a mountainside. About 90,000 people live there, in shanty homes. Made of tar-paper, cardboard, mud and discarded building materials, they lean crazily against one another – fires and floods are serious calamities.

Tourists can buy tickets for a guided tour of a *favela*, as well as a tour of the zoo. Not me, though. I have no desire to watch children playing in raw sewage on rutted paths that pass for streets. Mothers there who bear five children, I hear, are lucky if intestinal parasites don't carry off three of them before they reach the age of five. Echoing Gro's words, I hear Indira Gandhi: "Poverty is the worst form of pollution."

How much do foreign aid and loans help the poor? Too much of that money is raked off, you can be sure, by Brazil's political/financial establishment. Too much raked off, too, from the sale of resource concessions to foreign capital.

Must it ever be thus? Bill Blaikie, where are you? Didn't you once tell our House of Commons that countries are sold out by their own establishments? Yes, even Scotland, you said, when, 200 years back, Scottish lairds sold their crofters' farms out from under them so English nobles could raise sheep. Ach, that was a case of sheep eating people, and cause for Rabbie Burns to mourn:

> The English steel we could disdain
> Secure in valour's station
> But the English gold has been our bane –
> Such a parcel of rogues in our Nation.

Returning through the park, I buy a hot dog. But no ketchup – I'll not fatten the Heinz ketchup empire. Its head, a man by the name of O'Reilly, is an engaging Irishman, to be sure. He's a quaere fella, too, who once surprised his staff by exclaiming, "Why, half of these lies are true!" But he makes too much money, does O'Reilly. In 1990, he took home $75 million in salary, bonuses and stock options, to say nothing of the company car.

Ah, this People's Forum in the park has given me hope. Keen, zealous youngsters will go home, their awareness heightened, their energies charged, to keep in touch with one another and fight for what Gro calls "*the* ethical and practical challenge of our time – the achievement of the unified management of the planet."

On this, another ordinary day in the life of Mother Earth, her population rose by 260,000, even though 40,320 died of want. Which caused (or did it?) the Archbishop of Canterbury to opine, as reported in today's *Journal do Brasil*, "The quality of human life is more important than its quantity." His Grace added that it wouldn't cost the United Nations that much to make family counselling and birth control devices available everywhere. But His Grace was not so un-ecumenical as to lace into those religious dogmatists who won't let the UN do any such thing.

Dorothy and I have supper in our Hotel el Presedente. Its elegance has faded, but its rates are reasonable. Which is just as well, as I am paying for this trip out of my estate. Of course, it does lack air conditioning. But at least you can open the windows and experience the weather.

Which reminds me – another thing that happened today is that 1,500 tonnes of ozone-depleting chlorofluorocarbons leaked into the atmosphere, much of this coming from air conditioners and fridges. More bad news for sunbathers, as the ozone's protection disappears and their skin suffers the consequences.

Later, I venture into the night, walking around the downtown hotel district, *el centro* as it's known. Once this area was the proud centre of a jeweled city in the Portuguese empire. Almond trees planted in those glory days still shed their broad, orange-veined leaves (it is autumn here). But signs of decay are everywhere. The terrazzo-tiled sidewalks are cracked and filthy; monuments of empire in the public squares – fountains, statues of *conquistadores* with drawn swords – are chipped and blackened by time and smog.

I don't expect to see many street children on my peregrinations this evening. Hundreds of pre-teens, I was told, have been scooped up and carted off to country camps for the conference's duration. The government does not want the delegates dismayed by the sight of sidewalk-sleeping children.

Still, I see many. There are, after all, 12 million "lost" or "abandoned" children in Brazil. When a sandwich van makes a stop near me, numberless youngsters materialize from the shadows to clamour around it.

I take a seat at a restaurant's sidewalk table on a broad avenue below the ornate Teatro Municipal, and order a beer. At once, bright-eyed entrepreneurs, six or seven years old, surround me. Can they polish my shoes? Sell me Chiclets? Shoe laces? All are eager to learn some English words, these avid little scholars . . .

I finish my beer and resume my walk. A commotion draws me down a side-street. An excited crowd pushes around a bleeding robbery victim in the road. Then a small white van, its *beep! beep!* hardly heard through the ruckus, inches its way into the throng. Brisk young men in monogrammed smocks join hands in a circle around the victim, and then administer first aid. Any country would be proud of these smart youths, volunteers in Rio's *Cruz Vermelo*.

Walking onward, I see a movie poster. Under the image of a contorted head with black wires criss-crossing through the brain is the legend: "No soul; no strain." Yessirree, seems like that all-pervading American culture has worked its way to Rio. Even though this isn't Rambo himself, it's surely one of his offspring.

Away from the lights of the movie marquee, I notice

young bodies, too emaciated to command much of a price, are offering themselves for sale in dark corners. This is one of poverty's real horrors.

Returning, I am stalked and robbed. And, of all places, on the exit ramp of a large, well-lighted subway station. Well, I suppose it was my own fault for not looking over my shoulder. And I had carelessly stuffed a big wad of inflated *cruzeiros* in my right pocket.

Foolish me. There was a silent, quick dart at my back, a stiff body check worthy of a Pittsburgh Penguins hockey player, and a lightning hand liberated the contents of my pocket – an almost surgical operation that effected a much-needed transfer of cash from the rich North to the poor South – only about $30 Canadian.

About these inflated *cruzeiros*. The Brazilian government has exhausted its credit sources, both foreign and domestic. So what's to do? Print money, of course.

Two days later, we attend a reception at the Copacabana hosted by B.C.'s environment minister, John Cashore, and graced by the presence of David Suzuki who, like the White Queen that Alice met in Wonderland, has mastered the trick of remembering forward. Also present is Jean Charest, the federal environment minister, who unflappably fields questions from ardent Greenpeacers. On this just-another-day-on-Earth, another 140,000 fuming cars, trucks and buses hit the world's streets to begin pouring their noxious fumes into the air.

Later we taxi back to the hotel, the cabby gunning his bucket of bolts through streets packed with a wild melee of wheeled conveyances. Screeching buses rear up within inches on either side, their passengers clinging to the rails for dear life. But through the free-for-all, our cabbie sails serenely, like a soccer player of Pele's standing, dribbling effortlessly through his opponents toward the goal. He sings snatches of hymns, and from time to time devoutly crosses himself. Soon I, too, am making the sign of the cross.

There is a no-show here in Rio. He is Carlo di Ripa, the European environment commissioner. (Not long ago, Carlo was an Italian playboy in green shades and Guccis.) Carlo's no-show is his protest against the refusal of the Americans and their Arab allies to support meaningful curbs on the emission of toxic chemicals into the air. They insisted on watering down the Climate Convention, lest it be a "drag on business."

Carlo remains of the view that we *can* do something about the weather. He leads European proposals to tax unclean energy sources, hitting hardest the dirtiest – coal, gas, oil – and lightest the cleanest – wind, waves and sun. The U.S. will have none of that, even though its gasoline taxes are only one-eighth of those of Europe, and one-quarter those of Japan.

And U.S. opposition kills the Climate Convention. In the scramble of global competition, sales go to countries with less in the way of environmental regs. (As for Canada, what's the point of further raising gas taxes with cars now streaming over the border for fill-ups?)

The next day, Flemengo Park again, and another speech – this one delivered by Italy's environment minister. In the torrent of words, I make out one phrase – "propulsive capitalism." I couldn't get the rest. He was speaking in an official language, French, using Italian sing-song stresses. What *was* the pitch he made? Capitalism igniting run-away consumerism. Was he saying canoes are better for lakes and campers than power boats? That skis are easier on the land (and on your bones!) than snowmobiles? That manly body odors score better than deodorants and perfumes?

I do believe he is some kind of red. The way he moved his hands gave him away, as if he was saying capitalism was like a bicycle racer in one of the bowl-tracks where you ride the walls and wobble and fall if you don't pedal furiously.

But I do not believe he dared to mention the Italian railway system, or claim as a plus that it employs twice as many breadwinners per travelled mile as the European average. Probably he's not *that* red.

It is the following day, a day on which 140 species of life, some a million years or older, are doomed to disappear, and seven more actually become extinct, a result of the activities of one species: man. In short, just another day in the life of the planet.

Cross-legged on what used to be grass, a group of unofficial delegates are planning a march on the American delegation. It puts up at the Sheraton Hotel, far down the Copacabana. The group wants to demonstrate against the U.S. for refusing to sign the Bio-Diversity Convention. The lone hold-out. The U.S. president has averred that this convention does not "protect ideas."

Uh oh. Guess what? Our old friends the pharmaceutical companies are working Rio over as they have Ottawa. Ideas? Their idea is to patent and brand living organisms. The Gene-Tech Company already has contracts out in the Third World on 15,000 marine organisms. And half our wonder healers come from nature's storehouse.

The Brazilian government has chanced to express some disappointment with its big northern creditor. Its Amazonia is rich in the cunningest patterns of excelling Nature, in the Bard's words. Brazil wants to refine and market its indigenous barks and fungi and microbes. But if money power can buy up these potential enrichers under the rubric of protecting "intellectual property rights," Brazil might as well kiss that notion goodbye.

With that in mind, at breakfast today I asked a fellow named Kwidini, minister of sports for Zimbabwe, if Rambo fell under "intellectual property rights." Kwidini said he did indeed.

The next morning, I hear from the poet Petrarch, from his villa near Padua, across six centuries. He tells me that "to know the disease is half the cure." Later he adds: "It is part of the cure to wish to be cured." I think I know what he's getting at.

Another day passes, a day on which 180 square miles of forests, the "Earth's lungs," disappeared. That's an area one third the size of sprawling Los Angeles.

I am courteously received by Amazonian natives in the traditional thatched meeting-house they have built in Flemengo Park. They are bronzed, handsome, capable, and aware. They speak gravely, with sad eyes. Their rainforest homelands are being invaded.

In a way, they are luckier than natives south of Amazonia. They were invaded 300 years ago when piratical *banderates* struck inland from the Portuguese colony on the Atlantic as far into the continent as Peru's mountains. These desperados, with muskets and ferocious Spanish dogs, pillaged native villages, slaughtering those not worth enslaving to work coffee and sugar plantations.

Now, pushing into Amazonia come poachers greedy to capture alive rare wildlife – the animals and birds that, since time immemorial, have been the earth-born companions of the natives.

Come, too, the desperately poor, to fell trees to sell; to slash, burn and clear rain-forest land to farm and graze their cattle on.

And can the mega-agribusinesses be far behind? Yes, and with deeds to the land, to intensively cultivate single export crops, using mechanization and massive doses of chemical fertilizers. Land that for centuries fed native and settler families with indigenous, nutritious crops become company plantations. They produce for one reason only: to export. The first settlers, the natives, join the teeming urban poor in their cardboard and scrap-metal shanties.

Now who am I to question the laws of economics? They efficiently provide, I am asked to believe, goods and services for developing countries to export, and the means to buy their food on the world market. Thus our shelves are stocked with soya and sugar from Brazil, pineapples and bananas from the Philippines, peanuts from Africa, meat from Central America.

All well and good, if you are a shareholder in an international agribusiness. But not well and good for countries that lose their farmers and farmlands and can't make enough foreign exchange to buy imported food. Or even to pay off their debts.

I keep going back to what Gro said: "The world cannot save its tropical forests and their living creatures as long as international trade patterns force agricultural nations to destroy natural habitats to plant cash crops."

Speaking of foreign exchange, today world-wide currency trading reached a record $650 billion. Shows there is still money to be made!

Another day. Another 500,000 scientists go to work at making smarter, deadlier weapons – as many as go to work in non-military research and development.

I am in a chair outside the swanky Meridien Hotel on the Copacabana. I have a fine view of the beach. This is no place for an old fellow. The young in one another's arms make me muse ... Oh, dear, I should have taken better care of myself.

Suddenly, coming down Atlantic Boulevard, closed to normal traffic by red bunting, is a cavalcade of white limos. It sweeps under a pedestrian overpass where soldiers, silhouetted against a cloudless blue sky, finger automatic weapons. Around the limos, motorcycle police in blue helmets buzz like insects. Above them, a file of helicopters churns the air, armed soldiers crouched in their open doors. As the limos reach the hotel, the choppers hover above them like hummingbirds. Statespersons, black, in black suits and white ties, emerge from the limos and pick their way toward the hotel through a cordon of soldiers and police with wooden truncheons. This must be their lunch break! A respite from the speeches in the Rio Centrum. Who they are I never find out — possibly Prime Minister Bongo of Gabon and his retinue.

I can understand why there is a military presence today. But this extravaganza? I know that from time to time, *arrastoes* — rag-tag teenagers — leave their hillside *favelas* to swarm onto the beaches of the Copacabana, mugging and robbing. But they won't swarm today — not with this show of force!

It's a pity Brazil is so big on a military culture. The country's military build-up goes beyond just keeping the poor in line. Too bad it doesn't follow Costa Rica's example, and do away with its army completely. The Ticos, as Costa Ricans like to be called, are daft enough to believe that countries win arms races by dropping right out of them.

Meanwhile, Brazil's populist president, Fernando Collor de Mello — when he's not trying to stave off impeachment for embezzling public millions — likes to get his photo in the papers test-driving a Tiger tank, or at the controls of an F-18 jet. Have you, dear Reader, any idea how many

BTUs are burned to take an F-18 from zero to 150 mph in two seconds? No, nor do I.

And from what I hear, toxic militia-mania is not getting much mention in Rio Centrum as an environmental hazard. Though I can't imagine what plunders Earth's treasures more efficiently, or poisons our environment more effectively, than military activity.

I go to sleep. When I awake, Mother Earth has completed another spin on her axis, and humanity has spewed another 56 million tonnes of carbon dioxide into the skies.

Think of it: 56 million tonnes. That's ten times as much as we put up in all of 1900. By 2050, tonnage (and our thermometers) will be skyrocketing. Climatologists say world temperatures will increase by two or three degrees Celsius by 2050. With the slow seas rising, the sheer cliffs crumbling . . .

Meanwhile, there I was, in the Intercontinental Hotel's breezy, sunlit dining room, minding my own omelette, when I was overtaken by a hot flash of prejudice. Twelve Saudi Arabian delegates were shown to a table near mine. And I burned!

They are in tailored khakis, genial, smiling. Others defer to one in their midst, a prince, no doubt. He graciously smiles at their sallies, but his eyes betray the hawkish arrogance of great wealth.

All men, of course. Their wives are home in their desert kingdom, behind veils and walls. The menfolk rove the world's sybaritic spas, never wanting for anything, partaking of all the pleasant vices, seemingly never sated or bored.

My flush of prejudice is insalubrious. Why loathe them for being what and who they are? But what of their actions – can't I be riled about them?

These men represent the Imperial Power of Oil. Men kill

themselves over their tar-baby. It adulterates the air. Its sales multiply as its money chatters, influencing what we read, see and hear. Who really killed the Climate Convention? Need I ask?

The next day, my second-last in Rio, I hear proclaimed at the Rio Centrum, by a man who'd been given up for dead, Cuba's esteemed *Jefe*, that an important biological species is at risk: man.

Yes, the Earth Summit is concluding by hearing from heads of state, who've each been given seven minutes to say their pieces. Señor Fidel Castro walks to the podium. He's not in his familiar battle fatigues today – no, Fidel is decked out with gold braid like some admiral from HMS *Pinafore*. Silver-maned now, his gait slowed, the man still has presence.

Well, Fidel, I'll tell you who's at risk. You. Your friendly Evil Empire is no longer in the spotlight, and auditions are in progress for a replacement. The American congress has tightened its trade blockade around your little island, never mind the niceties of international law, and you and your compatriots are feeling the squeeze. Fidel, you are almost as extinct as a Bulgarian Communist with twirled moustache and baggy pants. But you just don't get it, do you.

And neither does your audience! On you go, grabbing these seven minutes and wringing every second out of them.

"Let the ecological debt be paid, not the foreign debt," I hear you proclaim.

"May hunger disappear, not man!"

Then, as if you hadn't been naughty enough, you take a swipe at the money boys.

"The hegemony of international finance, whose purposes are not peoples'!"

Rolling applause as you walk back to your seat, more

than accorded any other speech. Your listeners can't contain themselves. Even a chagrined President George Bush, waiting his turn to speak, is caught by the cameras putting his hands together soundlessly.

Later, Prime Minister Mulroney — our very own — announces in his speech that Canada will reduce Brazil's debt by $150 million. This is Canada's part in the "Swaps for Nature" program. Debt reductions for developing countries, under this program, are made if the money "saved" goes into environmental projects. There are only a few simple provisos. The developing countries must agree to be friendly to foreign capital; to open their markets; to privatize; and to pay their debts.

It is time for Dorothy and me to check out of our Copacabana hotel, and leave Rio, the Earth Summit, and the People's Forum in Flemengo Park behind. On this day, the poet Thomas Hardy, speaking to us from the beyond, gets in the last word:

> *We are getting to the end of visioning*
> *The impossible within our universe*
> *Such as that better whiles may follow worse*
> *And that our race may mend with reasoning.*

Really, Thomas. I know people tend to see the dark side more as they get older. And this year does mark your 152nd birthday. Still — if you were walking and talking in the People's Forum in Flemengo Park, you'd feel better. These people have hope. They've celebrated a marriage within themselves, a union of the socialist red and the environmental green. A creative minority, couldn't you say, carrying in their loins the seeds of a majority culture waiting to be born?

PRINTED IN CANADA